THE TODGER DODGERS

By

Jimmy Walker

To likeminded fantasists & the odd fetishist.

Acknowledgment

No book is ever written in isolation, and The Todger Dodgers is no exception. I am deeply grateful to my friends and family for their unwavering support during the long hours of writing, and for reminding me to find humour even when the words felt burdensome.

A heartfelt thank you to Noble Legacy Publishing for their invaluable guidance, steering this story from its first draft to the finished book. I also extend my gratitude to the editors and designers who meticulously shaped the rough edges into something worth sharing.

Lastly, to the readers: thank you for choosing to open these pages. Without you, stories like this would have nowhere to call home.

Table of Contents

About the Author

Jimmy Walker is a writer with a keen eye for humour and a natural ear for the rhythm of everyday life. His work combines wit, honesty, and rawness, bringing to life characters and situations that are as relatable as they are unforgettable.

When he's not writing, Jimmy can often be found observing people in cafés and bars, collecting stories from the streets, or sharing laughter with friends who inspire much of his work. The Todger Dodgers stands as a testament to his belief that the funniest stories are often the truest.

Prologue

When unfeasibly rich entrepreneur Sam Prentis, loses his genitalia to a rogue Rolls-Royce sprocket, he is sold on the idea of a prosthetic phallus by the coincidentally named Richard Edwards, A K A Dick ED. Richard, and Sam's gold-digging wife Judy, conspire to do away with their respective partners and inherit a fortune.

They load Sam's bionic replacement with explosives, primed to detonate during aphrodisiac-enhanced copulation, but something goes terribly wrong, or right; (depending upon who's looking at it). Either way, the conspirators are in deep trouble.

To add to their woes, a high-octane prototype is mistakenly dispatched to Annie's 'Treble A' Adult Shop in Glasgow.

. . . Following a compulsory cannabis 'top up' trip to Bongo Bill's and a spate of habitual shoplifting, pot head brothers Tam and Jeddah escape pursuit by ducking into Annie's. The theft of a prototype, and the rescue of a tailors' dummy from a builders' skip, sets in motion a string of unstoppable events? How could they have known that such a random act of opportunism would set them on a trip to the other side of the world and change their lives forever?

Chapter One:
P.I.G.M.E.

Had Mrs Edwards realized the extent of ridicule her son would suffer under the derogatory abbreviation of his given name, she might well have christened him William or George. As it was, she called him Richard after 'Tricky Dickie Nixon.' Add to that, early-onset alopecia, a psychogenic stammer, and an inordinate phallic inferiority complex, the young man was off to a decidedly bad start. Fortunately, what he did have was a 'very thick skin.' (He would need it!)

Throughout a withdrawn, soul-searching adolescence, despite diminishing self-esteem, it helped him to ride the storm of vitriol, until eventually, it lost its potency. Unfortunately, the hurt he thought he'd left in the schoolyard was to re-emerge at university. After falling asleep at a fresher's party, someone felt-tipped an eyehole on the top of his bald head, stretched his polar-neck jumper above the ears, (and it all began again).

That was to be the last 'freshers,' or for that matter, any other kind of party Richard was ever to attend until he sorted out his problems: intensive speech therapy noticeably helped his stammer, as for alopecia, Yul Brunner's baldness had become a macho fashion statement, so he simply shaved off what little hair was left.

Although not particularly underendowed, online exposure to 'overendowed' porn stars left voyeuristic Richard feeling decidedly bereft (as it does to most of the pervulation). Hoping to somehow level up the penile playing field, he spent every waking hour in the prosthetics and orthotics wing of the faculty.

It was there he first met 'Design and Innovation' undergraduate Janet. She too, had been nurtured on a secret stash of John Holmes movies. Just like Richard, the car-crash revelation that all men aren't similarly equipped set her on a quest for viable alternatives.

Researching the annals of erotic consumerism for an answer, she came across a collective of ancient phallic symbols in the British Library and eureka!

Back in the workshop, she produced several oversized

facsimiles on her three-D printer and punted them out to likeminded students.

With textures, contours, and skin tones of the real thing, the samples were jaw-droppingly authentic in appearance, (but as we know, appearances are all too often deceptive. Several disgruntled buyers, expecting at least some level of porn-land functionality weren't satisfied and demanded an immediate refund!)

Surfing for an online solution, she happened upon Richard's paper on gender disparity, and two worlds collided! He argued that when it comes to cosmetic enhancement, women have an unfair advantage. Siting liposuction, silicone boobs, blepharoplasty, rhinoplasty, genioplasty, and collogen lips as treatments readily available, he concluded there was nothing of comparable significance for men.

After seeing his nerdish Facebook image, Janet discarded her mini skirt and fishnets for a neatly pressed pinafore and horn-rimmed glasses. She scoured the bio-prosthetics wing and there he was, bent over his computer.

Shaking her head despairingly, forcing a smile, she lowered the lid of his laptop and offered her hand. 'Pleased to make your acquaintance, professor. I read your 'gender disparity' paper,' she said, and before he could object, added, 'I totally agree with your premise, and I think I might have a way of redressing the imbalance you expounded.'

Richard shook his head wearily. 'R-really?'

'It seems we're both looking for different answers to what is essentially the same question, so why not pool our expertise?' Janet looked him firmly in the eye and continued, 'All we have to do is transmogrify every woman's phallic dream onto a prosthetic drawing board, and we'll be onto a winner, don't you think?'

'Go on?'

'We live in a supreme age of vanity, professor, an age, as you contend, where men are largely overlooked when it comes to augmentation.'

'And?'

'And there's no stigma anymore, so why not take advantage?'

Richard closed his eyes for a moment, cupped his crotch protectively with one hand and shook her hand with the other. 'Pleased to meet you. I'm listening.'

'By manufacturing an idealized version, we could end the

phenomena of penis envy virtually overnight,' she said. 'With my design capabilities and your bio-engineering expertise, a sure-fire winner. Wouldn't you agree, professor?'

'C-call me R-Richard, and c-count me in.'

Janet counted him in, and under the trade acronym of PIGME, the 'Prosthetic Institute of Genetically Modified Engineering' was born.

The mutually enjoyable journey from drawing board to manufacture included several injection-moulded prototypes and one or two kiln-dried models from a potters' wheel that weren't quite up to spec. A succession of micro-circuitry and design modifications followed...Several wet runs, later it was time to launch...

Their polycarbonate slide-on hit the adult' libido market with a bang! The blurb literally sold itself and took the erotic internet world by storm. Facebook, Amazon, and Etsy overloaded, eBay and Shopify crashed, and the money came rolling in. So much so, to accommodate wholesale production, they rented a vacant industrial unit and hired asylum-seeking Sadiq to oversee the fully automated assembly.

Online orders came from far and wide; in no time at all the factory was running 24/7 at maximum capacity just to keep up with growing demand.

Richard and Janet took time out to tie the proverbial knot. There was never, what you might call, any 'real regard' between them; it was simply a marriage of greedy convenience. 'A tax-avoiding paper exercise to keep our money 'under wraps,' Richard said. Emphasising the word 'our' was his way of keeping Janet onside. With the foresight to secretly register the patent offshore (in her maiden name), she was way ahead of him.

Things were on the up-and-up-and-up: order book full, profits mounting at an incredible rate, but 'Sod's Law' will out. It didn't take discerning competitors long to realize that half-price facsimiles will always outsell the genuine article.

Combining child labour and conveyor-belt assembly techniques, almost overnight, the market was flooded with 3D clones from China.

The 'P I G M E' brand of penile enhancement was suddenly 'dead in the water.' The couple's meteoric rise to fortune over all too soon: red letters, bailiffs, final demands and cancelled overdrafts became the order of the day.   Resentment displaced what little regard remained and Janet began to refer to thick-skinned Richard by that abbreviation he so abhorred. 'You'd better get your thinking cap working, Dick-Ed!' she screamed, 'or you'll be wearing it in the bloody dole queue!'

Richard bit the proverbial ego bullet to tell her he still had a way of keeping ahead of the game. 'Calm down,' he said, 'I've been working on a new model with a series of innovative, ground-breaking improvements, ideal for the as-yet untapped amputee snob market.'

'Snob market?'

'The one where rich people won't buy anything that isn't obscenely overpriced!'

Once he had Janet's full attention, she lightened her tone to ask about the 'so-called innovative improvements?'

'A variance of skin tones and textures, a selection of functionalities, gonad cusps that slow-release oxytocin hormones. Each model can be modularly programmed to individual taste, unlike the emerging trends; encrypted, impossible to copy. As soon as we get a high-profile endorsement from a mega-rich penile amputee, it's game on! Just watch this space,' he said in a tone that won him a temporary stay of abandonment.

'Just where will we get a mega-rich penile amputee?'

'It shouldn't be too difficult, since the Duane Bobbic revelation, they're chopping them off like toenails.'

Janet couldn't quite get her head around the concept of 'modular programming,' but it sounded like a good idea, so she decided to run with it, on condition she could test-drive the prototypes.

She'd sampled all the so-called 'AI emerging trends,' over-indulged in a myriad of S & M virtual realities: whippers, flippers, well-endowed trippers, goers, slowers, and 'I'm not sure I knowers, but none really hit the G spot. 'Count me in,' she said.

. . . After weeks of hacking the A & E databases, the National Electronic Library flagged up the perfect subject. Richard gazed dreamily at the printout and smiled to himself as he read the admissions file for the twenty-sixth time:

Name: Samuel Prentiss
Sex: (Male)
Classification: Traumatic penile amputation
Age: undeclared

Occupation: Entrepreneur

Brief description of accident: The patient's genitalia became entangled in a motor vehicle mechanism, resulting in 85% penile & complete testicular loss. Amputated parts, crushed beyond recovery (Ground into mulch).

Richard squeezed his legs together and winced... 'Oooooooooooh!'

Vital signs: respiration regular. No loss of consciousness.

Blood pressure: 120/80

Temperature: 96.8

Heart rate: normal

Patient's demeanour: lucid, restrained. (Solus dolor limina).

Richard Googled the Latin superscript and sniggered to himself. (He often did that). 'Hmm, high pain threshold, eh, that could come in handy!'

On his way to the one-bed private clinic, he consulted his copy of 'Wannabe's guide to the filthy Rich' and underlined the reference to 'Sam Prentiss':Hobbies: money and classic cars; notoriously cutthroat in his business dealings. Eccentric self-made stationery and paper-clip magnate. Twopence halfpenny less than Elon Musk, (and counting).

'Oh, yes!' Endorphins turning summersaults, greedy mind racing at the thought, Richard subdued his stammering impulse with five minutes of controlled breathing and crept furtively through the clinic grounds to the tradesmans' entrance.

While the unfeasibly nonchalant eunuch absorbed the Dow Jones index, Judy, his even more relaxed, oversexed, and undervalued wife, sat refurbishing her fingernails at his bedside, practicing her seductive pout in a hand-held mirror. When the door opened, she refused to be distracted, but Sam frowned, tutted, and put down his Financial Times. The refracted sunlight had turned Richard's head into what Janet once called his 'alopecia Belisha' and lit up the room. Pinstriped suit and Oxford brogues, at odds with badly camouflaged acne and a hapless grin, completed the picture as he sidestepped the swinging door like an uncertain tap-dancer.

Sam peered over his reading glasses. 'Who the hell are you?'

'Richard Edwards, sir. I'm the t-t-odger fairy who's going to rebuild you, sir. I'll make you an offer you can't refuse, and I know you won't be disappointed.' He approached the bed tentatively to hand the stone-faced patient a card.

Sam shook his head. 'I made my millions refusing offers, don't you know.' He sat bolt upright and recoiled as Richard tottered to the foot of his bed, opened an attaché case, tugged his cuffs to show there was nothing up his sleeves, then raised his sample between outstretched palms like an offering to the gods.

. . .When sure he had captured enough interest, he tickled the stem before bowing reverently. Pressing an innocent-looking activation mole on the well-polished, bulbous end, he lay the penile prosthesis gently on the bedsheet. 'Wallah! Meet the Rampant Rod, our newest slide-on model, sir, myoelectric and multifunctional repertoire.' Producing the control module from his pocket, he continued with a well-rehearsed sales blurb... 'dye-cast in the colour of your choice, and of course made-to-measure, injection-moulded to any bespoke specification: spiral, conical, ribbed or simply glandular, it's up to you, sir, a matter of personal preference.' He pressed the activation button on his module.

When the great serpentine fiend undulated to life Judy's eyes widened and her jaw dropped; it was simply the idealisation of every phallus about which she had ever fantasized. She began to salivate, shuddered involuntarily to each nuance as the penile snake danced a horizontal rumba across the bedclothes. It bumped and buckled, twisted, turned, and corkscrewed. By the time it reached Sam's pillow, she had varnished most of her knuckle and was starting on her left wrist. 'Ugh,' she sighed dreamily, she just couldn't help herself...'it's beautiful, truly beautiful.

'Beautiful, is it?' Sam forced himself back against the headboard and kept his finger on the emergency button. 'Somebody get rid of this idiot!'

Judy's eyes milked over with repressed emotion; she moistened her lips as her face took on the characteristics of a pouting infant. 'Don't be so hasty, darling,' she squeaked. 'Let's hear what Mr Todger fairy has to say.'

Richard took the cue and winked in her direction. 'For a price, madam,' he nodded back towards the patient and grinned, 'we can match skin tones, freckles and texture, and you'll soon be reaping the b-bonkable and b-bankable rewards.'

Judy's face by now had turned a curious shade of puce. 'Bankable, you say?'

It was an incongruous moment for the entry of two burly porters. They looked at each other and then to Sam.

'For six hundred pounds a bloody day, I expect a bit of privacy, for heaven's sake. I'm the only bloody patient here!' he snarled. 'Get this lunatic away from me.' He took the offending object burrowing into his bolster in a stranglehold, and deactivated it by pressing gently on the glandular head mole. 'Hmm, clever piece of kit though. Get him out of here!'

Richard gasped in surprise and gulped. 'S-Six hundred quid.' (His asking price had just doubled). 'S-Six hundred bleeding quid a day, phew.' Lifted by his elbows and propelled feet flaying toward the exit, 'six hundred bloody quid a day?' he repeated. 'What about my s-sample?'

'My sample now, I think,' Sam said. Until that moment, he'd associated the words 'huge erection' with his Dubai building program. 'Animatronics have always been my pet fascination,' he mused. He held it up to the bedside lamp like a prized specimen, and Judy sprang to his side.

'And hedonics mine,' she mumbled under her breath as Richard was bodily hoisted from the room.

As he was deposited onto the tarmac, he scrolled the contacts on his phone to 'witchipoo-wife' and pressed call. 'It's not going to be as easy as I thought, but it could be worth it,' he whispered, 'this fellah's m-minted.'

Even though her husband's last six endeavours had not produced a single sale, Janet had to reluctantly admire his persistence. Anyway, she was in a win-win-win mood: if Richard closed the deal, she made money; if he didn't, then he was history. The third 'win' involving a certain offshore account, she kept to herself. 'You do what you have to, dick-ed.' She texted the reply, knowing full well he would anyway.

He hadn't had much luck recently. Last week's sales flop (pun intended), involved a castrated adulterer carrying his offending body part three miles, only for Richard to steal it from the ice bag while the patient was in pre-op. Then, like a rabbit from a hat, he produced a slide-on model from his sample case. 'Wallah, my emasculated friend, you wouldn't like this on your arse for a wart now, would you?'

The patient grabbed at the sample with one hand, his tingling, smarting crotch with the other. His mood swung from suicidal to euphoric in that single instant, and he sat upright. 'Can you. . .Is it. . . Will you. . .How. . .When?'

'Yes, I can, yes, it is, I might, and it's easy-peazy-ball-bag-squeezy, that's how. When's a different question!' Richard replied, but he discovered the amputee was waiting for his 'Universal Credit' back pay, and the sample vanished quicker than it had appeared. 'Sorry mate, no bread, no head, I'm afraid, no dough, no go, no mun, no fun neither, old chap. Now, while you might say I have the utmost sympathy for the poverty stricken, castrated unwashed, the world of hedge-funds and off-shore tax avoidance beckons.'

Then there was the 'game show' transvestite who tried to save a few bob by performing his own gender reassignment. (He won the booby prize).

Richard parked his car behind a nearby pub and made his way back to the clinic on foot.

Judy was inspecting the scrotal cusp in the natural light, she spotted him from the bedside window and turned to Sam. 'Don't be too hasty, dear, it would have cost nothing to listen to what the man had to say. You must consider my needs?'

'Your needs!' Sam laughed, 'if shagging half the western hemisphere can't do it for you, what good is a plastic do-dah?'

Judy thought about it for a second, and brooked no argument. She knew better than to complain.

Fact was, as long as it was kept off the record, Sam had never discouraged her infidelity. 'You're a piece of crackling,' he once said. 'Keep away the gold diggers and you're good for the corporate image, but the minute you go public you've messed up. I go pre-nup, and you end up messed up, tits up and skint. Take it or leave it.'

Judy took it, she knew it was nothing personal, just his infuriatingly tidy mind. 'Whatever you say, Sam.'

'Remember, discretion is the better part of Moolah?'

She knew exactly what he meant, ever since the day he found her squatting on the photocopier, she sensed the looming inevitability of penniless abandonment.

'Who's that for?' he demanded. When she refused to answer he pulled her from the machine and pressed the delete button. 'Do that again and you're history!' He looked at the carbon copy and sneered. 'That reminds me they're putting the Channel Tunnel toll up next month,' he said. He ripped the print out up and threw it in the waste basket, but Judy had already printed off a dozen copies.

. . . She never forgot Sam's stark warning, but at that moment her thoughts were on the object of lewd desire he was so fastidiously examining. Closing her eyes, she flexed her arse muscles, wiped the dribble from her lips and replayed the bed-top rumba in her mind. On a phallic fantasy that subsumed all reason she cradled the rod to her cheek and just about managed not to kiss it. 'Whatever you say, dear.'

Richard, on the other hand, had no real concerns about his wife's fidelity, Janet had spent so much of her adult life marketing designer aids, the whole idea of one-on-one heterosexuality had become a complete anathema to her. As far as Janet was concerned bespoke appendages were the future. When that particular niche market began to flag, she was easily persuaded to invest in Richard's new line in prosthesis for penile amputees. It seemed like a good idea at the time, but she was forced to conclude that men who tend to have their parts chopped off are for the most part skint. To put it her way, 'a castrated millionaire is about as rare as an honest banker.'

Maybe she was right after all, Richard thought as he crawled back through the long grass and bellied down opposite the private annex.

It's a class thing, until the privatized NHS does a U turn, the emasculated working class will just have to stay that way. But I'm in the 'last chance saloon' here. If I let this one get away, I'm history, he told himself.

Hard sell, soft sell, any b-bloody sell'll do!

Lamenting from a safe distance, he wiped away the tears, took a deep breath and stood up straight. In a hospital white coat purloined from the staff cloak room, he pinned his notes to an open file and sloped past security just as Judy emerged from the side room.

She put away her makeup and puckered a half-hearted goodbye to her mega rich spouse. 'Later, darling' she said.

Her dutiful air kiss was acknowledged by a dismissive wave of Sam's hand. 'Whatever,' he replied.

'Ungrateful b-bastard,' Richard growled as he watched her arse twitching, practiced waddle. 'Why haven't I got a page-three missus like her,' he asked himself. At that very moment his reflection in the glass revolving door answered for him. 'Oh yeah, well l-looks aren't everything.' He watched her hip-twitching sensual walk to the rest room and returned to the list of Sam's injuries with a new relish.

Severing of the following:

Internal artery: 'bloody nice arsery.

Right and left testis: 'dropped a bollock there eh, mega rich snob.

Epididymis: 'e.p.i.d.i.d.y.m.i.s,' he repeated in a slow sensual drawl. 'Oh, how I love that word.'

From a safe distance he followed Judy to the pub across the road, and once again found himself leering over his lever arch at her silicone implants. Umbrella lashes casting a Clockwork Orange shadow across downcast features, one foreboding sign he chose to ignore, the malevolent glean in her eye, another.

Seductively stroking nail varnish remover with long digits, a bottoxed bottom lip swelled in time to her breathing as Richard adjusted his tackle. 'Hello again,' he gulped nervously when she finally looked up. 'If this is the wrong time, please stop me. My name is R-Richard, as you may have guessed I specialize in penile prostheses.'. . . His attempt at an endearing smile was more of a pained wince.

'P.e.n.i.l.e. preposterous.' She bastardized the phrase in a mocking tone; her face crinkled in amusement as she pumped her tongue suggestively into her inner cheek and smiled. 'Penile-propergobfullous, that's literally quite a mouthful.'

Richard flushed. 'I'm sorry. More android than prosthetic, but this is probably too s-soon.'

'Not at all,' she replied, 'I've never dodged a todger . . .or a lodger for that matter, now sit down. Do you have a catalogue I can choose from, or is that the only model?'

'As well as the established models we have a few innovative prototypes.

'For instance, give me a for instance?'

Richard began to back off. 'Look, you're obviously upset. I'll leave you my c-card.'

'No, you damn well won't.' Judy was shaking her head with impatience, not with distain, and raised an admonishing finger. 'You'll answer my bloody question!'

Sensing a possible sale, Richard's voice gathered a lilt of confidence and he re-jigged his approach. 'We tend now to give are new models iconic names that you may find a trite fallacious.'

'Fallacious, there's another nice word, but what do they

actually do? Give me a blinking for-instance?'

'Funny you should say that, one model can be programmed to actually 'blink,' but mostly they all do the same thing, all be it in slightly modified ways. For instance, when the bible bashers moaned, we rebranded the 'P-Pope-headed-blurter as the 'Paisley-pounder' and sales went up by 20% overnight. Then we tried other headings.' It's all a matter of marketing.

Judy licked her lips. 'Headings? Do go on.'

'The Whitehouse range: the 'Trump-pump' and the Clinton-clip-on', onto the more contemporary 'Starmer Brahma' and 'Kinnock-kidders,' when there was an outcry of 'political incorrectness,' but still top of the price range and our all-time best seller we have the famous and inimitable 'Rampant-rod.'

He joined her in the furthest cubicle where she afforded a promising glimpse of thigh and suspender. 'Right,' he said when he finally managed to regulate his breathing. 'Quite a lot of your husband's .... quite a lot of it. . .of his. . .of it is missing, is it not?'

'They did manage to save one inch.'

'Which means that based on the average male appendage,' Richard smiled and tapped the keys on his calculator, 'he's probably lost about f-f-four inches?'

Judy shook her head and winced. 'Make that t-t-two. You've got me doing it now, but no matter, d-do go on.'

'Well, there's a very good chance that we can graft a modular form of our latest prototype onto the residual site.'

'Will it work like a proper one?'

'It's still at the experimental stage, but there is no reason why it sh-shouldn't.'

'Tell me more?'

Richard immediately went into 'stammer-free' sales mode. 'By splicing arousal electrodes from the penile stub to the prosthesis we can recreate erectile and orgasmic tension in synthetic gonads.'

'Slow down!' Judy's hormones began to pinball at the prospect.' it's not often I say it, but you must slow down.

Richard gulped another hurried breath and continued. . . 'Blood supply deluge cannot be replicated, that's where electromagnetic induction takes over. Once erectile nanotechnology engages, lateral motion automatically kicks in. You wouldn't know the difference....'

'Oh, wouldn't I now? Don't be too sure?' Lateral motion, I

must have one, she thought, but for the sake of appearance, swallowed a globule of saliva, licked her lips and nodded pensively. 'Hm, I'm sorry, I can't quite understand all this technical stuff, it goes right over my head.'

Richard donned his best patronizing frown. 'How did it happen, Mrs Prentiss?'

'I just never had the education that's all, and call me Judy.'

'No, I mean how did the accident happen?'

'Oh that? Apparently, he was leaning over the engine of his Roller at the time. Pubes wrapped around the armature or something and dragged his genitals in.'

'Ah, aghh!' Cringing at the image in his head, Richard had to force his mind back to the potential sale. 'Excuse me for asking, but your husband is the Sam Prentiss, is he not, paper clip monopolist?'

'Misogynist more like. I see you've done your research?'

'Everyone has heard of your husband, Mrs Prentiss, I mean J-Judy. Stationery baron, a millionaire when he was eighteen.'

'Stationary just about sums him up,' she laughed, 'and probably barren as well. What's your point?'

'Well, it just seems slightly odd that the countries' sixth richest man would be doing his own c-car repairs.'

'Hey, the same fellah recycles used postage stamps, darns his own socks for God's sake. How do you think he got so bloody rich?'

At the thought of such stinginess, Richard's mind flashed to Janet and her particular set of moneysaving foibles. He nodded in sympathy and made a note. 'Still, it must have been t-terrible for him.'

'Terrible for him! What about me? I mean, you'd think that having his gonads minced by a Rolls Royce Straight-Eight would provoke a suicidal inclination. Any normal man would have had a go at topping himself by now, or at the very least a nervous breakdown, now that would be normal.'

'I believe he used one of his own staplers to clamp the artery, what a guy,' Richard said, and turned to study her reaction. Button-popping implants, by now pushed up almost to chin height by folded arms, she was staring, salivating, licking her lips in that pseudo porn mode again.

The absence of compassion in her features might have been attributed to post-traumatic stress, but Richard sensed there was something else going on. 'What a guy,' he repeated with a sigh. To bridge the silence, he picked up his clipboard and began to recite the plagiarized details of her husband's injury, right up to the severing of the epididymis.

'That bloody Roller, eh?' she said when he had finished. 'When he said he was having trouble with his magneto, I thought he meant libido. I could have told him that!' She looked at her watch, then pouted towards the young barman leering in her direction. 'I actually considered having the offending sprocket mounted; even penned the inscription, if only he hadn't recovered? The hydraulics that ground his b....' (she ironically cleared her throat). 'But it wasn't to be, so I had to make do with a 'get-well card.'

'Look, I don't mean to embarrass you, but are there any photographs of him, of the. . .of his. . .before the accident?'

'I don't own a fast-action lens, honey and hey,' she laughed, 'it's been that long. Sorry, I can't even remember what it looks like, sorry, looked like, except it most certainly was not that long,' she said as a strange semaphore of sensuality was taking place with the young barman.

Richard had drunk too much too quickly, and he wasn't used to it. Judy was fluttering her stick-on eyelashes, puffing out her chest towards the, he began to feel superfluous, but had the presence of mind to confirm her email address before staggering from the pub . . . Looking back, he watched her totter open-mouthed to the bar.

Jaded thoughts bobbling somewhere between hope and trepidation, he slid himself back behind the wheel and rechecked his equipment. ,

. . . Largely sobered up by the time he arrived back, Richard entered the workshop with an air of manufactured confidence that Janet always saw right through.

Huddled over his bench, careful not to disturb the erectile and ejaculatory circuits, Sadiq was peeling back the scrotal seam from the last of the day's batch. With a huge sigh of satisfaction, he decanted clear peppermint oxytocin into the polyplastic testicle. Tucking away the circuitry, he hung the finished Rod on a rack next to the models he'd prepared earlier and slid the whole assembly into the sterile chamber. Only then did he allow himself the ten-minute break he'd so fastidiously earned. Cradling his cup of hot cocoa, he fought back tears of joy to admire his handiwork through the Perspex visor.

. . .As the last of the dough-like specimens disappeared into the pigmentation booth, the first emerged from the other side, skin toned, bell-headed, blue veined, and proud. Sadiq was always emotionally moved at this metamorphosis, but he liked the next part best.

. . . While one robotic arm plunged the synthetic mole into the gland head, another implanted the ultrasonic transducer deep into the scrotal wall. He involuntarily winced and girded his knees tight together whenever this happened. Before moving the rack of finished Rods to the cooling hanger, he replaced the jug of oxytocin emulsive in the refrigerator.

Richard pushed past him to hurriedly mount his own depleted slide-on onto the charging pod. 'Don't cry, Sad dicky, we're gonna be okay if I make this sale.'

Janet's voice suddenly cracked from the doorway. 'You're gonna be on the bloody dole if you don't!' Holding a handful of fibre optic urethras like a bunch of rhubarb, wearing an upside-down smile, and all-in-one tucked into green wellies, she shuffled from the back office. 'I'm not throwing good money after bad.'

'What a f-feckin boiler,' Richard muttered.

'What are you jabbering about?'

'Hi, darling, I was just saying I like your boiler suit. Is it new?'

Janet handed the depleted tubers to Sadiq and squared off to her husband. 'We have to face it, Dick-Ed,' she sneered, 'the slide-on revolution is over, there are too many cheap copies out there, and if you don't make this sale, we're kaput, over, finito. Capiche? The NHS can't afford our prices and not enough Glaswegian amputees are in BUPA.'

Richard knew just how to play her. 'Your genius has brought us this f-far, dear, and I know you're not one to give up,' he said. 'All we need is the first m-mug, I mean subject, and the sky's the limit. Let me tell you about this Sam Prentiss fellah.'

As impressed as she may have been by the Prentiss millions, it was when she heard that Sam was an internal combustion nerd, fallen fowl of a rogue magneto, that her ears really began to prick. 'Tell me more about him?'

. . . She listened avidly as Richard described Sam's classic car collection and his penchant for animatronics. 'Okay,' she conceded, 'one last roll of the dice then. You work on the wife, and I'll have a go at the combustion nerd.'

Chapter Two:
Tam & Jeddah

In a Caledonian backwater almost 300 miles away, 'hair-of-the-dog' late punters and early-all-nighters crowded around the only functioning A T M for miles. It was two minutes to midnight, and they shuffled about impatiently in the pouring rain. They were all waiting for that twelve- o-clock chime to signal the cash machine was ready to give up its Friday bounty of Universal Credit' lager vouchers.

The mood was borderline joyous until the oncoming police car 'wheelied' into overspilled sludge from a nearby blocked gully, then it turned ugly. Sergeant Rab McKenzie made that same happy detour every Thursday night, but the torrential downpour came as an unexpected bonus: he grinned lecherously as tailenders cursed, danced and dodged the gutter spray.

Two young brothers at the front remained unmoved and smiling, it would take more than a dirty water dousing to upset Tam and Jeddah. What they liked to call their 'Joint Seekers allowance' was about to provide them with a cheap day-pass from abject depression to a state of selective amnesia. It had been that way since their mother run off with a wayward transvestite.

In an action replay of so many Fridays before, benefits at the ready, the brothers cut off the main road, ducked down a dark alleyway, through a crack in the galvanized fence, across a field of sodden fly-tipped rubble, to an abandoned warehouse.

A Colonel Bogey knock caused an orange face to appear in the tiny first floor triangle of glass, and a string-line key to be lowered slowly into reach.

William McGivern, AKA Bongo Bill, fooled no one with his phony Rasta persona, truth is, he had never been further east than Barlinnie prison. It was there he shared a cell with Hissing Sid. Sid taught him the finer wholesale cultivation points of the most potent weed in Clyde side. Bongo's Rasta illusion was the worst-kept secret in Springburn, but keeping it was a small price to pay for a trade price deal of Glasgow's uncut and finest homegrown.

The majority of committed tokers would have gladly exchanged their own mothers for one of his loaded five-skinners. (In fact, several had made that very offer).

Bongo met the brothers at the entrance, crouched and peered furtively left and then right, and then left again, before ushering them through a pitch-black maze of passages and makeshift stairs. They paused expectantly on the landing, until a signature whistle caused Sid to creak open the access door. 'Shhhhhhhhhsh, ish in here,' he hissed, and waved them inside.

From a granddads' second-hand Sunday suit to a stuffed Artic fox, Bongo's Aladdin's cave was adorned from floor to ceiling with unredeemed pot pledges. One wall completely lined with burglarized DVD players, interlinked, recording a donkey-rigged Wee Wullie classic from a master next to Bongo's chair, another, adorned with what looked like a shopwindow display of stolen car radios.

In direct contradiction to unconvincing dreadlocks, Trumpite-tan and gold laden neck, a pair of bean-pole milk bottle legs folded together below Bongo's baggy shorts as he fell back into a seating position.

Balanced precariously on a makeshift perch, a one-legged parrot squawked over and over nothing resembling 'everybody must get stoned,' until that is, you were actually stoned and it became syllabic perfect. Either side of the grow-room door behind him, two Rottweilers snarled and strained at their chains. Bongo proudly watched as they ravaged a cannabis laced drumstick to pulp, then treated each to a calming head pat, whereupon they whined and flopped passively, tongues out, chin first, onto the pot crumbed floor.

'Sorry about de mutts, mister Little and Large, can'nae be too careful, der are one or two other crim's in de area a hear, now what can I do you for?'

'Something that'll blow our Caledonian socks off, dye'ken?' replied Tam.

'I have de very thing, mah wee frens,' he replied in a curious mixture of Bridgeton and Bridgetown. A clap of the hands sent 'Hissing Sid' tottering to the drying room.

Bongo liked to tantalize and impress favoured customers with a grand tour of his operation, so he stood and released a clamp to open the vacuum-sealed door. 'Come marvel at Hissin's works.'

A sudden rush of pungency filled the squat and sent Tam balking. 'What the feck is that?'

'Ah,' Bongo breathed in the pervading bouquet like a wine connoisseur, 'de future, me fren. You can forget your Red Leb and your good old Rocky; forget your Paki Black and your Zero-Zero, dis home grown will blow de feet off wit de socks! Dis no ordinary bush, what we have here is de hybrid about to put a thousand Moroccan farmers on de dole.'

'What is it?'

'A combination of sativa and indica feminized seeds ....'

'It's reekin!'

'Yeah, me frens, I'm undecided whether to call it Jock Strap or Skunk. What yah tink?'

'I've never smelled a jock strap that mingin,' Jeddah said, and bit his tongue.

Tam's eyelids unfolded into his skull as he tried to mentally screenshot the patchwork of pipes, cables and tinfoil that lay before him: a series of hoses drip-drip-dripped from a reservoir of nutrient-fed water, beckoning cannabis chutes upward, banks of incandescent lighting hung from the low ceiling, a great snake of flexi steel ducting traversed each of the grow beds to expel the foul air into a disused abattoir next door.

The constant whine of air filtration and humming drone of transformers gave the impression of a factory running to capacity, which to some extent it was.

'Wow, some wee lecky bill?' Jeddah said.

Bongo pulled the window blackout blind to one side and pointed to a conduit of cable emerging from a far-off flickering streetlight. 'Courtesy de national grid. Less of de talk, more of de toke. Come sample de latest ting.'

. . . Half a day, five spliffs and a Marley's 'Ganga Gun' later they had exchanged the majority of their 'joint seekers' allowance for a generous bag of heads. On a cloud of semi-comatose euphoria, they made their way homeward. Pausing to rescue a headless tailors' dummy from a builders' skip, in their exalted state seemed wonderfully fortuitous. 'This fellah's worth a twenty-pound deal in anyone's money,' Tam said, and Jeddah nodded.

The intention was to return to Bongo's with their newfound bargaining chip the following day, then the party could begin all over again. . . How could they have possibly known that such a harmless plan would set in motion a string of coincidences that would change their lives forever?

Via the offy and a Pound Shop, linking the manikin between them, two brothers swaggered through a tumbleweed of chip paper and empty beer cans singing 'I ain't got nae body.'

In any other town, it might have turned at least the occasional head, let us not forget, this just happened to be Glasgow: one-time European city of culture, ten PM, benefits day, circa 2015.

Distant police sirens, an intruder alarm, and several cursing, singing drunks provided an appropriate backing track to their discordant tones as they skipped merrily beyond singing. . . 'I ain't got nae bo-ho-ody and nae body cares for . . .'

. . .A drunk, upended from the nearby Slash Inn, suddenly broke their rhythm and shouted 'ME!' He landed horizontally at their feet, crawled his way upright along the length of Jeddah's body and turned ashen faced to the dummy. 'You'd better get this wee man to hospital,' he laughed, 'he's in a worse state than I am!'

A familiar light went on inside Tam's head, he paused and tapped the side of his nose with an index finger. . . 'Wait, bro, I'm having a wee special moment here. Let's get this dummy fellah home.'

Before he could protest, Tam stuffed the price of a pint into the drunk's top pocket and propelled him back towards the bar with a well-aimed arse kick. 'You're not the only dummy here, son.'

By now, cannabinoids had hijacked Jeddah's reason; his lips refused to form a single coherent sentence, and he could only mimic interest. Crafting his tone to give the impression he was listening, a lazy 'Aye, bro,' was all he could manage before falling into mumbled deliberation for the rest of the journey home. In detached confusion, he watched Tam drag the dummy torso, neck first, to a legs akimbo sitting position in the vestibule. Glaring down at the inanimate heap, he thought it only fitting to rearrange the limbs at a more respectable angle before rummaging for the skins.

Tam nodded his approval. 'First things first, bro.' He doused the neck area of the manikin with liberal splurges of ketchup and jam and stood back to admire his work.

During a generous engorgement of pound shop munchies, Jeddah suddenly remembered the drunk's last remark. 'In an even worse state than me,' he repeated, loading their second joint of a brand-new day, and began to titter uncontrollably. What followed was an interminable cycle of munching, giggling, choking, and toking, only interrupted by the gratifying hiss that follows each tug of a Tennant's pull ring. . . Eventually they both collapsed smiling, deep into their own technicolour dreamworld. . .

. . .Thump! thump! Thump! Jeddah screwed his head back into the carpet. Thump! Thump!! Not regular like a normal morning-after jackhammer headache, but intermittent, then nothing, and then Thump! Opening the corner of one eye to note that daylight had returned, he buried his head deeper. (If he could have clamped his eyes tighter, he would have).

Tam reached out and threw an empty beer can at the television. Thump! Thump! Thump! Sliding the fur from his tongue with his top teeth, he slithered into the hallway to watch the landlord's silhouetted fist banging on the frosted front door glass. 'Look through the letterbox, loser. We've been a wee bit busy sorting out the last Rachman!' he shouted and crawled back into the living room to turn up the volume on the TV cartoon channel. 'That'll stop the wee eejit demanding money with menaces.'

Jeddah glanced out at the lobby. By now, the dummy had fallen to one side. The cocktail of ketchup and raspberry jam had trickled down its torso to a congealed pool on the lino. He stopped giggling long enough to laugh in earnest, falling somewhere between a failing starting motor and braying donkey. Jeddah's earnest laugh was decidedly unfunny.

'Get teh feck!' Tam cried and smothered his ears.

That alone might have been enough to deter even the most vehement landlord, but coupled with the sight that befell him in the lobby, it took this one off his feet, propelling him arse over heels to the concrete pavement below. He cowered in the gutter, poking frantically at his mobile phone.

'Hello, emergency; which service do you require?'

'B . . . body in the lobby, bloody head cut clean off. De-bloody-capi-fuckin-tated I tell you. C.c.c....claret everywhere.'

. . .It was several hours before the Rapid Response Unit arrived to cordon off the whole block. Traffic was halted, perimeters taped, flak-jacket automatons manned adjacent rooftops. On the doorstep threshold every one of a ten-man squad vying for the back of the pack.

Seasoned policeman Inspector James Crosbie pushed his way through. National Service had rescued him as a teenager from these same mean streets, and for that he'd always be grateful. With a finger to lips he made the shush sign and pummelled the door.

'Police,' he roared in his best, toughest voice. 'Open up!'

'Yeah, right, that's so original,' Tam laughed. 'Look through the letterbox, and see what happened to the last Rachman.'

A steel persuader swung, the door burst suddenly inward and showered the headless manikin with splintered wood.

Taking a greedy hit on his third joint of the new day. Tam pondered the stampeding footsteps and coughed thoughtfully. 'Maybe we should consider paying off some arrears,' he mused. Before he could even think about how, he found himself spread-legged and pinned facedown to the sticky carpet. 'Feck sake, I canae move.' he wheezed as he was being frisked a little too friskily from behind. 'You'll no find the rent up there, Jimmy.'

Jeddah blew out his cheeks. He turned from his steaming brother to suppress a simmering giggle, but the fleeting glimpse of a warrant card stole all humour from the predicament and flooded his mind with potential alibis. 'If it's about shoplifting, we were in the Sarry Head on the sherbet at the time. Aye, and when that smash and grab occurred, we were at home sleeping it off, d'yeh ken?'

'Let go of me, I'm needing a pish,' Tam growled, but what he really needed was to dash to stash his stash of hash. Just as he was about to make a bolt for the door, the nervous fracas in the hallway slowly gave way to a spate of infectious giggling.

Panic began to subside accordingly when Crosbie appeared in the living room doorway. He was holding the headless dummy aloft, shaking his head, wearing a rather inappropriate grin. Except for the leg by which the manikin was held, all its limbs had fallen free. 'Exhibit A, I think, let's all go home.'

Sergeant Rab McKenzie leered at his two stoned suspects who were juggling expressions somewhere between affronted and amused. 'Aren't we arresting these two no-marks?'

James Crosbie thrust the torso into his sergeant's waving hands. 'Aye, that'll be right, and what do you suggest we charge them with, having a laugh?'

'Ugh?'

'Do you want to be writing reports all night just to get two pot-heads a fine they'll not be paying? No, well.' . . . He paused for the logic to register and turned to his sergeant. 'Let's just file this one under 'things aren't always what they seem,' eh?'

The brothers struggled to keep their faces straight as McKenzie clenched his fists and kicked the torso back into the lobby. Now that Jeddah had risen to his full height, he didn't feel so confident 'Shut it, yeh pair of eejit cowboys,' was all he could manage.

'Yippee Kiyay!'

'And get some bloody air freshener, yeh mingers!'

The flat emptied almost as quickly as it had filled, and two unhappy tokers were left with a fine mess to clear.

Jeddah cradled a dismembered plastic limb into the living room. 'The wrong arm of the law,' he laughed and held it in a Nazi salute. 'Zieg Heil, McKenzie, yeah barm!'

Tam jumped to his feet and tapped his nose. 'Don't move, I'm having another wee special moment here!'

A vicious hangover had displaced last nights' high, and Jeddah froze in bewilderment. 'Aye, and I'm having a coronary. 'He remembered his brother's wee special 'why not photocopy a few fivers moment,' but they only had a black ink cartridge. That dastardly plan won them three months in Barlinnie for passing monochrome currency. Then there was the sheep rustling scam that ended chasing spring lambs the length of Sauchiehall Street. As usual, Jeddah thought his brother's wee special moment was probably doomed; as usual, in the absence of an idea of his own, he agreed.

Clinging onto the plastic limb, he stood as motionless as his uncertain legs could manage. 'Sometime today, eh, bro.'

Tam re-emerged from the bathroom carrying a whiteish towel. Folding it into a triangle to cradle the dummy limb, he looped the makeshift sling around Jeddah's neck. 'Bear with me, bro,' he said, and threaded the sleeve of a combat jacket onto his brother's left arm, leaving his right arm hidden in the lining. 'Think about it, Jed, with our friendly limb here, you can roam hand-free past every booze shelf in town. D'yeh no ken, it's a shoplifter's dream?' He smoothed out the coat tail and sat back to watch.

Jeddah looked into the cracked mirror. Blindsiding Tam, he meandered past the kitchen table; using his hidden hand, he deftly slipped a can of lager beneath the jacket and smiled. He couldn't have ignored the simple logic of his brother's latest 'wee special moment,' even if he wanted to, and he didn't, so he didn't.

'Never saw a bloody thing, let's hit the road,' Tam said.

. . . Given the spiralling rate of petty thievery, the backstreet retailers of Springburn learned the hard way that nothing of value should be kept within shoplifting reach. At first it didn't deter Tam and Jeddah, but after a fruitless morning flat-nosing minimarket toughened glass, they decided to try their hidden arm in the City Centre.

In retrospect, their timing could not have been worse. With Giro cheque deliveries running late on the run up to the September weekend, a light-fingered army of petty pilferers had been predictably busy before they even got there. As supermarket booze stocks plummeted, security guards were under severe pressure to get results.

Little could the errant brothers have known that on that very morning, an eager-to-impress probationary guard was tailing what he thought to be an easy pinch towards the liquor shelves. Jeddah in dark glasses, hobbling along, dummy arm in a sling, while a seemingly uncaring carer steered him toward the whiskey display.

A little too unsuspicious for my liking, the trainee thought as a large bottle of Jameson's dematerialized right before his eyes. When the same thing happened to a giant-sized Smirnoff, he felt he had no choice but to intercede. 'Excuse me,' he yelled in his sternest, toughest voice. 'Can I nae have a wee word?'

'Here's two, piss off!'

An abandoned trolley sent him careering into a nearby two-for-one display. The odd couple broke into a free-for-all gallop and leapfrogged the checkout barrier into the car park.

Scrambling uncertainly to his feet, the guard looked up, realizing he too was caught on camera, had little choice but to at least give token chase. Despite limping to slow his progress, being slightly less stoned than the two miscreants ahead, gave him an advantage he did not need or want, and he couldn't help but gain ground. 'Get a bloody move on, mah wee jobee's at stake here,' he shouted after them, but every time he paused for breath, so did they, until it was getting ridiculous!

Jeddah could run no more; he fell back against a wall, curled his upper lip, and bared his teeth at his pursuer. 'You dinnae really want to catch me, bigyin, do you?'

'Violence is the first resort of a hungover mind, dya ken?' added Tam.

'Well then, why don't you go back to the manager and tell him you were outnumbered, we'll even supply a corroborating fat lip?' Jeddah added.

The guard sighed in cowardly concert, took time to consider his position, cupped his chin, and grimaced. 'Make it a wee black eye and we've got a deal.'

Tam took the plastic arm from Jeddah's sling and removed one of the contraband bottles. 'I still think blubbering through a wee injured lip would be more convincing, draw more sympathy, if yeh like, but it's your decision. Either way, it's worth at least a month on the sick and a feasible criminal injuries claim. In fact, we should be charging you!' He broke the seal on the Jameson's. 'Have a wee dram and think about it.'

The guard hobbled gingerly between them. 'Aye, and maybe even my P45, if I'm lucky,' he winced, 'but I still prefer a shiner.' Taking a welcome slug, he clamped his eyes and screwed up his face to soak up the impact.

Tam shuffled his feet into a baseball stance and steadied himself. 'Your call,' he said. He was taking careful aim with the dummy arm when an encroaching police siren caused him to hesitate . . . As the noise grew louder, Jeddah grabbed the false limb from him and replaced it in the sling.

Leaving the guard's contorted face whispering, 'not too hard now, ken,' the errant brothers backed off and tiptoed to a back-peddling trot. Tam looked back to see the guard cursing and punching himself in the eye. 'Sorry, pal,' he whispered, 'I would have enjoyed that.'

A series of back alleys and a disused railway cutting later, they emerged onto the Cathcart Road. Before they had time to relax, a refracted blue flashing light sent them scampering into the nearest outlet, which just happened to be Annie's Treble A adult shop.

Years of watching customers and cash register at the same time had left the eponymous proprietor, permanently cross-eyed. She was talking to Tam and staring at Jeddah's cradled arm, bent now at an impossible angle across his torso. 'Oooh, that looks sore,' she said. 'Can I nae help yeh, lads?'

Tam dodged the great fiberglass penis that swung from a mock-gothic arch above. Pushing between a gender bent peruser and foot fetishist, he peered through the scratch marks on Annie's blacked-out window. The security guard was sat in the back of a hovering patrol car outside caressing a formidable shiner. 'Just browsing,' Tam said. In an oft practiced manoeuvre, he stepped to one side to block Annie's view of his brother, and absently plucked

23

a sample from the 'pixilated pussy' rack. 'What's the crack with these gizmos, misses?'

'Built in whisky aroma that one. You can USB it into your computer, program it to personal requirements,' replied Annie, grateful for the chance to show off.

'Personal requirements?'

'That particular model oscillates, vibrates, undulates, and sibilates; it can twist, pump, turn, or spin according to your vulvae needs; it comes as solar chargeable, mains adaptable, digital, and analogue. Not bad for eighteen pounds fifty, don't you think? Ten per cent discount if you show your dole card.'

'Uhm, have yeh no got anything smaller?'

Annie cupped her chin towards Tam's crotch. 'Aye, son, I just might have a wee shrunk-wrapped model.'

While this was happening, Jeddah was busy trying to force the square peg pack of DVDs into the round hole of a false limb. As it was a matter of honour not to leave a premises empty armed, he abandoned the 'Debbie Does Dallas' boxed-set in favour of an intriguing brown paper parcel sticking out from behind the counter.

Tam was strangely captivated by the range of synthetics spread out before him across the counter, as Annie continued . . . 'You can have ribbed, solar heated, and self-lubricating, in pink, black, and polka dot. We also stock a selection of deluxe models, but they're probably out of your price range.'

Tam looked over at Jeddah, signalling for more time. 'Don't judge a crook by his brother, hen. What else do they do?'

'Well, they come with a memory stick carrying all the latest software. We call it the hard-wear software, get it?'

Tam didn't get it, but he had to carry on with the diversion. 'Aye, is that all?'

By now Annie was visibly annoyed. 'Well, they can suck, blow, moan and groan, wobble, gobble, flagellate and oscillate. They come in different flavours too: apple, orange or spearmint. You can even wear one on your head like a furry hat while it whistles Dixie, now are you buying or writing a bloody thesis?'

The police had given up their search in favour of the nearest butty bar, and Jeddah was winking frantically from the doorway.

'A bit over-spec for me, missus,' Tam said reluctantly. 'Sumo Sue does all that and more, for a bottle of Buckfast, but thanks anyway.'

Annie rubbed at the bristles on her top lip and shouted after the two furtive figures sidling back into the street. 'Aye, so I hear. I was thinking of reporting her as an unlicensed street trader.'

Through a series of railway sidings and abandoned factories, they finally made their way back to the safety of their Springburn tenement. Tam loaded a joint and stopped a clenched fist millimetres from his chin. 'Have you ever tried to knock yourself out, Jed?'

'Only every Giro Day for the last five years, bro.' He slid the stolen package from the dummy arm and read the label. 'Paisley Pounder, let's have a shufty.' Pealing back the protective wrapper he exposed a huge pink phallus. 'WoW! Cast yeh wee peepers, bro, Sumo would kill for one of these.' Sighing, he laid it on the coffee table with a contrived reverence. The hairs on his neck froze rigid as he held his breath to cautiously disengage the Velcro scrotal seam. 'Oooooh.'

Beneath synthetic gonads a complex arrangement of micro-electronics rolled out on a malleable circuit board, and his own testicles retreated deep into his stomach. He slotted in the batteries from the TV remote, carefully stuffed back the workings and shook the phallus to his ear. . . . 'That went right through me, that.'

'Aye, you wish.'

'Let's see what it does.' Jeddah stroked the stolen sample like a pet snake and laid it gently back down. 'C'mon, baby, let's see what you've got?' When nothing happened, he crossed his legs and slammed a clenched hand into the latex testis. At that moment he was fighting off a terrifying flashback of his last encounter with Sumo Sue. 'Bugger doesn't work anyway.' Squeezing the stem contemptuously, he watched spellbound as a plausible gland-shaped papal head sprang from the synthetic foreskin. 'How weird is that? A wee bit too psychosomatic for me,' he cried and tossed it to his brother.

Tam immediately wedged it into the waistband of his tracksuit and began to dance around the room. 'Nothing could be finer than to be in her vagina in the mor- hor-hor-ning.'he sang and prodded the reverend head with his finger.

The monster suddenly developed a tic, the tic became a twitch, the twitch a tremor and the tremor a full-blown paroxysm. As it wriggled downward, 'we shall never surrender,' bleated from a hidden micro-transmitter. 'Get it off, get the wee fecker off!' Tam pulled down his pants to get at it, but by then the Paisley Pounder had engaged between his buttocks. 'Arghhh, get the fecker offa me!' he screamed hysterically. The coffee table overturned as he danced around the room trying to extricate himself from the animated penis: cans were trampled, cigarette papers and sweet wrappers took to the air like a rabble of butterflies.

Jeddah grasped the offending phallus in a double handed stranglehold, after a serious struggle, he finally managed to twist it free. Flinging it to the floor, he stamped out. Wee shaaalll Neeeeeeeeeverrrr Surendeeeer . . .'The sac split and the batteries pinged out across the room. . .

The end of such a long, eventful day called for one last king-sized five-skinner. Tam fell on his back pulling up his pants, Jeddah built up with the last of their pot. A coughing snigger turned to giggle until they laughed themselves to sleep. . .Another arid 'morning-after' found Tam yet again scouring the flat for any smokable or drinkable remnant from the night before. 'Arghh, we're in need of lager vouches, bro, my wee tongue's like a sunburnt scrotum.'

A subdued 'Aye,' and 'nae wacky-backy either' was all Jeddah could manage from beneath the upturned coffee table.

While waiting for the next 'wee special moment' to arrive, Tam retrieved the spent Paisley Pounder from a clutter of empty cans and brought it tentatively to eye height. 'We have the technology; we can rebuild you,' he said, staggering his way to the kitchen. Securing two pickled onions into the torn sack with super glue, he stretched the shaft upright, but whenever he let go, it flopped, bell-end first, back onto the tabletop.

Jeddah unstuck his head from the carpet. 'I know just how it feels, bro. Maybe we can take it back and claim some kind of refund?'

Tam wasn't overly keen on the idea, mainly because it wasn't his, but in the absence of anything better, he decided to run with it. 'Why not, but leave the patter to me, ken?'

. . . A blurry-eyed hour later found them back outside Annie's sex shop. Tam was trying to catch her eye from the doorway, but a conspicuous browser had her full attention.

Features hidden behind the upturned collar of a dirty white mac; he was feverously pawing an item from the S&M shelf. 'I've got my eye on you, vicar!' she hissed.

Tam rapped on the glass. 'Hello, Annie, 'remember me?'

It took her a moment to focus. 'Aye, I ken you.' She started to polish a bronze phallus from the back counter. 'You're the Baz that stole my 'Paisley Pounder,' you wanker.'

Assuming she was referring to him, the pseudo clergyman half turned and a rack of spiked leather spilled from beneath his vestments. He tried to make good his escape, but Jeddah stuck out a foot that sent him tumbling to the pavement.

Tam made the sign of the cross, picked up the dangling contraband, and kicked his reverend arse onto the road. 'That'll cost you a few Hail-Marys, father.'

A redundant seafarer hurriedly replaced a DVD he was in the process of shoplifting, and scooted head down from the shop.

'We're both professionals in our own way, Annie,' Tam began, 'you sell smut and rubber things and we're committed petty thieves. We've all got to make a living, haven't we, so how about a partial refund for this?' He pulled the revamped Paisley Pounder from under his coat and pointed it at the We buy second (for the want of a better word, 'hand' goods) sign.

Annie sighed and shook her head in wonder. 'Whilst I must admire your industry, gentlemen, your sense of integrity could do with a wee bit of fine tuning.' The bronze phallus she was holding had been converted into a tazer gun. A squeeze of the testicular trigger sent 1000 volts into Tam's groin. . . 'Now that's what happens to misguided people who steal from me,' she cried. 'Those that don't enjoy it, that is.'

'Arhhhhhhhhh!' Tam found himself, next to the pseudo vicar face down on the pavement outside, grabbing at his crotch until his pelvis shuddered to a painful halt. Jeddah pulled him upright, and they slowly began to backtrack.

'Just hold on a minute,' Annie shouted after them, 'I ken that you two wasters need a swally. As you can see, I'm short of a couple of amoral, peak-time bouncers and you two fit the bill. What say we do a deal?'

'We're no bouncers, misses.'

'Well, what are you then?'

Tam struggled for the right word, 'erm....'

'C'mon, it's not a trick question.'

'Perpetrators.' He smiled and added, 'We don't do menials.'

'I'll make it worth your while.'

'How much?'

'A gallon a shift.'

'When's peak time?'

'Mostly Saturdays after confession.'

Tam looked at Jeddah and nodded his head. 'What about perks, we have to keep our hand in, ken?'

'Okay,' Annie thought about it and conceded, '50% of anything you can make from blackmailing the regulars. How does that grab you?'

'And extracurricular theft, after all, we have our nefarious reputation to protect?'

'What you do to the customers on your own time is up to you, hen, but we do have certain standards here. You can try out the merchandise during working hours, but no free samples, definitely no more shoplifting. Do you ken?'

Tam hadn't felt so elated since his Christmas Giro cheque came early. 'Any chance of something in advance?'

Chapter Three:
A Cockup Too Far

They had had some success selling their 'PIGME' concept to the phallically challenged of Glasgow. 'It's all good and well in the castration capital of Europe, but the English accept penile diminution all too readily,' Janet said. 'Propaganda victims of all that 'size does nae matter nonsense.'

'There is some common ground, either side of the border a celibate's bank account can be accessed through their partner's neglected libido,' was Richard's starting point. 'Show them what they don't have to be missing,' he told himself. Grinning lecherously, he pulled off the main road to check his tackle,

This was to be a swan song for the trusty appendage that had served him so well in the past. Although revolutionary for its time, it was doomed to obsolescence once the Mark V hit the market. 'Don't let me down, Rampant!' he shouted.

Picked up by the over-sensitized sensor, a broody moorhen 'coo'd.' It triggered the programmed reaction that pranged his slide-on to forensic rigidity. There was nothing he could do but wait for the program to reset, so he pulled over and turned his thoughts to things over which he had more control.

In the rich persons' mansion across the copse the lights were low, he trained his night vision binoculars on the one dimly lit window, and waited before firing up the engine . . .

Looking out into the fading dusk, Judy's state of arousal was anything but artificial, the trees bending in the breeze took on beautiful phallic shapes, the autumn moon a great red testis in the sky.

Pouting and licking her lips, she closed her eyes. The gas guzzling groans of Richard's three-litre Jaguar became heavy breathing, the screech of brakes when it came to a halt, an oh so familiar climactic noise.

Her doorbell rang. She glanced up and grimaced at the sight of his doleful expression leering into her CCTV camera, pulled on her pants and straightened her skirt. When she opened the door Richard attempted an endearing wink, handed her another business card and translated the acronym. 'Prosthetic Institute of Genetically

Modified Engineering, PIGME for short. Nice to see you again, madam.'

A less endowed salesman might well have had the door immediately slammed in his face, but with her eyes transfixed crotch-ward all the way through his introductory pitch, she was helpless. 'Call me Judy, she said, 'and I can tell you're pleased to see me.'

'I'm Richard, but my friends call me Dick.'

Judy couldn't suppress an involuntary guttural groan, and had to clear her throat. 'How appropriate, why don't you come in,' she said, after pausing for affect added. . . 'Dick.' Lifting a brow, she licked her top lip sensuously, pulled him inside and tripped him onto the couch. 'Oops, sit down. . . Dick.' She smiled and shimmied her arse toward the kitchen. 'Tea, or would you like something more potent?'

'Mrs Prentiss.' Richard cusped his crotch to obstruct her view before he began. 'Are you aware of the moratorium on binary replacement values?'

She shook her head from the doorway and stared open-mouthed. 'Uh, uh.'

'Well let me explain. . . I am obliged you see, by their 'glandular preference' mandate to consult with the spouse before any prosthetic selection takes place.'

The light that bounced off his forehead transposed a practiced Valentino smirk into a feckless, oddball leer, but it did not deter Judy in the slightest. Entirely consumed by something much more interesting, she genuflected nearer as he prattled on. . .

'Apart from the money,' he said, and stopped her in her tracks

At the mention of her second favourite word, Judy tore her gaze from his midriff to pucker her lip-gloss in the mirror. 'Money you say?' The whistling kitchen kettle once again triggered Richard's penile kinesis. She spotted the change and fell back onto her knees. 'Tell me about the money.'

Reminding himself to mute the sonic receptors as soon as he got home, Richard dropped the clipboard protectively into his lap and crossed his legs. 'Are you familiar with the laws of bio ethics?'

'No, only the laws of nature, Dick, anyway, laws-shmaws.'

A terrifyingly lurid smile was breaking at the corners of her mouth, and Richard squeezed his thighs together. 'No, well, I am obliged by their mandate on penile enhancement to consult with you

30

before we offer a genetically modified prosthesis to your husband.'

'Genetically modified you say?'

Although the initial cost might sound prohibitive, the potential benefits are incalculable, even if the procedure might be a bit dangerous.'

'Only a bit?

'Yes, there is always that risk with ground breaking bespoke surgery.'

'Ground-breaking. Don't you mean ball-breaking?'

'Haven't heard that one before,' Richard said.

'Potential benefits you say, do tell?'

'Remember Christian Bernard?' Transplanting made a multi-millionaire out of him. I'd be prepared to share that wealth in exchange for your cooperation.'

'Wealth you say?' She reverted to her best seductive twinkle. 'Do call me Judy.'

'Yes, if you can persuade your husband to undergo damage replacement surgery, Judy, we can. . .'

. . . She interrupted him and raised her voice half an octave. 'Damaged you say? Blown out of the blinking exhaust, you can't get any more damaged than that now, can you?' she laughed. 'You're talking about transplanting, aren't you? Just where do you find a compatible boner doner, Dick?'

'Yes, well no, well yes, well no, not exactly. We will grow DNA cultures from his spleen to biological reproduce compatible penile nerve endings which we then implant into a biosynthetic appendage.'

'Biosyn. . ?

'Half natural and half. . .'

She finished for him . . .'Plastic?'

'Polycarbonate syncophane, to be precise.'

'Plastic just the same.'

'A revolutionary plastic though.'

'Ah,' she said, 'you're in my ballpark now. I've had some great fun with plastic: rectangular and cylindric.'

Richard sighed and continued. . . 'Using state-of-the-art silicone aggregates, we can replicate the features and skin-tones of the real thing.'

'I already have several just like that. What's the difference with yours?'

'I don't mean to embarrass you, madam, but . . .'

'Embarrass me, I dare you. In fact, I insist.'

Rising to the challenge, Richard stood and took a calming breath. 'A normal phallus contains some twenty odd thousand nerve receptors. We replicate only those that serve a practical and climactic advantage.'

'Climactic advantage, you say?'

'Yes, thus eliminating premature ejaculation, erectile and most other coital dysfunctions, thereby ensuring optimum satisfaction'

Judy was by now inexorably hooked. 'Optimum satisfaction, you say. Where do I sign?'

'Not so fast, madam. Spleen cultures, however, will not tell us what his missing appendage actually looked like, for that, we need a detailed description from you.'

'I've got bigger prawns in the freezer!'

Richard began to sympathize with her husband. That particularly hurtful comparison had been hurled in his direction on more than one occasion. His voice took on the detached tones of a salesman, he checked his tone and his crotch. 'If you had, perhaps, a home movie or a snapshot we could then craft a facsimile and implant it onto the residual site.'

'Snap shot? I don't have a fast-action camera. She leaned over to accentuate her cleavage and began to giggle infectiously. 'Is the operation called a strapadictomy?'

'Oh, very original, haven't heard that one before,' he quipped.

Judy made herself a drink and poured him a similarly large one on the rocks. 'Get that down your neck, big fellah, I'm going to take you somewhere you've never been.'

Richard slurped the whiskey down in one nervous gulp, without further preamble she straddled him. 'This should be interesting. Never mind my screaming, make me have some.'

Pinned by a denier leg, he found himself jostling with her serpent tongue for an ice cube. 'Oh, God,' he cried.

'He's not going to help yeh, big boy. Less of the talk and more of the action.' The sound of her piecing squeal swelled the Rampant Rod to bursting point, and she went for it. Although a connoisseur and veteran of every penile aerobic in the book, she had experienced nothing to equal this. Appreciating that undulating plonkers are hard enough to find, Judy was understandably sceptical, but this one didn't just undulate, it wobbled, shook, trembled and throbbed, in between it pulsed, reeled, twiddled and pranged.

Knowing it couldn't be kosher, under 'scrotal reconnaissance 69' she traced a prominent blue vein flex right up to the tell-tale join. Rather than spoil the moment with specifics, she decided to make the most of it. Flipping to her feet and then over the kitchen table she was going to wear him out the old-fashioned way.

. . . The personal demo Richard was about to perform had left a trail of chaffed unbelievers the length of the Clyde and beyond, (but not today.)

The limb twisting, ball breaking show began in fine style, but after an aerobic hour, it was he, left purring in a crumpled, frazzled heap, wondering if it had been a bonk too far; or if at last he had found a kindred match for his animatronic deviance?

Judy reappeared carrying two more glasses. 'Don't blame yourself, I've never been out bonked. I'm an ego-nymphomaniac, Richard darling, pure and simple, and your machine takes the element of chance out of it.'

It was only at that moment Richard realized she was on to his secret. 'You mean you really don't mind!' he exclaimed.

'Mind, no way. I love it.'

'What about your husband?'

Sam loves vintage cars and money, and that's what he's good at. Let's just enjoy what you're good at, for now anyway.' Purposefully dropping an ice cube onto her belly, her distinctive squeal sound-activate the kinetic penile-oscillator as she squirmed into the carpet.

Richard gasped. 'At last, I've found the perfect match: someone who appreciates me for what I'm not.'

'You nearly got away with it dear, but you must never try to fool me again. Remember, I wrote the bonking book.'

He blushed and nodded his head like a scolded child. 'I know I'm not very attractive, I need an edge that's all. Sorry.'

'Don't be. That machine of yours takes the element of chance from it, and more than makes up for a decidedly yucky appearance.'

Richard blushed again. 'I'm not made of wood, you know.'

'Ah, but your best bit is. You can come up and see me anytime, darling, as long as you bring it along.'

'You really don't mind?'

'Mind, I'm chuffed to the vulva. Now tell me everything.'

'About . . ?'

'Your range of course. What else?'

Judy's eyes lit up and her tongue hung out as Richard went on to describe the various models. 'From the famous Paisley Pounder to the ecumenically blacklisted Pope-Headed-Blurter, that we had to take off market, there were several near misses, each of which I had the honour of test piloting,' he bragged. Talking about black-listed, did I mention the Obama brahma?'

'No,' Judy said and squeezed her eyes shut.

'Then along came the bionic slide-on Rampant Rod, rendering all its predecessors obsolete. It became a victim of its own success. Within a month they were punting cut price copies at every Sunday boot market in the country.'

'Oh yeah?'

'Yeah, knocking them out door-to-door in Brighton they were. The latest batch is different though.' Raising his eyebrows, he spread his palms for emphasis. 'All the refinements you've just had the pleasure of, controlled from an encrypted memory chip, impossible to copy.'

Feeling spent and strangely free to bare his soul, he told her about his adolescent alopecia, and how in the summer his bald head glowed.   Her silence was misinterpreted as concern, and he continued. . . 'Everybody laughed, so I skipped university' for the British library, it was there I met Janet. After a celibate courtship we married on Magnus Pike's birthday, but it just didn't happen between us.'

Judy was stifling a yawn, pretending to listen at the same time. . . 'Oh, and why was that?'

'One wedding night glimpse of my homo erectus locked an irrational fear of all but synthetic stimuli into my new bride's psyche? You see, she had been nurtured on a diet of 'John Holmes and Ron Jeremy' videos, and expected all men to be similarly endowed.'

Judy subdued the snigger that was dancing in her larynx. 'Hm, what a wonderful thought. I can only empathize with her there, but do go on.'

By now Richard had forgotten all about the sale. He told Judy 'by nature, Janet was a very creative person, who once carved out a good living in designer bedroom aids.'

'Aha, a woman after my own part.'

'That first slide-on model had so many hits, eBay crashed for a month and the money came pouring in, but that greedy bitch stole the patent!'

'Oh, dear.'

'Yet if it wasn't for me.'. . . Richard fought off the impulse to weep and just about managed to pull himself together. 'Anyway, the slide-on market is saturated now, all that's left are transplants for penile amputees.'

'You mean Sam isn't the only one?'

'You're kidding! Since Duane Bobic's castration, demand has risen by more than 600%. In Glasgow it's almost a fashion statement, I tell you they're clipping them off like toenails up there. Problem is, they're all on pension credits.'

Richard began to sob and Janet leaned into him. 'Don't fret, darling, you're the best salesman I ever, erm, entertained.'

'I'm nothing but her glorified bloody messenger. If not for me she wouldn't know a decent todger if it jumped up and bit her.'

'Have you got any that do that?' Judy asked excitedly, then corrected herself, tutted, shook her head and told him he had a big problem. 'Sam's penis was probably the least used organ he owned,' she said, 'he probably doesn't even miss it. Why not wait for the next amputee?'

'Law of averages says he'll be a Glaswegian benefit scrounger,' Richard replied slipping into self-pity mode. 'Anyway, Janet said I'm history if I don't close this sale.'

Judy could muster no real sympathy for a man, just like her husband, whose biggest asset was an undersized penis. 'Why not divorce the bitch: non-consummation and all that?'

'She's pre-nup filthy rich, and she stole the patent. What about you, why don't you get rid of Sam?'

'Same reason, I suppose.'

Richard studied her. After revealing his all, she hadn't ridiculed him, (well not too much). Had he at last found someone to listen, was she the soulmate he'd always yearned for? 'Judy, do you think the we, that maybe, you and I could . . ?

'Let me tell you, honey, falsie or not, nobody has ever rung my bell like that before, well not twice on the bounce anyway.' She pouted again and her nostrils flared. 'Do you want to go for the hat-trick? From the beginning if you don't mind.' . . . An hour later he lay sobbing in the recovery position, and she was bouncing on the balls of her feet, laughing at his suggestion that they elope. 'Come back when you're a zillionaire,' she told him.

'I have to go,' he said glumly.

'And I have to . . . you know what. So, what about one for the road?'

'Will you at least think about what I said.'

'Only if you and your animation double down for a finale.'

'Done.'

'You most certainly will be,' she couldn't resist whispering as she reached for the one part of his anatomy not completely flaccid.

. . .

Sam's survival might have been a gross disappointment to Judy, but there was an upside: if he had died there'd be no salesman, no Rampant Rod. She uncurled her legs across the couch to replay the video on her ceiling mounted screen.

Richard couldn't sleep that night either, every time he closed his eyes, a recurring psychosis pinballed delusions between grandeur and abject poverty. He flicked on his remote, TV always helped him not to think.

Click: ITV. Chris Tarrant was asking if he wanted to be a millionaire.

'Too bloody right I do.'

Click: The History channel. an old clip of the Hiroshima bomb somehow reminded him that liquid nitro-glycerine has a pale, oily consistency similar to...?

Click: Sky Cinema screening the Double Indemnity movie.

Click: Bid TV: announced a Viagra auction. . . an intriguingly wonderful plan began to gestate in his devious filthy mind and he reached for the phone. 'I need to see you right away,' he whispered and immediately set off back down the motorway.

. . .'Let's get this right,' Judy said. 'You graft a new penis onto a man who never really used his old one, a man who wouldn't know an orgasm from a wet hiccup, you plant a bomb in it. Am I right so far?'

'Yup. Primed to go off at the point of climax.'

Then with a cocktail of Viagra and oxytocin you persuade your old never-had-it, iceberg wife to bonk him?'

'Yup.'

'They blow themselves up in the process, and we end up with all their dosh. Is that about it?'

'Yup.'

'Are you insane?'

'It's all about timing you see,' Richard explained excitedly, 'Janet rediscovers her libido with a man who hasn't got a penis. It's quite beautiful really. If you think about it, a latter-day eunuch is the only person a woman with a phallic phobia could ever fall for. The only one who wouldn't make her feel inadequate. Don't you get it?'

'Not really.'

'Anything's achievable if you're greedy enough. Just think about it!'

Judy closed her eyes; her head began to shake cynically. 'You're having a bloody laugh,' she said, but his silence told her he was in fact, deadly serious, so she thought about it . . .Toes began to tap, hips began to twitch, turned-down lip's curled upwards as she mentally played out the scene. 'Wham bam, thank you Sam,' she sniggered. 'Instead of cumming they went.'

'In a climactic blaze of glory, yup. All you need is a high explosive, an industrial dose of pheromone and an evil mind.'

'Count me in!' Judy said, pirouetting onto the couch, 'but first. . .'

. . . Richard reported back to Janet the very next day. 'Sam Prentiss really wasn't interested in the sexual aspects,' he said, 'but he is an engineer in spirit, a technical approach from you might just swing it.' He was surprised at how easily Janet succumbed to such dodgy logic, in fact, she didn't need much persuading at all.

You see, she'd also done her research, establishing Sam the man was everything Richard was not: he was tall, clever, had money and hair. On top of that, he had once written a paper proposing modern sexual obsession is a fallacy promoted by the porn industry. Its conclusion held that copulation was over hyped, overrated, for the most part over too quickly to deserve its lauded status.

Janet would concur with anything that seemed to exemplify her own frigidity, so the next morning, clutching her Rolls-Royce workshop manual, a box of Viagra laced Cornflakes, and the vague hope of affirmation, she took off for the exclusive one-bedroom private clinic.

. . . After switching the cereal with contaminated flakes on his breakfast tray, she found him completely engrossed in the Dow

Jones Index. Clearing her throat for attention in the doorway, all she could manage was a nervous 'hello.'

'Who the hell are you, and what do you want,' Sam snapped after a cursory glance.

'My name is Janet. and I have something I think might interest you,' she replied. 'What are you reading?'

'Sam chuckled at her clumsy inquiry. 'An article on titanium matrix composites actually. Not that it'll mean anything to you.'

'Really, is that the micro-mechanist approach?'

Sam took off his reading glasses and turned towards her. 'You're familiar with composite engineering?'

'Only contemporary fatigue theories. My field is really animatronics.'

Sam looked her up and down and smiled quizzically. With her sensible shoes, calloused hands and unisex haircut, she looked more like a coal-digger than a gold digger. 'Come and sit down,' he said. 'What can I do for you?'

She decided to get the awkward bit out of the way first. 'I designed the prosthesis that my husband left with you yesterday, actually.'

'Your husband?'

'For my sins.' She shook her head apologetically, hesitated at the pile of trade magazines on the visitors' chair, but Sam had already smoothed out an area for her on the edge of his bed. 'A mistake,' she explained, absently opening the workshop manual on the page headed Magneto Coil Assemblies. 'A bad mistake.'

'Well, we all make them, dear. Sit down.'

Not wanting to spoil the moment with specifics, somehow managing to avoid the very point of her visit, her conversation skirted between automotive engineering and bioethics. All this time Sam was devising a gentle response to the question she was avoiding. An indefinable something subdued his natural pragmatism, and he just couldn't bring himself to cut her short.

'Look, Janet,' he said softly when she eventually paused for breath, 'truth is, I'm really not that interested in what your husband was selling, whether or not it would be worth the effort, I mean.'

Janet nodded in resignation. As she stooped to pick up her book the line of a sensible woolly vest peeked from beneath her khaki shirt. 'Nothing ventured,' she said.

By now Sam was looking deeper into her eyes than anybody

had before. Unfamiliar lascivious fantasies peppered the chemistry the aphrodisiac had already evoked. Never before had he felt this way. He grabbed her free hand and closed his eyes. 'Wait! One question for you, Janet,' he said. 'Can a phantom penis get an erection?'

'Fascinating proposition,' she replied rubbing the bristles on her top lip. . . After several 'um's and ahs,' she frowned. 'If a phantom limb can itch, I don't see why not. Erroneous re-growth to nerve endings can confuse the sensory cortex. Yes, the answer is yes, Sam,' she panted, and they nearly kissed. . .

It was just as Richard had predicted, the perfect dovetailing: virginal ice maiden and mister impotent. For the next three weeks Janet hardly left his bedside. For years she had been postulating her theory that the penis is an anatomical mutation too far, at last she had found someone to listen. 'As an instrument of pleasure, it is inefficient and unreliable, for procreation, completely unnecessary! It screams out for synthetic replication, wouldn't you agree?'

'A highly functional replacement, in theory is not a bad idea,' Sam said, 'it would certainly cement our relationship.' He took the Rampant Rod slide-on from his bedside drawer and laid it on his lap. 'With a couple of modifications. . . Of course, it wouldn't be a question of mimicking nature, more of refining it.' By this time, he was unconsciously caressing the plastic between his fingertips. 'Tell me more about the prosthesis, what would power it?'

'The belt clip battery pack was okay for the niche market,' she explained. 'Just another pouch on a leather fetishists' belt, then there was the extra plutonium testicle. We called it the pawnbroker, but unless you were born with only one gooly, it was a bit obvious. Then we came up with this.' She took the prototype from her sample case, tweaked the synthetic foreskin and lay it on the pillow. 'The whole thing is a power pack.'

Sam picked it up and fondled it curiously. 'You mean?'

'Yes, we perfected a lithium dry cell membrane that lends itself to the erectile properties and skin tones of the real thing.'

'What about recharging?'

'Well, this one has a bio thermal cell that will top up from the subject's own body heat.'

Sam fought off the rare pang of regret flashing through his mind. 'There was a time I didn't need any help,' he lamented, and confided that as a young entrepreneur he boasted a healthy sexual appetite. 'Just as I was beginning to put it into honest practice, I became unfeasibly rich.'

'Well, what's wrong with that?'

'Nothing, you might say, but from that moment things began to change. All the available girls were so besotted with my bank balance, they dispensed with the formalities of foreplay and went straight for the vitals.'

'Don't tell me. You couldn't rise to the occasion?'

'Correct, it was all too contrived, too clinical, thus the seeds of chronic sexual aversion began to take root.'

'Snap! I suffer from a similar condition, but for completely different reasons, I must say. How did you handle it?'

Sam told her that after he became mega wealthy, the only way to keep the bevy of bimbos at bay was to marry the shallowest of them. 'And that's where Judy came in, she was the perfect partner: no pretence of love or affection, just simple avarice and a singularly one-track mind.'

'Oh, and what track was that? Let me guess. . .money? Snap again, I've got one a home just like that,' Janet said.

Sam lay back and stared into her languid eyes. She was yinging his yang in a way he thought he'd lost forever, and he needed to show her just how much that meant to him.

For consummating reasons, he readily volunteered to guinea pig the world's first fully functioning animatronic graft-on. (Only if she agreed to accommodate the field test.)

Janet wouldn't have had it any other way. She rushed back with the good news. 'Sam Prentiss would like the final say in the design, but basically he is up for it, what do you think?'

'I think it's a result, but who will he try it out on?'

Janet's expression froze, her averted eyes answered.

'No!' he cried. He almost overplayed the righteous indignation card. 'You are my wife after all.'

Janet even managed a contrived blush. 'A purely theoretical experiment, I think it's my duty as a scientist, but if you really don't want me to.'

'Well, I suppose in the interests of science. . .' Richard was inwardly grinning, but for the sake of appearance, pretended to be nobly wounded. It was all falling into place when reluctantly relented. 'I guess we all have to make sacrifices.'

. . . Five minutes later Janet left for the hospital baring glad tidings. This conveniently gifted Richard the run of the laboratory, time to re-jig the carbon testicular valve to accommodate liquid nitro. Now all he had to do was implant a tiny blasting cap beneath the synthetic gland mole. 'Easy Peezy,' he gloated and pranced back and forth across the floor holding his state-of-the-art phallic time bomb in the air. 'Ball bag squeezy!' Pulling on the synthetic membrane was a bit like re-skinning a sausage. He took some time and great care to smooth out the wrinkles before kissing it and replacing it back on Janet's pod.

'Who wants to be a millionaire, w-w-w-w-w-we d-do,' he sang merrily as he took off back along the motorway to leafy Cheshire.

Chapter Four:
Twitching Hormones

The operating theatre was equipped with the latest in wide-angle-zoom cameras and a flat screen monitor on every wall. Each unaware of the other's identity, liaising only through cyberspace, an eminent team had been recruited: an anaesthetist from America to ensure a continuous flow of nitrous oxide, a neurosurgeon from Japan in charge of carbon nano-electrodes, a famous Strasbourg consultant to oversee every stage of the operation.

They were each paid enough not to enquire where the actual location of the theatre was or the identity of the recipient. In fact, their only aspect of the patient was a three-hundred-watt florescent blow-up of shaven pubis and a one-inch penile stub.

While Janet was scrubbing up, Richard installed a Wi-Fi camera behind the recovery room ventilation grill. . .

The cyber anaesthetist established that perfect balance between pain and consciousness by remote control, his every instruction specific and concise as the assembled expertise combined to synchronized order.

Janet sliced through the penile scar tissue to expose erectile nerve endings, then carefully peeled back the epidermis layers to clear a site for the laparoscope. Sadiq vacuumed the surplus gore from the groin join and swabbed the sweat from Janet's brow as she lowered the prosthesis carefully into position. Only then did the robotic arms take over to mimic the surgeon's exact movements with forceps and clamps. One by one, each nerve fibre was grafted onto the built-in micro circuitry.

Richard and Judy sat in the pub across the road. Watching the action from a split screen monitor, they understood why it's said an operation is 'performed.' With Sam under the spotlights centre stage, the whole thing was pure theatre. Co-star Janet at his side in a state of absolute concentration, captivated as she spliced bio receptive long fibres onto the severed nerves. Once completed to her satisfaction, her attention strayed from the blow-up image of Sam's new tackle to monitor his heartbeat on the electrocardiograph.

Seven hours later the anaesthetist turned off the nitrous oxide by remote control and Janet lifted the oxygen mask from Sam's face.

He was breathing on his own now, her thoughts leapt to the future.

. . .The next morning in the recovery room, the patient shuddered himself awake, unstuck his eyelids to stare crotch-ward through a comatose haze.

Janet unplugged the monitoring system. Carefully unpicking the sterile dressing, she looked dreamily beyond the unseemly blotch of stitching and gore and licked her lips. Thankfully there was no sign of infection, but just to be on the safe side, she doused the area in spray-on antiseptic, (and Sam didn't even wince).

By refusing to leave the patient's bedside she had unwittingly played right into Richard's hands. Her three-week cycle of catnapping, dreaming and ogling, interspersed with the application of analgesic and anti-rejection hormones, gave him ample opportunity to plan his end game.

Week four; the patient was well enough to sit up in bed, he rasped his fingers against newly sprouting pubic stubble with measured relief. 'What do you think?'

Janet's eyes milked over with emotion. 'It's beautiful, quite beautiful. Not a wrinkle in sight,' she finally managed to gasp.

'How long then before we?'. . .

'At least another forty-eight hours I'm afraid, darling.' Sprinkling on the rapid cell-growth hormone, she closed her eyes to drink in the erogenous epiphany that swept through her lower body. 'Then, my darling. . .'

During Sam's convalescence she had been uncommonly civil to Richard. Why not, she was feeling uncommonly happy now that her cupid's bow pinged so tantalizingly? What she was actually experiencing wasn't lust, it was a simple metabolic reaction to the aerosol that sprayed so liberally around the room through a doctored AC unit. How could she know that for the last month her twitching hormones had been primed with pheromone impregnated air?'

. . . Two anxious days later, Richard peered into his laptop over a dinner-hour shandy. 'It's happening. This is it!' he cried and Judy sprang to his side. Somehow befitting the occasion, ventilation grill slats had chopped the Wi Fi image into

segments. It drew them even closer to the screen to watch Sam, stretched and flexing wearing nothing but a licentious grin.

Curly sutures lay discarded on the bedsheet alongside clipped pubis; the air filled with the strains of Barry White. 'Girl all I know

43

is every time you're here I feel the change, something moves, I scream your name!'

Janet emerged from behind the vanity screen, puckering, scrubbed up and flighty.

Richard, who had rarely seen her without signature regulation overalls and green wellies, sighed and shook his head as she tottered towards her doom. 'Oh, my Lord,' he shouted, 'I think I'm going to be sick! So, this is it, ground zero, it's your own bloody fault!'

Judy jumped from her barstool just as the penile receptors kicked in. The cyborg prosthetic rose like a great pink obelisk and took her breath away. 'Oh my God, just look at that wonderful thing. What a bloody job you've done.'

Richard felt a pang of regret now the end was nigh, (only a little pang.) The site of his wife's ample buttocks quivering in the foreground as she gravitated towards her destiny was just too much for him. 'I just can't bear to look,' he said.

'You're far too modest, you're a bloody genius,' Judy whispered. With her attention locked onto the object of Janet's bliss, her own limbs began to buckle in concert. That old irresistible urge took hold, she planted a wet kiss on Richard's cheek. 'C'mon, big boy, it's only right.' Slamming down the lid of the laptop, she let out a well-practiced activating squeal. 'I've never done it in a public toilet.' She grabbed for his crotch to check that his rod had reacted accordingly. 'Well not lately anyway.'

Absently polishing a glass, the young barman looked up at the ceiling as his only two customers grappled into the anti-space.

. . . When they reappeared twenty minutes later, one was bandy legged, starry-eyed, wobbling, Judy was once again bouncing on the balls of her feet like a prize-fighter.

Just as Richard was about to reboot his laptop, the earth literarily did move. In an ear-piercing crash, the clinic windows opposite disintegrated to a swirling grey mist. Bar room tables trembled, glassware rattled, a feed snapped from the lager pump showering the room in a spume of white froth. The barman immediately raced to the cellar to cut off supply. . .He returned to an aerated weightless snowstorm that peppered the elated duo, stomping knee deep around an upturned table.

Claxton's and fire bells rang out in the background, the blackened, charred annex across the street was sealed off.

. . . When the fire brigade reopened the road and declared the building safe, Richard and Judy were skipping their way, hand in hand back to the car park.

. . .They returned to the factory to find Sadiq sat at his workbench staring at the laboratory telephone. Richard tapped him on the shoulder, 'I've got some bad news for you, old pal, Janet's dead. By the way where's that demijohn I left in the fridge?'

'Dead, what do you mean, dead?'

'Jam-crackered, deceased, finished with engines, expired, departed, cadaverous, blown to smithereens, son. Now where is that bloody demijohn?'

'I used it up on that Glasgow consignment,' Sadiq replied. 'Dead, you say, what about my Christmas bonus?' He could have been forgiven for topping up the last of the slide-ons with the clear, oily liquid he found in the refrigerator, but to mistake the blasting caps for a new batch of penile sensors, even for him, was a cockup too far.

Fighting off the panic rising from the pit of his stomach, Richard's eyes flashed around the room. 'I'll double your bloody bonus, Sadiq, if you'll just tell me, you haven't bloody posted them off?'

'First class, sir. With you spending so much time away, I took the liberty.' As though expecting a military cross, Sadiq pushed out his chest.

Richard kicked hm in the nuts and ran around in circles mumbling in a strange language. 'OhhellGodnobloodyshitnoahhhh!'

Attributing this violent behaviour to some kind of displaced grief. 'Don't hold it in, sir,' Sadiq said from his foetal position on the floor. 'Take it out on me if you want to.'

When Richard had finished taking it out on Sadiq, he bowed his head and fell to his knees weeping uncontrollably onto his shoulder.

. . .That was still the position when Judy returned from her solicitors the following day with even more bad news. 'I warned you about using too much nitro, now there's nothing left of the bodies. That means technically, they're only 'missing persons' who can't be pronounced dead till the coroner says so!'

'Where does that leave us?'

'In the proverbial.'

45

'But I'm skint!'

'So am I,' Judy said, 'but thankfully, the executor has agreed to release fifty K into our respective bank accounts to be going on with.'

Richard was too awash with self-pity to listen. 'Oh, my God,' he cried. 'You won't believe what this dimwit's done.'

Judy showed no sign of panic. 'Stop blubbering, you wimp,' she said calmly. 'Let's think this through! The bodies must have disintegrated in the inferno, so all we have to do is wait until the accidental death verdict, then we'll be rolling in it. Now what are you whinnying about?'

'A bloody phallic timebomb halfway up the M6, that's what!'

He told her what had happened and went on to blame Sadiq, but Judy cut him short, 'and you leaving half a pint of nitro glycerine next to the skimmed milk had nothing to do with it I suppose?'

'There is that, of course, I just didn't think.'

'That's your problem, Dick-Ed, you just don't! If any one of those nobs go off, we're both up shit creek, so turn off the waterworks and get your coat.'

. . .Throughout most of the five-hour drive north, Richard sat in strained silence. He was wondering how greed could turn to rancour so abruptly. It was Judy that did most of the talking, but not one word of consolation. On a few occasions she referred to him as a stupid, brainless twerp, but what really hurt was the way she kept repeating 'no wonder your ex-wife called you Dick-Ed.'

He cursed himself for ever confiding in her. 'You're so bloody superficial, Judy,' was the best he could do.

'Yes, but only on the outside,' were the last words between them until they arrived at Annie's Treble A private shop.

A dreary lateral sleet spat into their faces as they climbed from the car. It was grey, wet, windy, dank, it was Glasgow. Even though it was pissing down, lunchtime perv business was surprisingly brisk.

The entrance was flanked by Tam and Jeddah, who saw them as just another pair of yuppy pervs squeezing their way through a sea of rubber and white macs' to the counter.

Judy felt several superfluous pelvic thrusts on the way, but she didn't mind.

(No longer donkey rigged) Wee Wullie Riley, barged past

46

clutching his plain wrapper for dear life. 'Really!' Richard cried.

The erstwhile big man was much too excited with his acquisition to apologise. 'No, not really, Riley,' he said.

Annie was consolidating her squint between the till and the mooching mackintosh brigade when Richard introduced himself as the C E O of 'PIGME.' Attempting a placating smile, he handed her one of his ridiculous cards. 'There seems to have been a mistake, madam. That last batch we sent you . . .'

'I know, don't tell me, the cheque could'nea have bounced 'cos I've no sent it yet.' She looked over his shoulder at Judy who was holding small print up to an overhead red light. 'Batteries not included with that model, hen, but it's mains rechargeable. One of our best sellers, that!'

Illuminated notices were arranged alphabetically on an overhead digital screen and Judy concentrated on the A's:

'Able bodied seaman in need of splicing. . .Aberdeen Angus requires horn,' right down to; 'Arse bandit dreaming of large, special friend,' finally, 'Aztec looking for sun god to worship.' She mused admiringly at the giant fiberglass phallus (resplendent with pubes,) swinging invitingly towards the sampling rooms, and wondered how she had resisted such places in Cheshire. Genitalia screamed from sealed glossies that packed the shelves and sucked the moisture from her mouth. Samples filled every spare inch of display space; they came in black, pink, polka dot and translucent: crown heads, ball heads, revolving heads, expanding heads, long heads, short heads, angry heads, double heads, Pope and Paisley heads, but not one single Rampant Rod in sight.

'It's not about the batteries or cheque,' Richard said. 'It's about that last consignment.' Now that he had Annie's attention he continued: 'well it seems that some fool mixed up a prototype, and there's a problem you see. Anyway, just to be on the safe side, we are recalling the whole batch.' He tried to sound nonchalant, but his tone had risen to a conspicuous squeak, and he cleared his throat and coughed. 'Just a quality control thing,' he said. Assuring her there was nothing to worry about, he unzipped the sample bag.

Annie smiled. 'Isn't that a lovely sound?'

'What?'

'The zip, of course.'

Richard tried to clear the anxiety from his voice and carried on. 'If you can let me have the units you received in the post this morning, we'll happily replace them, and throw in six extra models for your trouble . . . 'Oh, and you can forget about the cheque.'

'Too late, Wee Wullie Riley, the big old baz that nearly knocked you on your arse on the way in, he just bought the last one.' Annie leered towards Judy who was holding up another sample. 'Self-lubricating, hen, built-in rotary tickalator, one of our best sellers that!'

'Do you keep a record of the buyers, Annie?' Richard pleaded hopefully.

'Nothing like that, pet. We're sworn to secrecy, highly confidential, it's why we call it a 'private' shop.'

'You mean you keep no records at all?'

'Am I speaking a different language?'

'But you must have something, madam!'

Not having been referred to as 'madam' since she was an actual 'madam.' Annie wasn't sure how to react, so she half puckered toward the mirror. 'Would you like the 'confessional box analogy' or the 'pervomiter confidential' card, either way I'm shtum,' she said before adding, 'I don't like you, hen, so shall we cut the piffle. What's it worth?'

Richard tried to frown and still look hurt, but couldn't quite manage it so he played the sympathy card and looked up with hound dog eyes. 'It's really important,' he said, 'I could lose my job.'

'Awe, hen,' Annie mocked. 'I'd hate to be responsible for that, and you coming all this way just to put things right.' She leaned down onto the counter and returned his wounded leer. 'I can be nobbled, so bribe away!'

'I'll tell you what, as well as forgetting about your invoice, you can have the whole sample bag. How's that, madam?'

Annie leaned across and grasped his hand. 'The way I see it, hen, is like this: if it's important enough for you to travel all the way up from South Fork to castration city, then it's worth a bit more than a bag full of plastic do dahs, and the name's Annie by the way, my 'madame' days are long over!'

Judy had gotten as far as 'Water sports and Wazamatoonies' before finally tearing herself from the digital notice board. 'A thousand pound for your trouble, another for the addresses, tax-free, Annie,' and we'll throw in the sample bag for this.' She was holding up a strange contraption of leather, chains manacles and studs. 'Do we have a deal?' she shouted across the room.

'That's one of our best sellers: automatic pre-molding mechanism, self-flagellating, batteries included! We've got a deal!' She traced her finger across the page. 'Rampant Rods, is it? What's wrong with the bloody things anyway,' she laughed, 'do they explode or something?'

Annie missed Richard's frozen response, she was too busy copying out the list, that she handed to Judy in exchange for the cash.

Their car pulled from the nearside curb and a silver Kawasaki motor bike spluttered to a halt in its place. Jeddah and Tam nodded across the threshold, they watched Gypsy leapfrog backwards to effortlessly ease the great machine onto its stand.

A head shrugged from the black visored helmet, a cascade of blue/black curls purposefully released as she pushed out her bosom and strode between them. 'You must be the new bouncers.'

Tam tore his gaze from her heaving breasts. 'There's bouncers and there's bouncers, missus. Are you buying or selling, I've just got to know?'

'Firstly, I'm more of a mistress than a missus, secondly, I never sell, I give, and I live here.' Leather fetishists grabbed at their buttocks. She pushed her way between them, jigged her shoulders and her boobs followed suit. 'Like you said,' she winked, 'there's bouncers and there's bouncers.' Clicking her heels, she ducked under the swinging phallus and made her way to the back stairs.

Chapter Five:
Size Doesnae Marra

Since the balls-up Richard and Judy had hardly exchanged a word. He was totally preoccupied with self-preservation and hadn't laid a rod on her. Not one to go without, Judy stripped naked, spread Annie's list out on the bedside table of a posh Kelvinside hotel room and ran her finger down the page:

'Angus McKay. Doorman: The Barras.

Wullie Riley; (Wee). 52 Springburn Heights.

Procurator Fiscal. C/O Municipal buildings.

Wang. Lead singer, Scallywag Boyzband.

'Now which one of these buggers is wearing our 'go straight to jail' phallic time bomb? We'll have to go through then one by one. Do you fancy a bonk first?' she shouted, but Richard had his mind on other things. 'What's wrong, cat got your dong?' When he didn't reply Judy hurriedly pulled on her leathers and left in search of the salacious relief her metabolism demanded.

She really had no choice, but Richard did, he decided to stay in the room and plot her downfall. Knowing full well what Judy required before she could eat, sleep, think or listen coherently. Mindful that any credible plan would have to include full-on climactic satisfaction he plugged in the portable charger, set the control to 'boost' and ordered room-service.

. . .They had raved about the 'Barras' in Judy's 'Grab-a-Granny' guide. It ranked a close second to Liverpool's coincidently named, (I'm not making it up,) 'Grafton Ballrooms,' in the 'copping off' index. Judy gave her instructions to the taxi driver with some apprehension. 'Are there plenty of single people there?' she asked, 'much social interaction, would you say?'

'The wee Elephant Man would'nae have a problem getting his leg over in there, if that's what you're askin', he quipped, and added, 'mind you, poor old Merrick was better looking than some of the punters.' Holding out his hand for the fare, he looked her up and down and smiled. 'Are you sure you've got the right place, hen?'

'Show us yeh tits, missus,' a lurking urchin asked as he was counting out the change, and Judy felt eerily at home.

'Yes,' she replied, 'this is the place alright.'

First on her list was consummate bluff, Angus McKay. Here was a man, at any given time with a dozen youth reclaimant single mums on the sniff, none of whom could ever penetrate his Kalvin Cline skiddies. Remaining so aloof in the face of such unbridled adoration was the very substance of his mystique.

Angus fought burgeoning mid-life-crisis with a cosmetic enhancement that would be envied in Beverley Hills. From the neck up: chin sculpture, collagen lips, capped teeth and baggage tazer'd from beneath his eyes. From the neck down: sculptured pumped up pecs and lipo-sucked beer belly.

Just like Richard however, his Achilles heel was the embarrassingly diminutive todger nature had so cruelly bequeathed.

Now that final artificial piece of his gigolo jigsaw, the ultimate slide-on for which he'd sacrificed six month's wages and tips, was his at last!

'You just cannae' go against nature!' he was warned by his GP when he complained about his measly endowment.

'D'nae give me that size doesn'ae matter shite, doc,' Angus had replied. 'You're talkin' to a man who went through four years of borstal training without taking a bloody communal shower!'

Carefully unwrapping his newly purchased acquisition, he carried it to his bathroom like a precious rose, and read the instructions over and over before soaking it in tepid water until it became malleable. Grinning like a lecherous libertine, he spread open the gossamer gonad cusp, girded himself and took careful aim!

At the very point of installation his shrunken enemy receded like a terrapin's head under threat, and there wasn't enough to slide his slide on onto. 'Oh shite!' he shrieked. An internal oscillator picked up the sound, the Rampant Rod reanimated accordingly and sprang from his grip. Diving to the floor to deactivate it, he rolled onto his back and coaxed his metabolism to semi-arousal by skimming through a collection of 'page threes.' This time his new slide-on slid on like a made-to-measure 'Matey.' There it would remain, capillary attraction and malleable cusp assuring adherence.

Tentatively reaching with his fingertip to the activation mole on the gland head, he was immediately overwhelmed. . .Just as the blurb had promised, his new acquisition stood to attention like a sentry, proud and magnificent to his touch.

Angus had never felt such exaltation, such majesty. No more

would he carry the rolled-up, hip-pocket hankie to fool admirers. For the short time that was left of his bereft existence, he would not pass a reflective shop window without thrusting out in self-adulation.

He was in the process of ejecting a 'grab-granny-night' inebriate when Judy caught his attention. Making 'moo-eyes' from the foyer and running her false nails from nipple to knee, she compelled him to inertia. Straightening his pants, he watched her sensuous waddle to the dancefloor to flirt her body through an eclectic contradiction of golden oldies and house-music. Her gyrations and pouting attracted pelvic thrusts from every granny grabbing chancer in the place.

Sumo Sue wasn't the only ungrabbed granny to feel threatened by this lewd intruder, she was the first to vocalize. Secretly willing her to revert to type and break the bones of the contrasting beauty that made them look so sexless, on-looking ungrabbed grannies twirled in their spandex and sneered.

'Keep offa mah man,' Sue grunted, 'or I'll rip yeh wee heed off!'

'Who's your man?' Judy shouted over the neon din, and the big girl scanned the room hopefully.

When a dozen grabbers turned away simultaneously in denial. Judy leered through the smoke and waddled toward her target. 'Don't worry, I'm spoken for.'

They came together like Nureyev and Fontaine. Tongue hanging chancers ogled from strobe-lit corners as Angus's medallion swung in perfect time to Judy's bouncing mammaries. She responded with a pelvic frenzy that sent hemline to thong height and several voyeurs rushing to the toilets.

Coolly padding his brow, Angus casually dropped a free hand to her arse. 'Dinnae' fight it, babe,' he said, delighted to feel no panty line.

'I'm here for the taking,' she said. 'Make me have some!'

After twenty minutes of implausible 'Dirty Dancing', Angus cut straight to his Glasgow chat up line. 'What finer way to end a perfect evening,' he gasped with hopeful candour, 'than with a good old fashioned sh . . .'

The speed of Judy's response threw him. She grasped his vitals before he could finish, led him bulge-first to the darkest corner, threw him against the condom machine and reached for his zip. 'My thoughts precisely.'

If Angus so wanted his maiden slide-on outing to be special, he should have tried out the Rod's emergency braking system under field conditions. 'Take it easy, lass, slow down, will you?' he begged. 'Let's go back to my ken, ken, ken Oh Oh Oh Oh Oh f f f f flippin heck!'

Not one to be outdone, with the touch of a safe-cracker, Judy gently tweaked the erectile mole. It sprang the Rampant Rod upward, and out popped the blasting cap like a wine cork. This had the effect of dislodging the microchip and shrivelled the Rod to a chipolata frazzle in less than one second.

Angus stared down in blind anguish. In a state of post-orgasmic lethargy, he scooped up the blasting cap mole from the floor and rolled it up in his trusty hankie. A blob of super-glue will make sure it does'nae happen again, he thought.

Judy stood up and sighed wearily. 'I think you've got a puncture or something,' she said matter-of-factly, and left him pulling at his trousers. 'Oh well, one down three to go.'

Had she known she had inadvertently deactivated the phallic time bomb, she'd have disposed of the blasting cap and that might have been the end of it, but she hadn't, she didn't, (and it wasn't!)

Unlike Angus, rather than cursed by nature, the next man on Judy's list was one time eminently blessed, and as unselfish with his Cumberland proportions as physiologically possible. Be it wannabe porn stars, one-night-standers or a selection from his formidable single-mum and grabbable granny stable, Wee (donkey rigged) Wullie Riley seldom, if ever, went without. But all good thing etc .
. .

On what he come to know as the night of the short knives, Wee Wullie was suddenly (donkey-rigged) no more. As he lay in a post-coital Jameson's' stupor, his long suffering wifey put pay to his philandering once and for all. In a cold rush of Bobbic driven gusto, she vented twenty years of anguish on that wondrous whopper. Wullie became a mere statistic. Yet another castrated stereotypical victim for which his city was rightly renowned.

On reflection, his neglected wifey would have preferred a smoother, more efficient finish than the serrated agony of a bread knife. Be that as it may, the bereft woman did not desist until her Lothario's great German helmet had taken the shortest route to the car park of Springburn Heights.

'Now that's what I call downsizing!' she said as it was squashed to a purple pancake beneath an early morning deals-on-wheels. In the background poor Wullie was swearing fidelity on the ghost of John Holmes.

On realizing his best friend was no longer fit for purpose, resentment rapidly gave way to self-preservation; all fantasies of revenge were banished by an overriding foreboding of what she might cut off next. The only thing he had left was a gruff voice, which Wullie was determined to preserve at any cost.

'I'll find a way of making it up to you,' he growled, but in the absence of a functioning todger, failed to see how? It was a big ask, but he was determined.

When his GP confirmed the NHS would refuse to fund a transplant, Wullie found himself scouring the sex shops for the next best thing. . . . . Three days later he set his newly acquired Rampant Rod to overdrive, and warned the neglected wifey to brace herself.

They never heard Judy at the front door, but she could hear them right enough; (wild rhinos would have made a less coital racket.)

Wullie had serviced bilious barmaids, polemic pole-dancers, even a blasphemous nun who chanted the Lord's Prayer backwards while they were doing it. He'd had squealers, squeakers, groaners and screechers: yelpers, woofers and tweeters, but nothing to compare with this.

Ten years bereft of orgasmic release transposed the wifey's Glasgow drawl into a strange braying yodel. A decade of climactic frustration culminated in an eerie, ghostly howl that would have put a herd of constipated wildebeests to shame.

Judy cowered into the corner of the lift, assumed the position ahead of the explosion that didn't happen, and listened to the cacophony from inside. 'Yahoo! Whahowee! Oweee eehaooo, wow, wow,

woooooooooeeeeeeeeeeeeeeeh!
Ooooooooooooooohaaaaaaaaah!

Although Wullie's newly purchased Rampant Rod was benign, in a final climactic irony, his wifey liked the dizzying heights so much she kept him there until his heart gave out.

. . . At the wake his fans would remark at how well he looked, 'considering?' To which the wifey would lament, patting her cylindrical shoulder-bag; 'Aye, it was how the old whoremaster would have liked to go.'

'In his sleep?'

'Not exactly.'

Angus purchased the whole shelf of adhesives from a twenty-four-hour garage on the other side of town. With his Rampant Rod tucked safely under the passenger seat, he parked up for a fish supper. After swatting off a couple of apprentice muggers under the Tobago Street arch, he checked his quiff in the chip shop window and blew a sloppy kiss through the steamy glass. 'Make mine a cod, Sue,' he winked, easy on the vinegar, I'm spicy enough.' Two young girls tittered as he passed. 'Dinnae' fret, babes,' he said, 'there's plenty to go roond,' he told them.

Ignoring the 'feck off granddad' jibe, he went straight for the bulbous girl who'd been trying to chalk him up for years. Sumo Sue swept the hungry faces in the queue for objections and stuffed the cheaper haddock into his hands. 'If you're bluffing again, McKay?'

Angus led the way to the car park describing the various acrobatics he had in store. Unfortunately, an unfussy joyrider had gotten there first, all that was left of his trusty Allegro was an oil slick and a flattened beer can. 'I'll be back,' he shouted and jogged desperately away holding onto his lacquered follicles.

. . .To perform a handbrake turn would require a functioning handbrake, something the Allegro hadn't had since the sixties, so the joyrider had to make do zig zagging in vain for police pursuit. Angus had left a sign in the windscreen saying there was nothing worth stealing inside, but it didn't stop the young lad from rummaging under the seat for anything not screwed down. His tiny fingers circled the hidden phallus, 'Feck me!' he cried, unaware that he'd just uttered one of the trigger words. The Rod sprang up like a charmed cobra and his limbs recoiled in fright. The car jerked to a halt at a busy junction and set him on an Olympian dash for his young life.

. . . Angus was at the wrong end of a long queue of drunken night people at Peel Street Police Station. Rubbing his ears and shaking his head, he studied the motley line at the sergeant's desk. The combined incoherence of their ancient Coptic cackle was incomprehensible to the un-pissed, which meant that he was in for a long wait. As a Barras door person he was more than familiar with this phenomenon, so he left them babbling and nodded his way to the front. 'Scuse me, officer,' he smiled, 'but as I seem to be the only one here from the planet earth, could I no report a crime?'

The policeman returned his fawning smile, curled it towards a sneer under his crooked glasses. 'Sobriety, son, doesnae' get you special privileges here, so take your wee turn behind the aliens.'

A drunk Angus had earlier head-butted in the Barras was now puking over his new shoes, and the sergeant began to chuckle. 'Ma hymen's gone!' an old crone screamed at his incident book when her time came. 'Ma wee hymen's gone!'

'Well, it's no been handed in here, missus,' the policeman replied without looking up. His phone rang and the waiting room reverted to incomprehensible mayhem. 'Anyone here missing a clapped out Allegro?' he roared over the din.

Angus tugged his foot from a sticky combination of Tenants and haggis and thought better of taking offence. 'Aye, that'll be me.'

'Away to the compound and see if there's any damage. 'With any luck it'll be a write-off.'

Unfortunately for Angus, it wasn't, but disappointment was tempered with the discovery of his slide-on still wriggling away in the footwell.

Sumo Sue couldn't believe her good fortune. Having unsuccessfully scoured the mean streets for near-sighted stragglers, much to her delight, here was Angus inviting her for a ride through that same fish shop glass. 'I have tae'know,' she babbled, 'It's not that I'm ungrateful, but why are yeh 'nae' on the vinegars with wee snobby spice? I'm no complaining mind you but I just have tae' know. Every loser in the Barras has KB'd me under the 'fat bastard act', and now the resident stud wants ma wee coogy.

She began to drool and stutter at the same time, Angus told her not to wonder and forced himself to almost plant a kiss just to shut her up. 'Who knows the wanton ways of a standing todger?' he blubbered into her shoulder fat. It was cheesy but it did the trick and had her reaching for his zipper where they stood. 'Wait just a wee minute, hen, I'm nae' sure the cultural city is ready for this,' he panted. 'Let's go for a wee spin.'

For reassurance he clasped the Rampant Rod firmly beneath the seat and adjusted his rear-view mirror, so he wouldn't have to look at Sumo's jabbering features. Her high-pitched wincing spurred the Rod to life, and he began to relax. With each sideways glance her body took on less bulbous lines, and by the time they left the city lights she was almost un-repulsive. Sumo undermined that particular allusion with the announcement that she was 'needing a slash.'

Trying desperately not to hear the Buckfast torrent on his rear wheel, he slid on the slide-on, the gonad cusp cusped, and everything seemed in relative order. 'Hey, babe,' he proudly thrusted up to the map light. 'Get ready for some fireworks!' (It was to be the understatement of his lifetime).

The old Allegro was obviously not designed for what Sue had in mind. Most of the headroom was taken up by her ample attributes. With her great arse jammed between the headrests, leaving just enough space for Angus to slither between her and the roof lining, he took a deep breath. 'Geronimo!!!'

. . .A high-octane explosion at the point of sexual climax might be how any self-respecting granny grabber, ungrabbed or never been grabbed granny for that matter, would want to go. Alas, this particular maiden outing would turn out to be Angus's last, and he took poor Sumo Sue with him....

First on the scene sergeant Rab Mackenzie, discovered the charred superglue tubes and decided it was just another glue-sniffing orgy gone wrong. 'Frozen in the act like dog-locked mongrels. Third one this month,' he told inspector Crosbie. (Their demise would not even make the tabloids).

That same evening, in search of the nightly bonk her metabolism demanded. Judy blatantly hitched up her skirt to a young Adonis at the hotel bar. When he introduced himself as 'Wang,' of the boyzband Scallywag she couldn't believe her luck. 'Are you staying at this hotel?' she said and pouted a sensual kiss. 'Small world.' Before he could react, a well-practiced hand gravitated to his belt buckle, a denier knee pinned his crotch to the stool.

With nowhere to hide, Wang grabbed the bar rail and clamped her advance between trembling thighs. 'I don't think I . . . I don't . . .'

'Don't worry, babe if you're too tired, I'll do all the work. Pressing her knee deeper, she puckered and undid his belt. 'I'll just put my lips together and blow, as someone famous once said.'

With fingertips millimetres from her prize, Wang's fat manager approached from the blind side, grabbed her arm and spun the barstool on its axis. 'You are a phony!' he cried, and Judy faced up to him with murder in her eyes. 'Not you, hen, you're not to know, but the only straight thing about this one is his bloody Beatle fringe. Pretending to be hetro again, are we? Well, save it for the teenyboppers,' he said and turned back to Judy. 'Drambuie does that to him, hen.'

'Oh sorry,' she said despairingly, 'but you know what it's like when you're needing a good old-fashioned bonk?'

'Don't I just, dear, don't I bloody just. I wish I could help but sometimes you've just got to go without. Anyway, here's a couple of freebies for tomorrow night's concert.' He handed Judy two front row tickets. 'You'll have no problem there, I'm sure.'

Before he could re-buckled Wang's belt, she was rushing headlong to the lift.

. . . Richard was asleep when she let herself in. Even if the atmosphere was strained, Judy's insatiable need overrode all contempt, it left her with no option. . .

After feigning token protest, in no time at all, her paste brush tongue had him whistling his way into the kitchen. He re-emerged sporting what had taken on all the characteristics of a tiny hand grasping a Cox Pippin.

'Don't you dare be gentle with me,' she cried. Knowing full well how the prosthesis would respond, she pressed her face into the skirting board and shrieked a hearty 'Yabbadabbadooo.' (The micro-compressor did its job and sprang the gland to bursting point).

. . .Three hours later, as Richard lay snoring, Judy threaded the depleted Rod onto the zinc candelabra: closed her eyes and opened her mouth as it played out a ghostly dance to a high-pitched whisper of rugby songs.

Chapter six.
Packed Lunch Box

'If we're going to track these Rods down, you'll have to take a more proactive part,' she told him the next morning.

'What do you mean?'

'Pull your weight! I've diffused wannabe Angus McKay, seen off (one time donkey rigged) Wee Wullie Riley, so it's only fair that you take on this Wang character; turns out he's a bit more your gay type.'

Richard wasn't offended, he'd be loath to admit it even to himself, but the thought didn't entirely abhor him. After seeing Wang's promo shots, he felt uncomfortably charged toward that particular end of the market. 'I'm just not sure,' he lied.

'Oh yes you bloody are, anyway, you can take a good look tomorrow. I've got two front row tickets.'

'I've never. . . I wouldn't know what to do. Would he want me to. . . or would he want to do it to . . ?'

'Whatever a woman feels about men or women, or a man about women or men, it's just a question of the route you happen to take, if you follow me'.

Richard didn't follow her, but the conversation was rendering him forensically horny. 'What if he doesn't fancy me?'

Judy held up a tiny bottle. 'Spike his drink with this. 'Butcher or block, fake it till you make it, but make sure he takes it.'

'What is it?'

'Rohypnol, tasteless, odourless, guaranteed to knock him for six. When he's out of it you defuse him, simple as that.'

Strangely intrigued, Richard lapsed into one of his slightly embarrassing 'same-sex-unsafe-sex' fantasies. . . It was still on his mind as they took their places in the front row the following night.

. . .Wang was only ever a packed lunchbox short of a very lucrative stage presence, he was about to put that right by sliding on his new slide-on backstage.

. . . The house-lights dimmed, curtains slowly raised and the audience hushed. A moody bass-line throbbed out a twelve-bar-riff as the neon spotlight twitched his kneeling figure to life.

The screaming delight of excited schoolgirls, (and boys) was picked up by Wang's rampant sensor, the tempo grew, as did his sensitized pride and joy. Under the blinding glare he sprang upright, looked down and strutted his newly bulging midriff centre-stage singing 'I just want your, I just want your . . .I just want your. . . '

He picked out Judy in the front row with a beckoning a finger: a lick of his lips, a buck of the hips and a flashing leer drove the crowd hysterical. 'Bo-ho-ho-body,' he purred. 'Come, come, along with me he he.'

Shredded denim and a practiced lurid smirk, wetted the pubescence of a generation that saw no more than a bleached toothed, midriff-bulging mass of testosterone.

With a trio of backing singers gyrating behind, he drove the audience to a panting frenzy with every pelvic thrust. . . After an hour of tried and tested hormone jerkers, the finale involved an orgy of open-mouthed thrusting buttocks and ripping denim. The music, lost far behind screams of hysteria.

House-lights flashed on, and the crowd went wild. Bouncers launched intrepid stage invaders back into the screaming hoards, and the concert had to be abandoned. The headlines had already been penned: 'An orgasmic success' read one tabloid, 'Elvis lives' another.'

The head doorman was under strict 'no entry' orders to the post-concert bash. All it took was the promise of a freebee to win him over.

On his third hand-shaking, cheek kissing circuit the rock-star made a beeline for Judy. 'Did you ever get the bonk you wanted, dear?'

'I always do,' she replied with a lurid wink. 'Let me introduce you to my friend,'

Wang immediately switched his attention, a hand snaked onto Richard's thigh. 'I'm getting good vibes from you,' he whispered. 'Wait right there.'

A makeup man appeared from nowhere, a continuity girl clipped a microphone to Wang's collar. The director raised his thumb to the waiting media, a spotlight beamed, and Wang turned to face a barrage of questions.

'There have been reports that the band is splitting up, can you comment?'

Flirting with the camera, Wang brushed away a wayward

wisp of hair and sighed. 'Right now, my fans are more important than band politics. We are all individual artists. I can't speak for them,' he said. Adept at the art of not answering, he smiled very, very sincerely.

'Is it true you are making a solo album?'

'I've been working on one or two things, it's true.'

'Do you take drugs?'

A condescending smile hid a racing suspicion he'd been busted, and he closed his eyes in silent prayer. 'Music is my drug,' he replied, and his fat manager mimicked applause.

'Do you have a lovechild?'

'Do you practice White Magic?'

'Are you gay,' was the last unanswered question before the party began in earnest.

Gutter press scribes couldn't quite figure out if waitresses were dressed as bimbos, or if in fact, bimbos were waiting-on, either way it made for good copy.

Paparazzi poised, the backing-band of three nubile child gods, hired exclusively for their testosterone levels, didn't disappoint: they pranced, puckered and skipped into the fray of hand-picked nubile groupies.

In reality though, Wang was the band, what little talent they possessed was his. Not that Judy cared for such hair-splitting, in a state of carnal nirvana, drinking in the damp musk from their young alluring limbs, she pouted uncontrollably and pushed to the front. (After all, it was her night off!)

Wang's new penile acquisition engendered a generation of transfixed, heterosexual hormonal fans. It had the effect of keeping him firmly in the closet; as such, all thoughts of ever 'coming out' were left on the backburner.

'You can't now!' his fat manager, insisted, 'not when we're on our way to number one!

The talk about 'closets' and 'not coming out,' impelled Wang straight to the restroom to check his equipment.

Perched on a strategically positioned bench, Richard was struggling with that same big question. There was a certain vulnerability about the cult figure that stirred him. Would it be so abhorrent? he pondered, only this time didn't immediately cast the fantasy away. After all, look at the poor guy.

Unfamiliar stirrings battled trepidation as he fought to refocus on the job at hand, and crossed the restroom floor to study his bulging target

Wang shuffled along to make room. 'You know I'm not straight don't you, is it that obvious?'

Richard wanted to tell him his sexuality was the worst kept secret in glitter-world, and he was a stupid twerp to think that anyone that mattered would care and he needn't be afraid, but he contained himself. 'You're gay? Live with it,' he heard himself saying.

Wang opened his vacuous eyes and smiled. 'It's my fans you see.'

'What about your fans? It didn't do Elton John, George Michael, Boy George or Bowie any harm did it, not to mention Freddie Mercury? Just be yourself and they'll love you all the more.'

. . . Judy broke the silence by bursting into the 'men only rest room.' Waddling her body between them, she turned to face Wang. 'Nice slide-on tackle you have, by the way.'

'How did?'

She silencing him with a trademark lip-slurping kiss and spiked his unguarded drink. When Richard began to remonstrate, she spun and did the same to him. 'Well, tatty bye for now,' she hissed. 'I still need what I need!'

Soon to be embroiled in a delicious dilemma of her own, she strutted her stuff back into the fray, singing, 'sing if your glad to be gay,'

Intrigued by the so-called 'toy-boy' analogy, she wondered if the drooling boyz band would live up to their tabloid image.

Still young enough to be turned on by simple innuendo, not too young, she hoped, to follow it through, the one at the top of her bonkable list still giggled at the F-word, (and she was more than up for the challenge. . .)

A pair of despondent wannabe groupies, who knew when they were beaten, turned their attention to a promotion 6 pack, and taxing the tour bus suspension with a couple of ageing roadies.'

By now a drug induced haze was dragging Richard's thoughts toward that big question. Thinking ahead, Wang reached over to stroke his bald head. 'I'm pretty sure what I want,' he said, 'by the way, what's your name?'

'Richard Edwards, but you can call me Dick Ed, everyone else does.' Fantasy, grounded in lust was daring to speak his name, and he perused the dancefloor for a heterosexual alternative, but the sight of Judy waving her knickers in the air had the opposite effect.

Can one ever truly know oneself? he wondered, and quaffed his quaalude-laced champagne in one defiant slurp.

Fat manager hurtled around the room like a teary ping-pong ball, crying 'he's doing it again,' (but no one was listening). A gender-bending crossdresser waved a perfumed hankie in his face, and Fat manager blew his nose in it. 'Do I know you, are you a performer?'

The young man hitched up his skirt and twitched his lips to a sensual smile. 'Oh, I can perform, given the right inducement of course. Are you a member of the Lavender Club?'

'Member, I wrote the bloody rule book!'

Talk of slide-ons and gonad cusps raised Wang's libidinous level to fever pitch, he invited Richard for a cooling dip in the penthouse jacuzzi.

. . . Telling himself it was just to 'liven up,' wearing nothing but designer thongs, an ear-to ear grin and a freshly slid on slide-on, Richard lowered his aching form into the tepid water.

Wang double-checked his gonad cusp and slid in beside him.

'It's all too beautiful.'

Richard had forgotten about the ballistic danger, wondering why he wasn't recoiling from the singer's gentle caress, he moved his buttocks to accommodate, and asked what Wang was staring at.

'Your hair. There's very little of it.'

'So?'

'So, think about it: we've got a subdued punk, a jelled mod and a designer blonde. A retro skinhead would make up the full set.'

'But I can't sing.'

'And?'

'Can't dance or play an instrument either.'

Wang rasped a palm against Richard's head stubble and thumbed his chest. 'As far as my backing group is concerned, talent is a positive disadvantage. Ditto anything else that takes the limelight from yours truly!' Richard began to slip beneath the perfumed bubbles and Wang pulled him to the surface. 'Kapeesh?'

With the 'Small Faces' singing in the background, Richard heaved up a mouthful of bath-oils as he was eased from the water. The sheepskin rug curled into his skin, and he drifted to an ethereal place as Wang slowly towelled him dry.

'To Itchycoo Park, that's where I've been.'

Yes, he was in a land without castrative nightmares, dreaming; a land where there was no Judy, where his small to medium standing, like his sexuality, mattered not.

'Tell yeah what I'll do. I'd love to go there now with you.' This time Richard didn't turn away; face aching with pleasure; sheepskin fleece hurried his breath. Opening his eyes to erotic sensual shapes blasting back from the mirrored jacuzzi, he braced; gone was all resistance, he needed to be plundered, purged. He watched the reflection of an extremely Rampant Rod bearing down towards his upturned body, somehow at that moment it didn't seem to matter.

Wang was singing along now. 'We'll get high high. We'll touch the sky high.'

The ultimate irony of being anally inseminated with a bomb of one's own making defied contemplation. A black gaping abyss opened before him as he prepared to meet his maker. 'It's all too beautiful!'

. . .The next morning, it wasn't so much that Richard was glad to be alive, more that he did not feel soiled. In the cool light of day his sexuality, unlike his backside, seemed less in crisis than in disarray. The artificial bliss of still being alive had effectively trumped his earlier misgivings, and he smiled.

. . . To kill two birds with one stone, Judy had spiked both their drinks. The acid test of which would have brought a whole new meaning to the phrase 'slipping a mickey.' Richard pictured the headlines: ('Sex aid king found in teen idol's arms with backside blown off) and shuddered. How could he give her the satisfaction of knowing how close she had come to success?

Back at the hotel all he would say on the matter was 'Wang's slide-on did not contain the bomb,' and left it at that. 'Who's next?' He was trying his best to sound calm, but his hands and knees were twitching.

Chapter Seven:
The Lavender Club

Richard ran a finger slowly down the list of Annie's customers: "The Procurator Fiscal, him and the fella I spent last night with are both members of this Lavender Club."

After a token show of reluctance, not wanting to sound too keen, Judy nodded her head. 'The Fiscal's a bonded fetishist I hear, haven't had one of those for yonks, but you've still got a part to play.'

Here was a man who had spent most of his life denying one reality or another, but he'd read the blurb, and try as he might, he couldn't get away from the sensation the words 'Lavender Club' evoked in his groin area. 'It's okay for you, you're a three-way deviant, I'm lucky I still have a part to play with!'

Judy laughed, and Richard pretended to. 'What if there was a way around it? It might be risky,' he said, 'but not as risky as playing Russian roulette with exploding whatnots.'

'A way around it, such as?

'Such as disarming the rod without touching it.' Richard had his chemist thinking-cap on, trying to impress her. 'If we could introduce a neutralizing agent orally, something that would pass through the bladder and dissolve the synthetic detonator, the nitro-glycerine would simply be peed up against the wall.'

'And just how do we do that: I submit, your Worship, that if you don't want your testicles to explode, you'd better drink this?'

Richard gave her a bitter look. 'No, I thought we could put it in his glass when he wasn't looking. You know how that works, don't you?'

Judy's guilty expression confirmed his suspicion, and he took his own insidious plot off the backburner. 'Forget the neutralizing agent, too risky. I'm going for a walk,' he said. Slamming the door behind him, he left her watching the adult channel.

. . . Before dawn he had extracted enough mercuric chloride from the hotel barometers to kill a tartan army. Fantasizing about the circulatory collapse and the painful throes of Judy's death, he dismantled half a dozen of her Quaalude capsules and refilled them with the deadly tincture. After that, he planned to deflect all suspicion of foul play toward the Lavender Club.

. . . The next morning, he rang to ask about membership.

'I've already seen your credentials, but remember we have a deviant dress code here,' Wang said, and emailed Richard the rules.

. . . Judy liked the touchy-feel of leather on skin, and picked out her favourite figure hugging mini. Complimented by peek-a-boo top, spiked collar, and thigh length sado-boots, she was ready for anything!

Richard went for the kitsch anarchist porcupine hair wisps, stone-washed vest emblazoned with 'Feck the Establishment' and freaky face paint to compensate for any lack of wear and tear.

The converted Clydebank warehouse in a cobblestone backstreet had been made-over years before. From the outside it was nothing more than another abandoned storage facility. (Inside told a different story).

A colourful transvestite waited at the entrance with his introductory spiel. 'Here's the rub, we couldn't get a liquor licence, so we registered as a florist. You buy a £100 buttonhole and the drinks are free all night. Clever or what?' He pointed to the dress code poster on the wall behind them. 'Read it and weep, but remember, every flower tells a story.

Sprig of heather: dominant type.

Tulip: submissive.

Daffodil: open to all offers. (M M.)

'I'm liking it here already!' Judy proclaimed with delight. Dancing a jig, she bought a sprig of heather and a rose.

Caught up in the occasion, Richard never read the small print, and opted for a golden daffodil, simply because he liked the poem.

A swirling mist of cannabis incense rummaged at their ankles and infused the stairwell with the illusion of forbidden depths,

.   Wang was waiting to stop them on the half landing. Turning first to Judy then to Richard, he giggled. 'Well just look at you two, I can't believe it! You look so, well damn it, I can't put my finger on it, but I will later.' He mimicked a tickling motion with his index, giggled again and handed them each a luminous green glow stick. 'This is so we can find you if you get into trouble.'

'What kind of trouble?' Richard asked.

'That's for me to know and you to find out. If you're lucky!' he added with a smirk. 'Give our new guests a couple of Brown Hatters,' he told the heavily made-up barperson, and the crowd made way.

Judy took a slurp and began to twitch to the eclectic mix of 'Hard Rock' blasting from the overhead speakers. With her back to the bar, she took in the surroundings.

. . . But for a single adjoining door to room 284, brick-lined walls completely encased the basement; oozing condensation they gave off a musty tang of mildew that seemed somehow to suit her mood, suit the occasion.

. . .Caught up in the moment, a troupe of dancers pranced across her vision in various stages of undress.

Hands waving in the air, bow legged on a beaded leash, the fiscal was impossible to miss. 'Your arse is mine!' a familiar wild haired imp wheezed, and the crowd made way. The imp shot a menacing snarl in Judy's direction before delivering a property-marking kick to the Fiscal's backside. 'I'm your mistress, you dirty little smeg of Glasgow putrescence, deal with it!'

Judy's refracted kiss in the giant phallic mirror caught the Fiscal's attention. He put out his tongue and panted and she did the same.

Feeling strangely liberated, Richard remained at the bar 'F-ing and blinding' about the 'imperialist conspiracy' and the 'hidden agenda to keep 'us all' subjugated. 'The fackin' bosses are tryin' to fack us, innit?' he shouted. Falling somewhere between Australian soap-bimbo and dying feline, his failed cockney twang attracted almost as much attention as his daffodil buttonhole.

A circle of curious misfits parted for the huge, tattooed ogre who barged his way through and pushed his face to Richard's. 'What we need is to fack our way to power, staff 'em where it 'urts until they have our coffee-coloured children!' With decidedly cabbage breath, he curled his lips to huff between a toothless gin, and Richard tried to smile.

Gypsy let the prickly sensation of a chocolate-topped cocktail invade her senses before skulking low to the business side of the dancefloor. In her haste she misjudged the wide safety berth Judy's studded collar required, and impaled a protruding thigh on one of its spikes. With one arm meshed in gothic tattoos, the other in mock leather, Gypsy pulled her injured leg free, with no attempt to stem the flow of blood, she raised her whip hand high.

Judy closed her eyes to accept chastisement. 'Don't you dare be gentle with me,' she muttered.

The S&M queen lay down her whip, shrugged and ordered another drink. 'I'll see to you later, spiked lady,' she said and melted back into the crowd. 'Where are you going?'

Judy just shook her head and strutted across the crowded floor to the washroom.

Florescent locks underfoot, the green-faced imp was pulling up her drawers in a cubicle doorway. 'You certainly get around, hen.'

'It's you Annie! What the. . . what. . ?'

Annie gathered up her tresses and snarled. 'Don't knock what you haven't' tried, posh girl. What are you doing here anyway?'

'I think you know.'

Annie repositioned her headwear. 'Yeah, but I wouldn't mention it to the Fiscal if I were you.'

'Why not?'

'That Rampant Rod I sold him was a dud, the mole fell off and it shrivelled to a frazzle,' was her last decipherable utterance before her voice became a muffle beneath rubberised head-wear.

Judy was elated. With the last bomb inadvertently deactivated, she was free for the ribaldry ahead. In a rare quirk of generosity that was about to save her life, she handed Annie her stash of spiked Quaaludes. 'I won't be needing them now,' she said. These will take you to a better place. (How right she was).

Gypsy was flicking her miniature nine-tails in the restroom doorway, 'Time's up posh girl!' She beckoned Judy to a darkened corner with a playful bite on her shoulder.

Judy sighed, 'ah, that's just what I need.'

'Needs must, I suppose.' Gypsy said, 'but what about your punkified mate?'

'Oh, him,' Judy looked back towards the bar, 'bugger him.'

The eighteen stone, rose wielding gronk who was jamming Richard against the bar with a poignant tail of outing, was of that very mind. 'I found it very difficult to tell me mum, she had her suspicions when her knickers started going missing. 'Just a puberty thing she thought, but she was so wrong.' He gripped the neck of his bottle, slurped greedily, and his voice transposed to a strange piercing cackle. 'I say balls to what people think! If you're lucky enough to know what you want,' he gasped, 'and you're big enough to take it, take it! D'you ken!'

Intoxicated by this unexpected kinship, Richard looked up

from his pinned position and told the gronk just what he wanted to hear. 'You're certainly big enough!' he said. A homicidal glint flashed his way, inherent cowardice began to battle with his alter ego, and he bit his top lip and grimaced.

Judy disengaged her peek-a-boo from Gypsy's mouth to note that Richard still had his arms pinned. Ignoring his 'please help me look, she asked about his buttonhole.

The Romany beauty sighed and licked her lips. 'A daffodil? You've obviously heard of S&M.'

'Of course.'

'Well, a daffodil signifies M&M.'

'Sorry?'

'Multiple Molestation, baby, in other words the wearer requires a severe gang-banging.'

An ear-piercing screech caught Judy mid-giggle and stopped her cold. The music suddenly stopped and someone hit the house lights: Annie and the Fiscal were locked in an impossible frenetic embrace on the strobe lit dance-floor.

'Give them some space!' Wang roared, as he tugged at Annie's polyplastic ears. The silver beaded leash broke and sprung a thousand plastic balls into the crowd. Some lost their footing; thinking it was part of the show, they joined the neck clutching pair at their feet.

'Yeah, let's get this orgy thing going!' the gronk cried from the bar.

The fiscal was choking out his last dying gargle. Wang asked for someone to give him the kiss of life, unsurprisingly, there were no takers. Someone remarked that Annie's mask was better looking, and the crowd backed off.

'That's it! everybody out!' Wang shouted, but an inertia of morbid intrigue had taken the onlookers. Agape and muted they froze, until the magic word 'police' emptied the building like a leper's bell.

Many domineering and submissive appetites would go unsated that evening, not least the gronk's or Judy's. Along with Richard, they were caught up in the frenzied slipstream back up to street level.

Chapter Eight:
The Beautiful Game

It was grey, wet, windy and dank, it was Glasgow, and an off-beat carnival of misfits shuffled despondently along in the supper strewn twilight. Absorbed into familiar territory, the numbers dwindled until only Richard and Judy remained.

Springburn at five in the morning with no sign of a taxi, is not where you would want to be on a good day, but dressed like a pair of trippy hippies, you'd be lucky to survive till breakfast. There were no early risers, just an abundance of late revellers making up the bawdy mob that inevitably surrounded them on the high street.

Jeddah poked Judy's peek a boo with a nicotine'd finger. 'Hey c'mon here, Tam, here's the posh lass that bunged Annie in the Treble A. Just look at those wazzoomies!'

Judy didn't flinch, she simply stuck out her chest defiantly. 'Don't touch what you can't afford, dickhead.' Richard thought she was referring to him and shortened his neck. 'You're not the only dickhead here!' she said.

Her posh Sloan accent cut through the ramblings of the baying mob, it did no more than provoke a venue debate for their hatching fantasies. The brothers, only still at large because Bongo wouldn't serve them up any credit the night before, saw it as their last chance of sexual adventure.

Tam tried on his best Sean Connery: 'D'yeh no fanshy an orgy then, kid? My bro and me have our own wee pad,' he drawled.

Judy took a deep breath; try as she might, she just couldn't bring herself to say 'no.'

Encouraged by her reticence, Jeddah shooed at the leering gang. 'Catch yeh selves on, we saw her first, ken?' Clenching his jaw, he tried to face them down, but they were in no hurry to move, and the standoff began.

The arrival of a police car broke the impasse and skidded to a halt alongside. Sergeant Rab Mackenzie was just in time to diffuse the situation in his unmistakable parlance. 'Away tae feck!' the big highlander shouted and waved his manacles towards the brothers. 'You two, back to your wee hovel or you're for the Bar L.'

Tam and Jeddah took him at his word and joined boardy

onlookers as they melted into the background.

Mackenzie couldn't keep his tongue from dry lips as he helped Judy into his police car. 'Do you know it's a criminal offence to expose yourself in a public place, lassie?' he said.

Still unsure she was ready to be rescued, she looked down at his crotch and smiled. 'So is carrying an offensive weapon, officer.'

At this point Richard didn't look too much out of place on the street: greasepaint had solidified to form credible scar tissue on his lower jaw, blurry-eyed and leary, he appeared just about as battered as the rest.

'See you? Away tae feck, yeh baz, before ah break yeh wee heed!' McKenzie told him when he tried to climb into the car behind Judy.

'I'm with her!'

Of course, Judy denied all knowledge. 'I don't know him, officer.' She slammed the passenger door shut, the police car sped away leaving Richard suddenly alone, at the mercy of the strange scary mob. Shortening his neck again, he fell-in limply behind. As they cruised the parks and shop doorways trying locks, badgering dawning winos, Richard limited his lexicon to the odd 'aye' and an occasional 'ken.'

Despite various attempts he couldn't escape the tail end marauders, whether tying a lace, pausing to puke or pee, or taking a wrong turn, Tam was invariably there to steer him back into the clutch.

By some small mercy he survived the rigours of cursory interrogation. He found himself in a six A M Sunday huddle at the bar of the 'Slash Inn', a pint of Tenants thrust into his uncertain grip.

Claiming to accommodate early morning Barras marketeers, the Slash Inn was one of several bars to circumvent Glasgow's licencing laws. Now, as well as the odd market trader, they were serving up early morning chancers and after-hours lock-ins.

There was no natural light in that particular windowless lounge. Were it not for breakfast TV blaring from the corner, and morning sport's pages spread over tables, it may well have been midnight?

'It's your roond,' Richard's new-found escort informed him before he had raised his first glass. Trying to decipher his unintelligible posh response, Tam tapped his empty on the bar and smacked his lips. 'Mine's a Tenants, son.'

Rummaging in his pockets, all Richard managed to come up with was a placating grin and a cash card. It invoked a look of borderline idolatry from Tam.

He steered his newfound blurry friend to the adjacent hole-in-the-wall to extract ten crispy ten-pound notes. 'They call me Tam, ken?' he said and offered to go to the bar.

'Aye, Tamken, they call me dickhead; short for Richard Edwards.'

Here was every Tenant-head's dream; a cash-card-carrying-punk, who could only speak a few words, the main one of which was 'aye.' (His popularity spread in concert).

The old soldier, who moments before had ridiculed him, now paid sycophantic homage to the dropout punk culture. Young bucks, who turned to smile at the potential sponsor for their 'Old Firm' binge. 'Today it's big match day,' he was told, 'today we stuff the Hun bastards!'

'Aye,' Richard replied, his eyes, by now glazing over. 'Aye, Tamken.'

Tam spotted his benefactor flagging, in the interest of continuity, he slipped his last 'upper' into Richard's glass. They all pretended not to notice when his accent reverted to its 'Sloan twit' resonance. It didn't matter to the recipients of free lager, suddenly it mattered not to Richard. While his audience of grateful drinkers were happy enough pretending to listen, he conjured up a vestige of pasted on pseudo revolutionary from the night before.

Not since the 'Big-yin' had meandered in during the making of a Clyde side documentary, had they been treated to such a combination of generosity and gutter humour. Making the best of both, they harried around for favour, until the most natural thing in the world for Richard was to make a speech. Through the distorted veil of Tenants, he thought he sounded like Richard Burton, when in fact he sounded more like Googie Withers. Without the working-class twang, it lacked any semblance of credulity, but while the beer was flowing, they didn't care.

'Aye, lad,' they all agreed when he slurred about lighting fires in the 'revolutionary underbelly, 'and where better that an old firm game?'

'Aye, lad,' the old soldier said.

'He's talking a lot of sense,' said Tam.

To a collective sigh of relief, Richard eventually faltered. As he slowly disappeared beneath the bench, the soldier grabbed the last of the notes from his limp hand and cheered. 'Tenants all roond!'

. . .By lunchtime the lounge was a bubbling mass of green and white, but the kitty had once again run dry. It was time to shake their snoring sponsor to life.

'For god's sake tell him we don't want another speech,' the old soldier said. 'Just his bloody PIN number!'

The barmaid, who could see what was going on, on another day might have ignored it, but there was a certain vulnerability about this strange punk that made her want to intercede. She bent down with her spew scoop and disinfectant spray and whispered in the old soldier's ear; 'leave the poor fool alone, laddie. Have you no shame?'

'Aye plenty,' he replied with a sneer, and tapped Richard gently on the cheek, 'but a wee bit short on lager vouchers at the moment.'

Amid the growing PIN number demands, Richard sat up, wiped the carrots from his chin, and stammered he was needing some air.

Tam kept him upright as they stumbled from the building into Market Street. Sunshine blasted at Richard's dewy eyes, and his first inclination was to return to the haven of shadow. 'What time is it, I thought it was night-time?'

'Liquid lunch time, son.'

. . . After a gallon of coffee in the nearby 'Greasy spoon, Richard began to feel suspiciously human. From the smoke smudged window, he peered at the endless tri-coloured river of heads flowing towards Park Head. 'I'm sorry,' he said. 'I can't go to the match with you. I need to sleep.'

'Aye, son. I know what you're needin.'

Once again Richard allowed himself to be led like a pet dog through the Barra's market centre. It was there they ran the gauntlet of homicidal enemy fans parading their Union battle standard.

'From the mountains and the glens, we are on the march again sounding out the battle cries so famous

And we're here to stake our claim, we're the greatest in the game, as we rally, rally, rally round The Rangers.'

They found Jeddah dancing around the bootleg DVD display liberated earlier from the Treble A top shelf.

'You've met my new pal,' said Tam.

'Aye, how yeh' doin', son?'

Richard belched. 'How come you're so, so alive?'

'He's carrying,' Tam said, 'just what you're needin.'

Jeddah suddenly stopped dancing. 'Let's see how much you've got then?' His serious change of tone caused Richard to unquestioningly turn out the contents of his pockets, it amounted to no more than a crumpled five-pound note and small change.

'He's got plastic,' Tam said.

Jeddah's expression went through several stages of disappointment, and ultimately satisfaction as he fumbled in the gusset of his tracksuit. Pulling his fingers free clutching a tiny polythene bag, he looked right into Richard's eyes. 'Get some of that down yeh wee neck and you'll be pucker, then down to the old hole-in-the-wall for the wee balance.'

'I don't. I can't'. . . Richard's protests were ignored and Tam clamped his nose. Jeddah emptied half of the bag's contents onto his gagging tongue before he could pull away.

The amphetamine sulphate dissolved on his tongue, leaving a chemical aftertaste required extinguishing. (Apart from that he still felt like dying).

Via a second visit to the cash machine, they re-entered the gloomy 'Slash Inn. Richard began to sense a gnawing ache where his stomach once was; his teeth began to grind as he accepted another pint, only this time it hardly touched the sides. Football songs abounded, while he waited to interrupt, his hand drummed frantically on the tabletop, his feet began to shuffle in the sawdust.

'Celtic, Celtic that's the team for me

Celtic, Celtic on to victory

They're the finest team in Scotland I'm sure you will agree

We'll never give up till we've won the cup and the Scottish football league.'

He slammed his hand onto the table for order. 'I do feel that the tribal antics of football crowds are a microcosm of the unrest of the working classes on the whole,' he said in one breath.

Every head in the place turned to him in hatred. 'I'm going,' the old soldier said. 'I can take nae more! All the free lemonade in the world is nae' worth this shite!'

Guessing that he was heading for trouble, Richard immediately changed tack. 'All coppers are bastards,' he shouted at the top of his voice, to which the old soldier took great offence.

'Any more talk like that and I'll pull yeh wee feckin head right off!' he said.

'Why, you're not a copper are you?' Richard asked, seriously.

'No, son, I'm a bastard!'

A swift exit and several even frothier pitstops later, Richard was feeling decidedly lively. They joined the long train of supporters on route to Park Head where a bung of fifty notes to the steward ensured their entry through a service door.

The underground labyrinth of dark tunnels emerged inside a swaying bank of bodies bedecked in green and white. A whistle blew, 60,000 fans roared; Richard was lifted off his feet, carried forward ten yards, then ten yards back to his starting point. Once or twice through the myriad of heads, he caught a tiny glimpse of turf, heard a far-off whistle that invariably prompted screaming controversy. Every bone-crunching foul, a fair tackle, every fair tackle, a sending off offence. Labelled a 'blind bastard' by 30,000 experts at every decision, the referee just couldn't win!

Tempers flared, passions rose. Richard didn't hear the halftime whistle through the din. More than ready when Jeddah fed him another dab of white powder, he began screaming at the top of his range. Leaping up he landed back on his arse in a pool of trickle-down urine. Then it began all over again: cursing, cheering, deafening noise of 60,000 cursing fans willing the ball into the net.

Richard didn't actually see any of the play. Too polite to ask the mob in front to sit down, he took what he could from the baying crowd: some jumped into the air, some waved their fists and issued death threats to nobody in particular. Tam and Jeddah just sang along until the fulltime whistle blew.

After the goal-less draw the police had prayed for, the trio travelled back through the same underground labyrinth, escaping the warfare outside and returned to what had now become their local. Singing and threatening anyone who wouldn't join in, Richard began to understand why they call it the 'beautiful game.'

After his brief sojourn into hooliganism, the boosting effect of amphetamine sulphate wore off, and he reverted to his pre-match 'aye and ken' vernacular.

Between nauseating flashbacks and post-match analysis that went completely over his head, he had learned one or two' community songs' that questioned the parentage of King William of

Orange.

By midnight they had run out of drugs, but while Richard still held a solvent credit rating, he could not be ditched, so the brothers took him back to the tenement to sleep it off. . . (For the second time in a single day Richard felt eerily close to death).

While two new best friends raided the fridge for 'a few tinnies,' he lay sweating and shivering in a stomach-churning foetal ball. As the buzzing in his ears dragged him toward unconsciousness, the tiny residue of speed still in his system fought any inclination to sleep. This was bolstered by a lack of appetite that his empty, yawning stomach contradicted. Most terrifyingly of all, his small to medium standing had shrunken almost out of sight!

Tam sat him up and pressed a can between his shaking palms. 'Get that down yeh' wee neck, son, it'll pull you together, trust me, drink enough and you'll feel better.' Against all instincts, Richard forced a can to his quivering lips and filled his mouth with the foul-tasting brew. Urged on by Jeddah, he tried again and then again, eventually the taste was not quite so repugnant. . . Three cans later had him once again practising rebel songs and swearing allegiance to the shamrock.

'You two are gangsters, right! How much would it cost to do someone in?'

The brothers burst out laughing.

'I can afford it you know. I'm potentially very wealthy.' By now beyond the point of revival, his voice was trailing off, he slipped to the floor in a semi-comatose heap muttering 'really I am.'

Tam and Jeddah needed a little earner and they looked at each other eyes wide. 'Really!' they said in unison.

Chapter Nine:
Where the members hang out

For most of the early shift at Peel Street police station, recent events would provide banter for a week. Not so for Inspector James Crosbie, who'd been up all-night scrutinizing security tapes from the Treble A sex shop. He was zooming in on a group of frolickers comparing equipment under the great swinging penis, when his sergeant ambled in and quipped over his shoulder, 'Is this where the members hang out?'

Crosbie began to choke on his bacon butty and quickly ejected the disc. 'Here's one from the Lavender Club.' Reloading the machine, he fast forwarded past the image of Judy having her breasts attended by a born-again Amazon and McKenzie stopped him.

'Rewind a bit . . .Stop! I know peekaboo, if that helps, and yes, they are real, guv, I've seen them close up.'

Crosbie was taken aback; he cleared the crumbs from his beard and studied the 'stilled' frame. 'How do you know her?'

'Rescued her from a gang of 'shite hawks' near the club this morning; took her home.'

'Why?'

McKenzie picked up the untouched half of his boss's sandwich. 'I couldn't leave her there, could I, surrounded by barm pots?'

Crosbie searched for the frame that showed the late procurator fiscal and Treble A Annie tangled on the Lavender club dancefloor.

'What about these two?'

'It's not the first time someone O D'd on booze and sex drugs, is it? It's all the rage in these places, so I hear.' McKenzie said.

'Ugh, ugh, make that mercury fulminate.'

'Mercury fulminate, you mean they were poisoned?'

Crosbie held up a sealed exhibit's bag containing the discarded Quaalude capsules. 'This peek-a-boo. Where does she live?'

'Staying at the Hilton, guv, up here from England on

business, she said. Shall I bring her in?'

The inspector looked pensively at his watch before replying. 'No, let's play detective for a bit. I fancy a wee posh dram, how about you?' As they left the building he was still chuckling. 'Where the members hang out, indeed, ha ha!'

A very smart commissionaire saluted and directed them to the lounge. McKenzie was first to the bar. 'I'll get these.' Crosbie was taking in the plush surroundings when he heard his sergeant complaining: 'Eleven pound for a couple of drams!'

The barman laughed cynically, 'the war's over sir,' he quipped, and went back to his obsessive glass buffing.

'Take no heed of him, can'nae take him anywhere,' said Crosbie, nodding towards his sergeant, then he wiped the smirk from the barman's face by flashing his warrant card. 'Now, son, this young posh lady,' he pulled out a head and shoulders video-print. 'Do you know her?'

'Oh yes, Judy, I mean, Ms Prentiss. Who's she, what's she done?'

'Does she use this bar?'

The barman nodded towards the staircase. 'Ask her yourself, Columbo.'

The two policemen turned to watch Judy's Betty Davis entrance. More respectably dressed this time; with a stamp of confident indifference she approached, jacked up breasts and swagger claiming the attention of everyone in the room.

'Hello, sergeant, how nice to see you here. I still owe you one, remember?' She smiled, pouted, and turned to the open-mouthed inspector. 'Haven't had the pleasure.'

Crosbie had his badge at the ready. 'No. I'm sure I'd remember, Ms Prentiss. Shall we find a seat?' Leaving McKenzie to collect the drinks he took her arm and steered her to a nearby table.

'Whiskey and soda,' she shouted over her shoulder, puckered, fluttered and licked her lips as she sat down. 'Call me Judy, what do I call you?'

'Inspector Crosbie,' he said tersely. He'd taken an immediate dislike to her and wasn't about to hide it.

'What exactly is it you want, mister policeman?'

'First of all, I want you to tell me exactly what business it is you have in Glasgow?'

Judy opened her jacket to reveal a plunging neckline,

puckered and fanned her face.

'Are you too hot, Ms Prentiss?'

'Oh, I can be, inspector,' she said, and leaned forward.

'Let's get one thing straight, Ms Prentiss. 'I am not as other men, whereas I can separate my penis from my brain when occasion demands. I am conducting a serious investigation into the suspicious deaths of at least two people, so forget the Mae West impression.'

'As the great woman once said, ''It's better to be looked over than overlooked,'' she sneered.

Crosbie took a moment to enjoy her pique. 'Now being a tolerant sort, permissive you might even say, I wouldn't dream of judging the sexual peccadilloes of others.' He paused to drag his eyes from her cleavage and began to lose the thread. . . 'As long as privacy is respected and those improprieties are legal. That's not to say, of course that these ....' he cleared his throat and continued .... 'habits don't appall me. Now what exactly is your business in Glasgow?'

'Well, Mr. D.I. self-important Crosbie, for the want of a better description, you might say 'adult' business. You are an adult, aren't you?' It was her turn to enjoy the moment. When he didn't respond she ran her tongue around her open lips and smiled. 'All you said is well and good, but if you rise so high above your primal urges, detective.' She leaned back in the chair to refasten her jacket and whispered, 'why were you staring at my tits just now?'

Crosbie left it to McKenzie to conduct the rest of the interview, from that point on he checked every body signal, every nuance of her tone. Judy confounded his sergeant with a series of inconsequential half answers, and Crosbie put an end to it by tapping a finger impatiently on his watch.

'What exactly were you doing at the Treble A sex shop, and later the Lavender club?' he snapped.

'Oh, you know, business and pleasure. The sex shop was the business bit, the Lavender club, pure pleasure I'm afraid.'

'We're going round in bloody circles here, so I'll ask you again, what exactly is your business, Ms Prentis?'

'Pandering to sexual inadequacy, addressing the shortfall, that sort of thing. Too complex to epitomize in a single answer.'

Rising from the table with an indifferent air of arrogance, she swished across the floor waving a cynical goodbye with manicured fingertips. 'Now if you're done, I have an appointment.'

'Lying in her teeth, Rab. I want everything you can get on her,' Crosbie said.

'Like what guv?'

'Everything: Companies House, Revenue Commission, CRB, Interpol, Scotland bloody Yard, the lot. Get me the membership book from the Lavender Club, the Treble A accounts, and security tapes for the last three weeks.'

'But.'

'Just do it, Rab' . . . Later that day, the file Crosbie uploaded from his inbox left him shaking his head in disbelief. He printed it off, called McKenzie, and they dropped it on his boss's desk.

The Chief Super thumbed through to the coroner's verdict on the last page and put down the file. 'Two people die in a gas explosion at a private clinic in Essex. Accidental death, James,' he said. 'What's it to us?'

Crosbie picked up the report and shook his head.' It leaves both Her husband and His wife potential millionaires!'

'So?'

'So, the day after they both visit Annie's adult shop, Annie and our Procurator Fiscal die in each other's arms in the Lavender club?'

The Chief shrugged. 'There's probably no connection, these things happen. We have a very powerful LGBT lobby here, James. There are adult shops and private clubs in almost every town in Britain, and they all have their rights.'

'Yes, but that's not all,' Crosbie said. 'I've looked at the CCTV footage from Annie's sex shop and guess what?'

'What?'

'Our very own Procurator and the infamous, no longer with us, Angus McKay were regulars there too.' Crosbie gloated for a moment at his boss's apparent puzzlement and waited for the penny to drop.

'Who the hell's Angus McKay?'

'The fellah with his plums blown off in a burnt out Allegro last week.'

'I remember, James, yes, the poor sod who come a cropper with Sumo Sue?'

'That's the one. They put it down to glue-sniffing, spontaneous combustion. You just couldn't make it up.'

McKenzie interjected, 'Angus was more of a lady's man, the

only thing that he'd be sniffing would be underwear.'

The Chief frowned. 'We can do without the levity, sergeant. We've all got to be P C in these matters, so just stick to the facts!'

'. . . Forget about underwear, I certainly smell a rat,' Crosbie told his sergeant later. 'You'd better get out there and find out what the hell's going on,'

'Where do you want me to start, guv?'

'Get me a list of all Annie's customers and match it against the Lavender members. Tell me the truth, Rab, have you been bonking the posh lady?'

'No, sir but I wouldn't mind.'

'Well don't even think about it, son, she's poison that one.'

'No, sir, I mean yes, sir, I mean no.'

'Oh, and posh poison's partner; this Richard Edwards character, see if you can locate him!'

. . .Once again, Richard awoke alone in his own vomit, and staggered from the tenements to the nearest hole-in-the-wall for his daily limit. Somehow, he managed to find his way back to the Slash Inn, where he brought up the subject again. 'I was serious last night you know,' he told Jeddah. 'About doing her in, I did mean it.'

'How much are you actually worth?' Tam said.

'Potentially…'

Upon hearing the six-figure number pound signs began swirling in the froth of Jeddah's pint, and an avalanche of possibilities gridlocked his opportunist mind.

Struggling for a response that would guarantee the optimum Lager vouchers without involving the actual deed, he re-established credibility by asking, 'Does it have to look like an accident?'

'No, it can't look like suicide though, there's an insurance get-out clause you see.' By now, all humour had left Richard's tone. 'You can even make it look like murder, 'as long as they don't pin it on the beneficiary.' He jammed a thumb into his chest for emphasis and rushed off with his hands clamped over his mouth.

'Let's ask him for a grand up front,' said Jeddah, 'and then dump him.'

'A grand's grand but why not five?' replied Tam.

'Why not ten?'

Before Richard's return, the asking price had peaked at a hundred, troughed at five, and levelled off at fifty thousand pounds.

'We're gonnae' have to put a wee show on, he's not a complete dick head, even if that is his nickname, he wouldn't part with his PIN, remember?'

Tam intercepted Richard at the toilet door and steered him back to a quiet corner. 'Listen,' he said sternly, 'this is a serious business.'

'Aye, and we'll be needing some exies up front, Jeddah added.

Richard nodded sincerely. How could the poor man know that the seeds of swindling had already been sown when he asked, 'how much?'

At the last-minute Tam bottled the deposit back down to the original five thousand pounds. Before Richard could say, 'is that all?' Jeddah jumped to his feet. 'Sure, son, that's right. Yeh nae dealing with amateurs, this is a serious business.'

Richard told them he'd have to check a few things first, but essentially, they had a deal, and he would meet them the next day with the 'necessary.'

'Aye, son, you lay the sling. Bring the readies here tomorrow, and we'll set the wheels in motion.'

'Aye, Tamken.'

Jeddah tentatively rubbed his palms together. 'Something on account?'

Tam kicked his brother under the table, but Richard was too busy emptying his pockets to notice. After he had left, Jeddah threw the wad of tenners onto the counter and shouted for 'order! The best things in life are free,' he sang.

They commenced a cramped jig between the gathering barflies. 'But you can keep it for the daft cockney, I want money,' they duetted in horrible disharmony (but it didn't matter.)

'That's what I want.

That's what I wa ha ha ha ha hant.

That's what I want!'

. . .Richard arrived back at the hotel. He was shaking uncontrollably and dressed like a hobo, so understandably the commissionaire was skeptical.

'Away to feck, soft lad,' he growled. Smiling apologetically at a passing guest, he dragged Richard back down the concrete steps by the scruff of his neck. 'If it was nae daylight, I'd be breakin' yeh wee heed, yeh paraffin fecked up lamp.' He whispered the words with a polite smile for onlookers, then casually dropped Richard over a dwarf hedge onto a pile of kitchen waste.

Dusting off his hands, he rushed to open the taxi door and reverted to his elastic I wouldn't mind a tip smirk. 'Good afternoon, madam.'

Sergeant McKenzie raced from the foyer to pull Judy out of earshot as she stepped from the cab. 'Where's that wee boyfriend of yours?'

'What do you want him for?'

'I've got reason to believe he might be able to tell me what the feck's going on, that's what!'

'It's funny you should say that, sergeant, he's been acting awfully strange lately. We could go up to my room and . . . chew it over.'
,

Peering from a gap in the brambles, Richard clamped his hand over his mouth (while Judy puckered) . . .

From his refuge in the refuse, he saw how meekly the sergeant raced on ahead to politely hold the doors, watched as Judy breast-brushed seductively past, and vomited into the kitchen waste.

The basement door creaked open, Gypsy upturned a bin of swill over Richard, and yanked him to his feet. 'Who the hell are you, and what are you doing in my midden?'

He wiped off the faded veg and finger-combed the fish bones from his hair. 'It's a bloody long story,' he said.

His posh accent won him a cautious stay of abandonment and an invitation into the sluice room where she gave him soap and a towel, then held him at arm's length like an irate mother. 'Haven't I seen you somewhere before?'

'Yeah, the Lavender Club.'

'You need a good scrub, but I've got some dirty linen of my own to sort out first,' she said and left him standing there.

Richard sighed, he collapsed onto a pile of soiled whites, and into an overdue, troubled sleep,

It was dark when Gypsy roused him with a cup of strong tea. Hands on hips, she stood back and watched while he forced the scalding liquid to his lips. 'What exactly were you doing in my midden?' she demanded.

'I'm supposed to be staying at this hotel.' He offered an unrequited smile through the steam and shook his head.

Gypsy looked him up and down. 'Ah, I've got you now: radical punk dropout with the spiked leather girlfriend?'

'That's right. What about you?'

'S & M queen, actually,' she replied with a curious smirk and bowed. 'This is my day job, and at this very moment, your peek-a-boo girlfriend is in the penthouse straightening a bent policeman. I think you'd better leave. Now!'

The striking figure towering above his five-foot nothing frame, thumbed towards the door. Richard gritted his teeth to stop them from chattering and finally managed to gasp, 'Let me explain, nice lady.'

Gypsy needed answers too, she jerked him upright, nodded doubtfully, and poured another cup. 'So, explain.'

For such a big woman, she was lithe like a cat. Arse muscles twitching beneath the starched white pinafore, threw his sexuality back into a state of hetero turmoil. She joined him at the table, lowered her boobs, flicked back her hair and flashed her teeth. 'This had better be good!'

And it was! Obviously, the truth was out of the question, so he spun her a tale of boardroom treachery, with himself an innocent victim of Judy's ruthless greed. Stumbling through such a contradiction of one-sided detail, she realized he was making the whole thing up, but let him carry on regardless. By the time the epic ended they were both smiling.

'No one could accuse you of letting the facts spoil a good lie,' she said, 'I knew as soon as I saw your daffodil you were unstable.'

'I think a wallflower would have been more appropriate.'

Adding to his confusion, Gypsy told him he wasn't wearing enough leather for a wallflower. 'If that big Jake had got his way,' she shrugged and paused. . . 'Well, you wore the daffodil!'

He shook his head questioningly, and Gypsy laughed. 'You didn't know, did you?' She went on to explain the significance of the flower.

Richard gasped. 'Multiple molestation, you say! Wouldn't that mean. . . Oh, no, I'm not, I mean, I don't. . . Look, I'm basically straight,' he managed to stammer, then thumped the table too hard and cradled his hand....'I've really got nothing against 'gays,' in fact, to be honest, I think that I might be just a bit 'gay' myself.' Gypsy rubbed his shoulder. 'Coming out can always be painful.'

The thought hit a nerve. Richard squeezed his eyes shut, and it was all he could do to keep from weeping. 'Coming out,' he said. 'I'm not sure I've ever been in!'

'Let's just say you had a lucky escape. You really didn't know, did you?'

'No, but I'd wager Judy did!'

'You'd win.'

'You're very understanding.'

'No, I'm not, I am very anti-Sergeant Rab McKenzie.' She spat out his name with anger. 'He's been passing your picture around the hotel. At this very moment, he's screwing the bitch that I was hoping to screw, who's trying to screw you. We're having no luck at all, are we?'

'Can I stay with you?' Richard asked. 'I'll pay you well. I've got plenty of money.'

Gypsy immediately agreed, regardless of the 'magic word,' she would have anyway; there was something about him, something beneath the surface, something refreshingly sinister. 'We're about the same size, I've got some spare leathers,' she said, and his eyes lit up. 'I meant motorbike leathers!' When she told him where she lived, his paper cup crashed to the floor.

. . . In the control of a force greater than his will, he climbed onto her machine and clung to her waist like a petrified limpid. Glasgow blurred by in the evening breeze as they cruised through the drizzle, and he was loving every minute of it.

Skidding to a halt outside the Treble A, Gypsy undid the clutching fingers locked around her waist, Straddling the great Kawasaki machine, her leather-bound leg cleared the handlebars by a yard. She helped Richard to dismount and beat a path between a clutch of 'white mac voyeurs comparing fetishes in Annie's shop window. 'Out of the way, wankers, we're closed till further notice.' Barging her way through, she pulled down the shutters and slammed the door in their leering faces.

While she was used to negotiating the pitch interior, Richard obviously was not, and groped his way into the path of the six-foot fiberglass penis swinging perilously from above. Gypsy laughed and pulled the huge phallic icon to one side. Helping him to his feet for the second time that day, she hoisted him effortlessly into a fireman's lift. 'You're having no luck with big pricks, are you?' she said, and dropped him onto the upstairs bed.

85

Chapter Ten:
The Recovery Position

Judy left McKenzie panting on the penthouse divan while she calmly polished her nails. "I know you're aware that I'm potentially a very wealthy woman. I also know you've wondered how to separate me from some of it. Am I right?"

Taking in every syllable as she stripped his conscience bare, Rab's eyes opened wide, his ears pricked, but he remained still.

'Well listen to me,' she continued, 'if you think that you can do it from between the sheets, forget it! You're not that. . . in fact, you're almost as bad as. . . well, never mind. Put it this way, you are not the end of my orgasmic rainbow, sarge, let's leave it at that.' Without turning, she grasped him through the bedclothes. 'But don't worry, darling, I happen to own the patent.'

Curiosity overtook initial shock, and he turned to see her calmly polishing her cuticles on the throw-over and grinning to herself. 'What do you mean patent?'

'I mean, I can rebuild you, sarge, but first things first.' She pouted, and looked him straight in the eye. 'First I want you to do away with Richard.'

Rab sat up straight and shook his head. 'I'm not sure I heard you right. Are you suggesting that. . ?'

'Stop!' Puffing at her fingertips, she raised a palm to stroke his face. 'There-there, sarge, anything but phony indignation. You know you heard me right. I want you to kill him, or at the very least have him killed, and for that I will pay one hundred K cash. If I'm wrong about you, then arrest me!' She held up her wrists symbolically; when he didn't move, reached back down beneath the quilt, 'or failing that. . .

Till then his most contentious bribe had been an occasional freebie from Sumo Sue. Thus far, corruption had been confined to altering the odd statement to ensure a conviction, or in some rich cases, an acquittal. To that end, he had of course, indulged in risk-free actions such as shredding the odd file, losing a vital piece of evidence, or, on occasion, fibbing on oath, that sort of thing. Rab had been known to 'accidentally' truncheon a manacled prisoner (to defend himself, of course). He'd snapped the odd wrist, ground the odd testicle, all in the line of duty. Even if not averse to the odd assault in custody, essentially, he saw himself as a law-abiding cop who had never considered himself to be corrupt. (But for a hundred K in smackers?)

This was different, in that it might involve some personal risk; this job would have to be farmed out.

What worried him more than the actual deed was how Judy could have been so right about him. Greed had indeed kicked in. In fact, he was deciding just what he could offer when she propositioned him. He caught her eye through the open bathroom door, touched a finger to his lips, and returned Crosbie's latest missed call.

His boss wasn't happy. 'Where the hell are you, Rab?'

'I'm at a friend's place. What is it, guv?'

'Why the hell can't you answer your bloody phone? I've been trying to reach you all day!'

Judy waddled into the room carrying a brown paper parcel and Rab's eyes widened. 'Sorry, sir, I've been sort of, erm, undercover.'

'What do you know about this Wang fellah, lead singer in a band called Scallywag?'

'Nothing much, some say he's a closet gay, but that kind of thing goes with the job. Why are we interested in him?'

'He wears a sexual aid, purchased from Annie's sex shop, that's why,' Crosbie said. 'It's all over Facebook.'

'Like I said, guv, it goes with the job.'

'Yeah, but you'll never guess what club he co-owns.'

'I'll be there as soon as I can, I've a couple of things that need to be taken care of first,' he said as Judy smiled and ducked under the sheet.

Crosbie had the I T girl track his last incoming call, and twirled his pencil. 'The lying sod! the lying conniving sod!' he told the wall.

Jeddah was punting out his wares in the Barras market when Rab crept up behind. 'Hey, do you have anything I can dance all night to?' He clasped one half of the cuffs around Jeddah's wrist before he could run. 'I think it would be less conspicuous if you emptied your own gusset, don't you?'

Jeddah searched disinterested passing faces for support and

the immediate area for a weapon before resorting to a textbook, hollow denial. 'I din'nae ken what you mean.'

The policeman produced a small pair of garden secateurs from his hip pocket. 'Now, I know exactly where you keep your drugs,' he said, 'but I've no particular wish to investigate your scrotals.' He waved the snippers in the air. 'So, unless you'd like a dodgy short back-and-sides?'

Jeddah delved into his trousers with his free hand. 'I've paid you once this week!'

Rab savoured the moment before putting away his snips. 'Leave your stash where it is, son. I'll meet you and your wayward brother in the Greasy Spoon in one hour.' Dragging Jeddah's arm with him, he checked his watch, 'In an hour, if you ken what's good for you.'

'Aye, but. . .'

'Ours not to reason why, son.' Rab yanked his arm forward, unlocked the cuffs from his own wrist, and slinked away smiling.

As it turned out, the brothers were on time; McKenzie was half an hour late, and made them wait even longer while he pushed to the front of the queue for a sticky bun. Unfazed by the contemptuous leers that followed, he sat slowly down opposite the brothers.

Feeling decidedly braver in the company of his sibling, Jeddah offered his manacled arm across the table. 'Take this feck off me!'

Rab smiled and clamped the free end to the tubular centrepiece. 'Don't use that tone, wi' me, son, especially when I'm here to make your fortune. Now shut the feck up and listen! How would you pair of no-mark chancers like to make ten grand?'

'Oh, yeah, and what do we have to do for that, kill someone?'

'Got it in one! It can look like anything except suicide, as long as it doesn't come back to me.' The brothers looked at each other incredulously. It was an almost verbatim re-run of yesterday's conversation with Richard, but they couldn't share their sense of deja vu.

'Who is it?' Tam was consciously trying to sound authentic, but Jeddah remained stoic: wrist shackled, eyes fixed.

'A short arse fool called Richard Edwards, A K A dickhead. You know who I mean, don't you? I rescued the little punk's girlfriend from you last week.' Rab studiously chewed on his bun,

88

and hesitated. . .'You haven't topped him already, have you?' he asked hopefully.

Tam laughed. 'No, we took his cash card for a spin a few times, but he cottoned on. Where is he now?'

Rab scrutinized them before accepting their ignorance. 'I'll find him for you.' Discarding the half-eaten remains of his sticky bun, he freed Jeddah from the cuffs. 'Now I hate to say this, but it's either do the business, or I'll nick you both for supplying.' Tam smiled, but Jeddah remained tight-lipped. 'Me or Barlinnie, take your pick!' was the policeman's bottom line.

'You didn't say why you picked us.' Tam was looking at his brother sardonically, but he was speaking to McKenzie.

The policeman tapped him playfully on the cheek and spoke as you would to a naughty toddler. 'Because, my fine wee friends, you know the little bugger, and you're a greedy pair of amoral nobody chavs! Am I right?''

Tam pulled away. 'We'll be needing some exies up front, sort of a retainer?'

'Aye, how much?'

'A grand?'

McKenzie threw a twenty-pound note onto the table and laughed on his way to the door. 'Get tae feck! I'll be in touch,' he shouted over his shoulder.

Jeddah rubbed his wrist. 'What's happening, bro?' The man's a lunatic if he thinks that he can get us to commit murder for him. Not for a twenty-pound deposit anyway, the cheapskate! What can we do?'

'We humour him, that's what.'   They were locked in a whispered huddle across the table when Richard sat between them, patting his breast pocket. A bulging brown envelope lifted the mood considerably, and quite naturally they reconvened at the Slash Inn bar. Coupled with the lubricating effects of lager, camaraderie took over from confusion, and it wasn't long before they had to confide.

. . . Richard sat back, content for them to think that he was analyzing the information, before announcing, 'Judy put him up to it.' He decided not to tell what he had heard from Gypsy, enjoying instead, the feeling of intellectual superiority his rapid conclusion implied.

'How do you figure that out?' Tam asked.

'It's the only possible scenario; if either one of us croaks, the other inherits a fortune. The question is, what can we do about Sergeant McKenzie? She's obviously bonking him.'

If Richard expected plaudits for his great powers of deduction, he was sadly disappointed when Jeddah stood and rubbed his belly. 'Anyone fancy a fish supper?'

Chapter Eleven:
A quiet Life

James Crosbie spread the files out 'tarot fashion' on his boss's desk. 'An explosion at a private posh London clinic leaves two rich people missing, presumed dead.'

'And how is that our concern?' the Chief said.

'Add to that, Annie and our Fiscal, Angus McKay and Sumo Sue, six in total.' Crosbie twirled his pencil and waited for a reaction that didn't come.

'And?'

'And now my sergeant's 'having it off' with one of the prime suspects.'

'What do you make of it?' the Chief said. (He felt obliged to say something).

Crosbie threw down his pencil. 'All these occurrences are unusual, even by Glasgow standards. That's without the common denominator that binds them.'

'Which is?'

'The Lavender Club.'

'So, what do we do?'

'We find out what the hell is going on there, that's what!'

The Chief Super shuffled the paperwork as though missing a document. 'What have you got, James, a few bizarre deaths in a bizarre city? We've got gang warfare on our streets and September weekend coming up, guaranteed to provide us with a couple of real crimes!' He shook his head, boxed the papers into a neat bundle and handed them back.

As he stood to end the meeting, Crosbie tried one last time to put his point across. 'There are links between them, links that. . .'

. . . 'What, sex and greed, that links us all doesn't it? We can't look under everyone's bed, James, and we don't want any scandals, not with the elections coming up!'

'Elections!'

'We all have our secrets, James. Lots of people play games, naughty games you might say that sometimes go wrong. Trust me on this.' He opened the door. 'We live in an age of designer violence and designer drugs, and you want a special squad to investigate a couple of fatal sexperiments!'

'There's a lot more to it than that. You know as well as me!'

The Chief stood to end the meeting. 'Oh yes, I forgot, an unexplained explosion on the other side of the bloody border!'

Crosbie knew it would be futile to pursue the matter, he'd spent half his working life talking to bosses who just wanted a 'quiet life.'

As he turned to leave the Chief Super' stopped him. 'Look, maybe you are on to something. I envy you in a way, James. Unlike me, the big picture does not distract you. I have to suffer these infernal budgets and manpower audits. If I had to choose between an open coroners' verdict and drug cartels, give me the gangsters every time.'

Crosbie was already closing the door, 'It's a number's game,' his boss shouted, after him, but it was his turn not to listen. He downloaded the 'phallic extension' blurb from the PIGME website, and couldn't help but be impressed by the sheer range. Printing off the bumph of an item that caught his attention. he made his way to the Pathology Department in the basement of The Royal.

He and Debbie had been more than friends for many years, but it was 'Debbie the Pathologist' he was there to see. His stoic expression confirmed that his visit was purely police business, and he handed her the printout. 'Glasgow's sole stockist dies in the arms of our Fiscal, after he bought one of these contraptions from her. What the hell's going on?'

Debbie sat down and clicked her tongue the way she did when she was on to something. 'Anything else?'

'Yes, Angus McKay, one of Annie's last customers, burnt to death in the arms of a well-known soiled dove.'

'Ah, Sumo Sue, I examined her remains. A bit old for 'glue sniffing,' I thought.' She reached into the drawer and laid two transparent exhibit bags on her desk. 'One contains the charred remains dislodged from Angus McKay's cadaver, the other an intact sample taken from the late Fiscal. The match is undeniable.'

'Why didn't you call me?'

'If I rang you every time something unusual came along, James, I'd never be off the damn phone! Anyway,' she added. 'Unusual at first, now the circumstances are downright intriguing.'

Crosbie slumped back into the chair and crossed his legs. 'Tell me about Exhibit A?'

'You're not going to like this, James, but it will be worth it I assure you.' She mounted the polycarbonate prosthesis taken from the Fiscal over an Eiffel Tower paperweight, puncturing the polythene cover in the process. 'Now,' she said when she was happy with the angle. 'Say something dirty.' While his expression pleaded for a clue, Debbie smiled. 'It has a receptor sensitive to certain vocal stresses, alpha soundwaves that trip a hidden pump to action.'

Crosbie felt it was some kind of practical joke. 'Are you telling me that if I talk about sex?' Right on cue the prosthesis sprang to rigidity and rendered him speechless.

Debbie pointed to the small print in the sales blurb. 'The combination of the letters E and X, create that throaty consonance recognized by the micro-sensor. They call it the French Connection. The 'UCK' guttural sound is another example.'

During the ensuing silence, the Rampant Rod slide-on reverted to its flaccid norm, but Crosbie's tension didn't.

'Touch the mole,' she urged. 'Go on, touch it.'

A clinical prod with his pencil returned the phallic monster to its proud bursting state. 'Well, I never?'

'I should hope not, darling. Apparently, these things are all the rage in Brighton.' She laughed and read from the printout blurb: 'peppermint emulsified, self-lubricating, thermostatically controlled, sound activated. I could go on but you're blushing.'

Crosbie remained in silent thought until Debbie removed the object of his discomfort, then repeated 'well I never!' It was the best he could do.

She liked the way his eyebrows apexed when he concentrated; enjoyed the strange dichotomy of a man who'd seen so much of the world, reduced to jelly by simple innuendo. He just wasn't good at intimacy. In fact, it had taken him years to plant a tentative kiss on Debbie's cheek, but she was touching forty now, the vague promise of that solitary kiss was no longer enough.

He caught her stare, then shied away and quickly changed the subject. 'Judy Prentiss,' he said, 'wife of millionaire Samuel who died the same way as Angus MacKay'

'What about it?'

'Turns out she was in the Lavender club the night the Fiscal come a cropper with Annie. What do you think?'

After too short a time she threw the papers aside. 'I'll tell you what I think James, shall I?' She called up her diary to cancel her appointments and closed the laptop. Rounding the desk, she kissed him full on the lips and nestled her face into his shoulder. 'I think it's high time we slept together, don't you?'

After a late blossoming and an uncertain spate of empty affairs, it had been a long time coming, and he hoped he could still rise to the occasion.

Debbie poured him a glass of red and stood back. 'Watch this space,' she said. Without another word, she stripped off her clothes in the dappled fire-glow and crooked her finger to the bedroom.

Feeling none of the morning-after unease, he surprised her with an unsolicited kiss on the neck as he helped with a stubborn hook.

Chapter Twelve:
Hypothetical wealth

Richard's hypothetical wealth took second place to Gypsy's deviant duties. 'It's all very well counting your chickens, but some of us have a paying job to go to,' she said, dropping him roughly on the bed. 'I'll be back later.'

He pretended to sleep, but there was still a rogue Rampant Rod to locate and deactivate. No sooner had Gypsy's 650 Kawasaki roared back into the night, than he was downstairs in the adult shop.

His eyes took a little time to acclimatize to the pitch interior and he dodged the same swinging phallus that had knocked him over on the way in. Fumbling away, groping blindly in the dark, he located the light switch and the world around him changed in the blink of an eye. Suddenly he was surrounded by a plethora of erotica, not an inch of display space wasted, genital prosthetics beckoned from every angle and he began to weep with joy.

High on a top shelf, above the dross of pubic curls and wisp, a line of stentorian slide-ons stood to silent attention. They were not his own models, but professional curiosity will out; he probed and kneaded each one to life before tossing it casually over his shoulder. Within minutes the floor below was a writhing sea of humming plastic. 'Bollox to cheap copies,' he sneered.

The distinctive jangling of keys stopped him in his tracks. A moonlit shard through the window scratch-marks highlighted a familiar image. Turning off the lights, he pricked his ears and crouched low as Judy pushed open the door. 'There's bound to be something in here that will help you, sarge,' he heard her whisper, and what tiny resolve he possessed buckled to panic.

A shadow loomed across the sea of dancing plastic and Richard froze, ducked for cover behind the great hanging fibreglass phallus, and gulped for breath.

The only sound above his own pounding heart was McKenzie swearing at his useless torch and stomping around in the dark. 'Feckin police issue bloody feckin rubbish.' Under the 'roller' effect of a hundred dancing sex toys, groping perilously close to the light switch, he lost his footing and crashed to the ground cursing and swearing.

Richard used the distraction to clamber inside the hollow swinging phallus, just as Judy clicked on the lights. Cramming his cheek hard to the penile eyehole, he watched her slow sensual approach. Licking her lips, twanging the elasticized bridle strap, she puckered. (His own testis retracted deep into his stomach!)

Squirming for a foothold through the mass of vibrating plastic, McKenzie grabbed protectively at his own groin, but by now Judy's mind was elsewhere.

Smiling like a child in a chocolate factory, she plopped easily into Annie's chair behind the counter, turned on the TV and selected her favourite 'Wee Wullie' DVD. 'Stay down there until you find something that fits,' she told McKenzie.

From inside his penile cocoon, Richard could see her face, bathed in the small screen glow, her wobbling jaw dropped, and she was dribbling from the corners of her mouth. An airborne fibre-particle tickled his nasal cavities, he had to daub his nose painfully against the rough inner-surface to stop himself from sneezing. Whistling around his sinuses for release, the imminent reflex that would have provoked his discovery and for all he knew, his execution, was somehow resisted. 'Ah, Ah,' ah'. . . He squinted his nostrils, contorted every facial muscle for control but it was a battle lost. 'Ah. . . Ah. . . Ah'. (Lucky for him, the Wee Wullie soundtrack was bleating out remarkably similar noises).

Carrying Richard's old anarchist tee shirt in one hand and a framed photograph in the other, McKenzie raced down the stairs shouting, 'he's been here!'

It spoiled the moment for Judy, she tore her gaze from the action. 'Shut up, this is the best bit,' she squealed, and turned her attention back to what was happening in porn land. 'Go for it, girl!'

'Ah ,' Richard moaned in almost perfect sync with the sighs of the impaled, small screen nymphet. 'Ah, ah, ahhhhhhhhg!'

McKenzie lay the framed photograph onto the counter. Judy looked down at the Gothic scene of whips and conceptual trophies on a dungeon backdrop. Gypsy was bedecked in leather in the foreground and it tipped Judy over the edge. 'Ah ah,' ah' ah'aaaaahhhhnnnnnnn,' she cried, fell back, took a deep breath to recover, and paused the video tape. 'How appropriate, but it won't take Inspector Crosbie long to make the connection.'

'Aye, he's nae' fool,' McKenzie said.

'Yes, well, we shall just have to dispose of him too then,

96

sergeant, shan't we? For which we can safely say I will be doubling your fee, on completion of course,' she said, and casually pressed the 'play' button. 'Oh, I love this bit,' she groaned and turned up the volume.

McKenzie could appreciate why she might want his boss dead, but there was still one thing that puzzled him. 'Why is the pipsqueak, pseudo punk so bloody important?' he asked but Judy wasn't listening.

'Come here, wee man.' She pulled him forward by the crotch. 'let's see what you got, then.'

While they were otherwise engaged on the countertop, Richard scurried free and crawled slowly back upstairs. With measured control he tiptoed to the bathroom, slid open the window and delivered the bellowing sneeze of his life to the Glasgow night air. 'A'a a achooooooooo!' Fortunately for him the noise reverberating through the underbelly of the city, did not distract Judy and the policeman from their lustful ministrations.

Shimmying down the drainpipe to the alley below, Richard tiptoed to the main street, to be swallowed up unnoticed by the marauding night crowd, and cautiously made his way to the Lavender Club side-entrance. The transvestite barperson opened the door. 'I knew you'd come back, they always do,' he said.

Richard barged his way through to the foyer. 'Speak for yourself,' he shouted. This time he made it a point to read the rules and purchased a simple daisy, which he understood depicted no more than the wrong time of the month.

Without another word he made his way downstairs where a colourful barperson was issuing capes and infra-red pistols for the next session. Wang waved 'hello' and beckoned from across the crowded dance floor. Richard followed him to the threshold of room 284 and peeked into the darkness. Shuffling expectantly beneath a hail of zigzagging strobe lights, a gaggle of caped combatants jostled for pole position.

'It's a simple game based on the Lazer-world principle,' Wang said. 'Instead of infra-red beams, we use something else.'

It all looked very tame to Richard. 'What else?'

Wang ignored the question. 'And you have to be naked to take part,' nakedness can be a great leveler, don't you think? Take off your clothes and you're just the same as everybody else.' he said, and looked down. 'Well almost.'

By now truly intrigued, Richard just had to ask where Gypsy came in.

'Oh, she's here to make sure the rules are obeyed. Look for yourself!'

A purple spotlight flared to life to focus on her. astride a giant black phallus. On the same lines as a mechanical rodeo ride, the great steed bucked and reared in accelerating motion. In skin-tight leather, thigh-high boots and little else, she held on to the synthetic foreskin with one hand, the other waving the business end of a power hose in the air. 'Wee ha!'

This is the best bit' Wang said. He clicked his hand-held module dial up a notch and the great phallus jerked wildly. It shuddered to an abrupt halt, and Gypsy gushed out a torrent that sent a hoard of marauders arse over heels. 'Show's over for now!' Wang shouted and turned on the house lights.

Richard was curious to know what the participants got out of it. 'Apart from wet,' he joked.

'Oh, it's much more than that on a Friday,' Wang said.

During her second vodka break of the night, Gypsy listened intently to Richard's account of what had happened in the Treble A, and agreed that it was no longer safe for him there. 'Go back to the hotel and wait for me in the sluice room,' she told him.

. . .That same night on the decidedly rougher side of town, Jeddah was emerging from the mother of all binges, (insolvent and hungover). He creaked himself upright and rummaged the room in a fruitless quest for any remnant of drugs or alcohol.

. . . An hour of self-pity and thirty seconds of soul-searching later, he took off in search of his rich benefactor.

The hood and stubble that blended so well in Springburn had the opposite effect on the posh side of the city: heads turned in distain, suits gave a wide berth. Oozing conspicuousness, he cut across a flower bed and skulked towards the exclusive hotel. Climbing the steps three-at-a-time, he took a breath and nodded. The giant commissionaire, was wearing a hostile 'who the feck are you' frown and Jeddah attempted a placating smile. 'Hi, I've an appointment with a resident.' He tried to walk nonchalantly by, but the toe of a size ten boot sent him tumbling back to street level.

The commissionaire snarled and brandished a threatening fist. 'Appointment with a resident, aye, and my arse is a cream bun!' In an effort to clear the steps in one leap he fell back on his arse.

Jeddah poked a derisive finger, just like Richard, he ducked low behind the nearest hedge and watched the big man scramble to his feet. 'Swivel on this, yeh lacky.'

A colony of kamikaze bluebottles circled the rancid air below. Overspilled cabbage-leaves fluttered in the swill of decaying vegetation; a cockney twang croaked from beneath. 'How did you find me?'

Jeddah touched his nose as a sign of intuition, and scampered down the sluice room stairway to brush the offal from Richard's hair. 'We have our methods,' he said.

As the squawk of a wild cat spun the commissionaire on his heels, the midden door opened behind them. 'Keep low, and get in,' Gypsy hissed. 'Moggies eh, Charlie!' she shouted through the privets.

The commissioner's polished boot missed a darting feline by a street. He stood on one leg to buff a toecap on his calf and lamented. 'Yeah, bloody moggies eh; moggies and jakeys!

Gypsy pulled Richard inside by the scruff of his neck. 'I'm glad you found your way here, wee man?' Scanning Jeddah from head to foot, she recognised him from Annie's shop door. 'Aren't you the bouncer?'

Jeddah looked down at her heaving breasts. 'Like I said before, hen, there's bouncers and there's bouncers. Jeddah's the name, minder's the game, right now I've got a contract with the wee man.'

Richard went on to describe in great detail the conversation he heard from inside the fibreglass phallus. Judy put a contract on my life, so it's just as well I put one on hers, isn't it?'

'Don't you move, big fellah,' Gypsy said, 'this wee man's in need of a good scrub.' She led Richard to the linen room next door, sluiced him down and settled him beneath a pile of freshly laundered bedding. 'Get some sleep,' she said, and put his filthy clothes on a bio-boil.

When she returned Jeddah was aiming his favourite finger. 'What we have here, hen, is a case of too many crooks spoiling a good'n. I saw him first, so I think that should get teh feck or. . .'

Before he could finish, Gypsy had his vitals in a half twist. . . 'It'll be a dry day in the Sarry Head when the likes of you can intimidate me, so, I've got a deal for you! Either we work together, or you get tae' feck, Capiche?' She backed him onto the sink, turned her vicelike grip to a caress and softened her tone. 'Look, if we play this loser along, we can all do okay. Have you seen how much he's worth?' She reached down and pushed out her tongue.

The glint in her eye made him tingle from diaphragm to crotch as she shrugged from her overall. He grabbed the pipes behind his head for support and a pair of velvet handcuffs appeared from nowhere. 'I've no wish to be gentle with you, big fellah,' she said. Clamping his wrists to the cold-water pipe she undid his trousers. 'However, there are certain rules to this particular game, stop means don't stop, pain is joy. I will dominate and humiliate you until you are truly purged!'

Jeddah's protests, by this time were inextricably confined to a series of dehydrated croaks as Gypsy circled catlike. 'Bollox, to that,' he growled.

'If that's what you prefer, big fellah, if you're very lucky, I'll take you to a place where you won't have to pretend.'

'Oh aye, and where's that?' Despite her nakedness Jeddah couldn't rise to the occasion: dumbstruck and terrified he was still trying to figure out the rules, and the opposite was occurring. 'Wait a m-m-minute,' he managed to stammer. 'I didn't, I'm n-not sure.'

Gypsy continued to lick her lips. 'I know, don't tell me, you feel vulnerable and exposed, that's the whole point, don't you see? I'm only taking you to where you secretly want to go.' Before pumping her screwed up knuckle deep into his solar plexus she slipped the leather hood over his head. 'There, that's better, isn't it?' she said and punched him again.

Trousers at ankles, his upper body lurched forward with enough impetus to yank the enamel sink from the wall behind. It spun in a great arc over his head to knock Gypsy unconscious on the solid slate floor.

The cascade of ice-cold water on his arse fired him to his senses and he fell forward, kneaded his thighs into her groin for purchase and bit the key chain from her neck. After an age he somehow managed to unfetter his hands and crawl to the door.

With one last look at Gypsy smiling lewdly, writhing under the impromptu fountain. 'Hmm,' she groaned from beneath the torrent, 'you are good!'

'Feck this for a game of soldiers!' he shouted and stumbled out back through the midden (pulling up his pants on the way).

At that very moment sergeant Rab McKenzie was cautiously

dislodging his head from between Judy's skull-crushing thighs. Grabbing him by the hair, she twisted his face upward. 'What do you mean, a man like Crosbie doesn't just give up. What's he up to?' Searching her mind for a cheap solution, she spread her legs to let him breathe, but in the absence of a eureka moment she reverted to type. 'Tell me everything there is to know about your detective inspector; He's top of the hit list now!'

'Well, he's a divorcee who lives alone, a stickler for detail, he's got a 'sort of' lady friend that works in the morgue and she's very, very bright. That's about it.'

'Works in the morgue eh, that could come in handy, and lives alone. I'll bet you didn't know the vast majority of fatal accidents occur in the home?' she said with a smirk.

McKenzie tried to grimace and smile at the same time, which if you think about it, can't be easy with a great pair of thighs re-clamping your face. . . When the kernel of a truly insidious plot began to take root, she released her grip. 'Get a move on we've got work to do,' she panted, 'faster, deeper and harder!'

. . . 'You're going to need his front door key, a screwdriver and a little bit of bottle,' she told him later.

While he admired her resolution, he couldn't help feeling like a puppet in her play. 'That sounds doable,' he said after she talked him through the detail.

'Once your boss returns from his philandering, he turns on the light switch and creates the dead-short that ignites a house full of methane. Result, another tragic domestic fatality!' She bowed and waited for applause.

Finally, Rab gave in and clapped. He had to hand it to her, she was beautifully evil. 'I love you,' he said, and she pulled a face behind his back.

Rab McKenzie fished for the spare house keys Crosbie had taped beneath his desk drawer, and checked that there was no one at home before letting himself in. After turning off the main power supply, he carefully unscrewed the plastic faceplate from a light-switch situated just inside the front door. With moisture dribbling either side of the pencil torch between his teeth he deliberately and slowly, fixed a single strand of copper from the 'feed' side of the circuit to 'earth.' Refitting the plastic cover, he smeared his prints with spittle wet hands before backtracking to the kitchen. In the borrowed communal light, he snapped the ignition electrode from the cooker hob before turning on the gas jet. A desperate frown spread across his features, he held his breath, agonizingly flicked back the main breaker, and left as innocuously as he had entered.

Judy suggested he should be as far away as possible when the bomb went off. 'I could go and see my mum in Dundee,' he said.

She thought it was a good idea. 'It'll work out well, your boss will be history when you get back. Remember you must behave normally.' She pushed him towards the door, 'that means carry on acting stupid!'

By now he'd ceased to occupy her thoughts, they were on the big picture. Judy had to find Richard, and the only clue to his whereabouts, his apparent connection with the Treble A adult shop. Donning her leathers, she hailed a taxi.

The forensic report on the Prentiss fire concluded spontaneous combustion following chemical impregnation was the most probable cause, and that nobody could have survived.

Crosbie tapped Debbie on the shoulder. 'Apart from residue amounting to little more than ash, no trace of human remains, a tad unusual don't you think, even after such a ferocious fire?'

'Not unusual, unprecedented! So where do we go from here?'

'You've got some leave coming up,' he said, 'what do you say to some quality time in London, do some shopping, see a show? I'll book the tickets.'

Debbie was as usual, way ahead of him. 'Anything but 'CATS,' she said, 'and we could even investigate a certain chemical explosion while we're there'....

He put his arms around her. 'You know me too well,' he said, and amused himself at the prospect of undoing her bra.

She smiled at his reticence in the mirror before planting a 'that's enough' kiss on his beard and gently pushing him away. 'I do know you, James, better than you think. I've been studying you for years, remember? To be honest though, I'm just as curious about this whole thing as you are.'

'Yes, but I'm still not sure where McKenzie fits in.'

'Right, the first thing to do is tell him the investigation is closed; give him enough rope. The rest we play by touch.'

'Touch, I like the sound of that,' Crosbie said, and pulled her into the bedroom. . .

The following afternoon found them 200 miles away. They were sitting in the pub across the road watching the demolition crew clearing up what was left of the Prentiss clinic. 'Correct me if I'm wrong.' Crosbie said, 'we suspect someone of something, but we don't know who, or of what.'

'What if nobody died in the explosion?' Debbie said.

'Then who would stand to gain. Sam Prentiss was rich anyway and the life insurance was negligible?'

The young barman, who couldn't help overhearing, told them he was on duty when the bomb went off.

'Did you notice anything unusual?'

Sensing interest, he sat down like an old friend. 'I should say so, the only two customers that day were sitting right where you are now, looking across the road just like you when it happened. After the big bang, I came up from the cellar and they were dancing and laughing. I tried to ring emergency services, but the explosion had blown out our phone lines. I went to three bloody boxes before I found one that worked. By the time I got back they were gone.'

'Didn't you tell the police?'

'I told them alright, and some baby-faced constable said I was being hysterical!'

Debbie asked if he'd mind looking at some photographs and he immediately identified Richard Edwards and Judy Prentiss. 'Curiouser and curiouser,' she said, 'I think what we may have here are two conspiracies, possibly three.'

'Assuming you're right, and nobody died in the explosion, let's look at the people we know are dead,' Crosbie said. 'We've got the Procurator Fiscal and Annie, Sumo Sue and Angus McKay. Beside the fact that they're all with their maker what else do they have in common?'

'All Glaswegians with a predilection for sex toys?'

'What else?'

'Annie's Treble A adult shop, yes, and what connects the sex shop to all the deceased?'

'The Lavender Club,' they said together.

Chapter Thirteen:
Utmost discretion

The Chief didn't mind his Detective Inspector's informal attitude when they were alone, it was when he acted that way in company that rankled. Of course, because Crosbie was aware of this, he did it all the more, but always fell short of taking, or giving, offence. The cat-and-mouse game they had played for years was set aside as soon as he saw his boss's distraught expression.

'We've known each other for years,' the Chief said, 'and for years, I've provided locker-room entertainment for most of the men. But you're not like the rest, James. I've always been able to depend on your discretion.'

Crosbie was never one to suffer needless preamble, but this was obviously a very delicate situation, so he sat back and waited for his boss to work up to the point.

'We all have our frailties, James, and I know that you're not one to judge.' He sighed and waited for an affirming nod of the head, then emptied the contents of a large vellum envelope onto his desk.

With the Chief's stare burning into the top of his skull, feeling he was under some ultimate test of self-control, Crosbie looked down at the bundle of photographs. . . If ever there was a time in his life to call on every nuance of his being to subdue a reaction, it was now.

During his service days he thought he'd seen everything. On shore-leave with shipmates who might not see the next dawn, he'd even pushed the probity envelope himself. After that, his time in the Vice Squad was augmented with sights that would remain vivid forever, but the spectacle of his Chief Inspector, regaled in frills in an act of ridiculous depravity with the late Fiscal and a mouth foaming green imp, beat them all!

To brace his laugh muscles and divert his breath through his nose, he clamped his teeth, evoking a series of short starting motor snorts.

Jaws locked tight, he perused the wall, the ceiling and the floor, focusing anywhere but the pathetic man sat dolefully opposite. Finally, he squeezed his eyes shut, turned the photographs facedown, and managed to suppress the impulse long enough to chortle one word. 'Blackmail?'

The Chief nodded solemnly. 'I'm desperate, James. I don't know what to do. I'm due for retirement next year, as you know.'

Crosbie regained enough composure to ask the obvious question. 'What do they want?'

'Money of course, more than I could ever afford!' The Chief replied, and threw the typewritten demand across the desk.

'Right, the first thing we do is get this lot to forensics,' Crosbie said.

Stuffing the photographs under his coat, the Chief shook his head. 'Not these, James.' With the evidence out of sight his expression lifted from a hang-dog frown to a constipated smile. 'The wife's seen everything, she's thrown me out and I need to ask a big favour. Could you put me up for a few days? I'll understand if you say no.'

Crosbie's reaction settled on the cynical side of sympathy. He reached beneath the desk for his spare keys that didn't seem to be exactly where he had left them. 'Stay as long as you like, I don't live there anymore.' He opened the door for his boss, who was understandably anxious to leave. 'Try not to worry too much, sir, if your wife knows already there's only so much damage they can do!'

'Oh, I'm not worried about her, James, she's a member of the club too, but can you imagine what the tabloids would do with these pictures?'

Crosbie could imagine, and he was glad when the Chief had left his office so he could have the best laugh he'd had in years. When his eyes had stopped watering, he wiped them dry and spread out the ransom note on his desk: 'Fifty grand in tenners or I go pubic.' He had to look twice before spotting the typo, and burst once again into laughter as he picked up the phone. 'Debbie, we've just got to meet for lunch.'

Chapter Fourteen:
Passion-filled city limits

In the passion filled city limits on an old firm match day, a quiet drink is impossible, so they opted for the fifteen-minute drive to Kelvingrove. Crosbie was brimming with the news, but managed to just about keep a straight face recounting the details of his meeting with his Chief Inspector. When he showed Debbie the hilarious ransom note they both burst into laughter.

Finishing her drink in one gulp, she handed him the empty glass, 'Same again please.' Leaving her on tenterhook he went to the bar and returned with two large ones.

Providence, coincidence or serendipity? Call it whatever you like, but on today of all days, two miscreant brothers just happen to settle in the very next booth, one nursing his crotch, the other a pint of Tenants. They were talking about 'that bastard McKenzie:' add a casual mention of 'Dick ed Edwards,' and Crosbie fished for his warrant card. 'Of all the bars in all the world,' he drawled in a weak Rick Blaine. . . Ten minutes later a posse of uniforms were frog-marching the brothers from the building.

'What in tarnation are you up to?' Debbie asked. When he told her what little he knew, she couldn't wait to hear the back-story.

. . . Jeddah looked for support but Tam had collapsed into fretful sleep on the single cell mattress, so he pressed his mouth to the Judas hole. 'Wrongful arrest, get me a feckin brief!' he shouted!

. . . Five minutes later the cell door opened, a hand drew hm out into the corridor and turned the key behind him.

'What's going on? Are we under arrest? What the feck are we supposed to have done? I want a brief!'

The duty sergeant gathered up the slack from Jeddah's shirt in his giant fist and marched him down the corridor, 'All in good time. Our Detective Inspector would like a wee word with you, laddie, if you're nae' too busy that is.' On the short journey from the dingy bowels of Peel Street police station not a gaze was exchanged, nor another word spoken, until the large policeman dropped the prisoner into the interview room chair.

Crosbie looked up from his desk and waited for recognition. 'You!' Jeddah gasped. Remembering the 'tailors dummy' shoplifting debacle, he tried desperately to recall any recent misdemeanors. 'We've done nothing wrong, what the feck's going on?'

Crosbie rose to his feet, raised a calming palm to allay interruption; aware of the eyes that traced his every step, he walked slowly to the window. 'Jethro Clarence O'Connell, AKA Jeddah: soft drug junky, petty perpetrator, apart from that a pretty nice fellah. I wonder if your scally friends know your middle name.' He took a pack of cigarettes from his pocket. 'Here, son, have a smoke, let me tell you a wee story, if you like, a latter-day parable. This parable, laddie, this story, involves a miscreant, but likable, son of Springburn; you! In fact, it could be said that you are the main character!'

Jeddah fumbled nervously with the cellophane wrapping, eventually he managed to light one up. Under Crosbie's admonishing finger, he refrained from stealing the pack. Enjoying his smoke too much at this stage, he decided against token protest. Furthermore, he'd seen the movie where an irate cop slaps the cigarette from the impudent prisoner's lips. In the circumstances nonchalance was out of the question, it left him with little option but to feign interest, and nod in silent concert while his nemesis continued. . .'this story concerns a young likable but misguided lad who picked the wrong pub in which to discuss police corruption. You again! There's a whole confusing plot that isn't relevant at this point, which no doubt, you will lie about later, but I digress.'

'I don't know what you're talking about!'

'I'm not completely heartless, Clarence, my boy. You need to retain some semblance of street cred,' I ken that, so I will allow you one more symbolic denial.' Crosbie checked his watch. 'But only one.'

'I don't know what the feck you're talking about,' Jeddah repeated and braced himself.

'That was it, son I'm afraid.' Crosbie smiled, unlocked his desk drawer and prodded the cigarette packet inside with his pencil. 'It's surprising the incriminating fingerprints that are left at the scene of serious crimes.'. . . Ten minutes later he turned off the tape recorder. 'Let me recap: rich boy Richard Edwards offers you and your brother a great deal of money to kill ex-girlfriend, Judy Prentiss?' (Jeddah nodded). 'Then sergeant McKenzie offers you a greatly reduced amount to do the very same to Richard Edwards.

How am I doing?'

(Jeddah nodded again). 'Aye, greatly reduced.'

James Crosbie twirled his pencil and shook his head in disbelief. 'You just couldn't make it up.' He opened the drawer and tossed over the cigarettes before bringing up the subject of exploding sex toys, of which Jeddah denied any knowledge. 'I believe you,' Crosbie told him, 'My problem now is, if you so easily betrayed your benefactors, what would stop you from doing the same to me?'

'Eh?'

'C'mon, Clarence, it's not a trick question.'

Jeddah winced at the use of his middle name. 'Because I'm shit scared of going to the Bar L?'

Crosbie plucked Jeddah's spent cigarette end from the ashtray with his fingertips. 'That was the right answer, but I'll keep this DNA-soaked exhibit just in case.'

'What'll I tell our Tam?'

'Whatever you like, you might even try the truth for its novelty value.'

Tam was still asleep when Jeddah returned. 'D'yeh want the good news or bad news?'

'Good news first.'

'We're free to leave?'

'Bad news?'

'We're out of pot and lager vouchers,' were the only other words uttered all the way back to Springburn. Tam put his brother's foul mood down purely to the lack of chemical stimulus, but he had problems enough trying to figure an angle to be worried too much about that.

Even though head over heels in lust, Rab McKenzie was thankful to be elsewhere when the bomb in Crosbie's flat went off. Judy, on the other hand, was disingenuous enough for both of them. Bidding a begrudged farewell at Glasgow Central, she had already decided to ditch him. She pondered the hypocrisy of a kiss, and kissed him anyway. 'Do be careful,' she said, but what she really meant was don't do anything stupid, you jumped up over-grown cretin.

No sooner was he on the platform than she was on her way to the Lavender Club to deal with her own unfinished business.

. . . The expensive décor was paid for by the profitable sidestepping of Glasgow's bylaws. Judy's personal taste was not affronted by this clash of Mock Tudor and Anne Summers. On the contrary, the lurid mishmash of debauching taste was a fitting reflection of her own hypersexuality, that's why she found it so appealing.

The latch gave under her weight. A distant throbbing bass, swirling smoke and a bevy of semi naked dances beckoned, but like an itch in constant need of attention, her body gravitated toward room 284. She paused in the doorway. Under the random hail of needle spotlights, the pitch-fibre walls inside glistened like a diamond seam, but it was something else that caught Judy's attention.

Inert beneath a red silk cover, its lines were unmistakable, and coital cavities began to fill. Running her eyes, then hands over the veiny colossus commanding centre stage, 'magnificent,' she gasped, 'truly magnificent.'

In full S&M ensemble, Gypsy pounced from behind a gossamer screen and threw back her head. 'I knew you'd return,' she laughed, 'they always do.'

Thrilled by her own daring, Judy edged closer and reached under the scarlet cover to confirm her hopes. Heart pumping against rib cage, she unconsciously licked her lips and tugged away the shiny silk. 'What does it do? How, what?'

'It does a lot of things, but mostly it simply is. You climb aboard and you do it, if you see what I mean,' Gypsy smirked her reply.

To be in control of such a beast would sate any number of Judy's Freudian hang-ups, the ultimate power trip, the cure to her penis envy. It was this very mix of technology and erotica that had so captivated her in the past. 'I've seen it's like before,' she said, thinking of her beloved Rampant Rod, 'but never on this scale. I must try it!'

Gypsy effortlessly flicked her into the air, to land with an arse heaving bump astride the great steed. 'Let's see what you got then.'

The two women looked at each other in an unspoken standoff.

Pipes hummed under hydraulic pressure as Gypsy slowly turned the dial. 'Hold on to the foreskin!' she shouted.

The bucking phallus began its journey through a random

cycle of jerks and bumps that launched Judy flaying into the air to land with a jaw-dropping pelvic crunch.

It made Gypsy's eyes (and other bits) water, so she turned the machine to level two. 'Easy peazy, ball bag squeezy!'

Judy kicked off her shoes to grip the swinging testis with bare feet. 'Whaa....whooo!' Lurching forward, she split her lip on the marble-hard gland. 'Whaa....whooo!' she woofed and spat, but kept her firm grip.

By this time contempt had conceded to admiration, and the lines of Gypsy's face softened to a reverent glow. 'That's enough, you've made your point.'

Judy had different ideas. Libido had sensually aligned with the random undulations setting her thighs afire. 'More, I must have more, faster and more, harder too!' she shrieked. The taste of her own blood excited her further. 'More, you feckin bitch, more!'

Having reached the peak of its normal range, the machine squeaked under the strain. Gypsy was angered, only she had dared to go this far before. 'You asked for it!' Rage had overridden a rare protective impulse, and she turned the dial to warp factor.

The great phallic steed bucked, reared and clanked, and for several frenetic minutes Judy's power was supreme. 'Giddy-up giddy-uppp giddyyuupp Yeeeeeeeeeeeees!' The hydraulics howled in protest. . . Friction ground overworked bearings to seize mid-cycle and the machine skrunked to a sudden halt. It catapulted Judy into Gypsy's arms, crashing them both to the rock-hard floor.

She scooped Judy into a cradle position and kissed her chaffed thighs all the way to the hospitality lounge. . . It was on those same sex crumpled sheets, that Judy confided she was going to kill Richard.

'Why?'

She spun from the bed. 'Oh, you know, business, pleasure, greed, revenge, the usual stuff. I'm going to kill him, but before he dies, I need some information. Now, where is he?'

'I could lure him here for you?' Gypsy said, 'but there's no need for actual violence. 'I could make him talk a different way!'

'How?'

As a Freudian slave to her subconscious, she suggested that the anticipation of pain held its sublimity in a way that conscious reality never could, but Judy disagreed.

'Gobbledygook!' she cried and tugged the catgut from

Gypsy's shiny caliper. 'It's far better to give than to relieve.' She went on to demonstrate some very interesting interrogation techniques. They spent what was left of the day comparing fetishes, indulging in some interesting hybrids.

. . .The interior surfaces of James Crosbie's flat were so impregnated with a lethal mixture of fossil fuel; no living organism was spared. Scurrying in the rafters ceased abruptly: ruminants fell dead from asphyxia induced methane inhalation, an oxygen starved cheese plant turned black in the hall. The tiny amount of gas that did escape added little to mitigate the odours already permeating the tenement.

The old dear upstairs suffered (she thought) a return of her dreaded migraine and promised herself a visit to the doctor's, otherwise there was no outward reaction.

Not wanting to spend his first night in Crosbie's flat alone, the Chief made a decision that was about to save his life by taking a well-trodden detour to the park gates. He'd met some wonderfully deviant friends there in the past.

Trundling homewards arm in arm with a mortar smudged bricklayer, the Glasgow temperatures plummeted. Crosbie's central heating thermostat picked up this change, activated the central heating ignition and BOOM!'

Turning the surrounding air into a searing ball of flame, it incinerated every internal surface before burning up all the available oxygen and snuffing itself out.

The next morning Crosbie stood flummoxed in the doorway. He was wondering why the forensic crew were taking so long in his kitchen when the Chief Fire officer put a hand on his shoulder. 'Did you ever have a problem with your cooker, inspector?'

'No, why?'

'Seems the failsafe ignition failed; electrode looks to have been broken off.'

'Someone trying to do me in?'

'You're the detective, what about this?' He drew Crosbie to the remains of the charred switch in the hallway. 'Look inside, the wiring has been compromised. If the central heating hadn't beaten them to it, the next person to turn on the light would have been barbequed.'

Crosbie instructed his exhibits' officer to chisel the complete unit away from the wall and bag it.

Thinking about the shiver in his backbone, his Chief couldn't stop from shaking, 'The resources you wanted, they're yours, James, whatever it takes,' he said.

Crosbie showed no emotion beyond twirling his pencil angrily. Looking at the blackened ruins of his flat he tried to muster his self-control with the first verse of Kipling's 'If'.

Before he could finish, Rab McKenzie bolted up the path wearing an 'off the peg' frown, which quickly changed to surprise. 'You're okay, sir?'

'Yeah, I'm fine. Any idea who might be responsible for this?' he asked, but the best that Rab could manage was a grunt as he looked from face to face.

Crosbie watched as his sergeant made straight for the site of the suspect light-switch. . . Listen, Chief,' he said when they were alone in the car, 'not long ago I had just two suspects and no crime, now I'm spoilt for fecking choice! These photos of yours, I know they were taken in the Lavender club. It looks like someone is running the blackmail scam from there.'

'What are you thinking, James?'

'If there were a bomb threat the building would have to be evacuated, and we could go over every square inch of the place, right?' He read the concern on his boss's face and added, 'I will personally see that any compromising material is destroyed. Like you said, sir, "we all have our frailties,"'

There was nowhere for the Chief to go, he knew it and he picked up the phone. . . An hour later 'emergency services burst in to the Lavender Club. 'An anonymous phone call,' the commander said, 'from the anti LGBT League, I'm guessing.'

Gypsy and Judy were disentangled and conveyed to the Treble A apartment to continue their sexperiments.

Crosbie and Debbie donned flak jackets to merged their way inside with the covert surveillance team. They threw a switch in room 284 and the great black phallus kicked into motion. Debbie flushed in strange confusion, but did not recoil. Standing her ground, she followed its contortions like a snake charmer.

Crosbie scanned the yearning faces of everyone secretly wanting to mount the beast. Just where is the line between curiosity and perversion? he pondered.

. . . Before noon the techno-gremlins had installed the very latest in intrusive technology to every room in the building, it was controlled by a remote 4 G network and relayed to a nearby mobile hub.

When the bomb-squad gave the official all-clear Gypsy and Judy returned to their favourite place, to carry on where they had left off.

(This time they were being watched!)

The odd key word, such as 'kill' and 'Richard' filtered through, but that was all until their lurid exhortations petered out. 'You go home and get some sleep now, I've got a plan,' Judy said. She waited until Gypsy had left 'and made the call.'

. . . After a full-on action replay with Sergeant Mackenzie on that very same bed. Judy released his vitals from a half twist, and selected her favourite studded hood from the Lavender's rack. 'When Richard arrives, tie him up, put this over his head, and leave the rest to me,' she said and picked up the phone.

The sly timbre in her voice told Richard she was up to no good, and he'd be needing protection. He found it perched on a Slash Inn barstool. 'There's something not right. Will you come with me?' he asked, 'mind me as it were?' After a few scoops of false courage and the promise of a generous bonus, Jeddah raised his empty glass and nodded.

. . . Half an hour later McKenzie was creeping up behind Richard in the Lavender club foyer. Jeddah leapt from behind the life sized cut out of John Holmes with a well-aimed kick that sent the policeman to his knees. 'Touch for that, yeh no mark!'

McKenzie's mouth was taped shut, hands and legs bound, leather hood tugged over his shaking head before they kicked him into room 284.

The foreshortening effect from Judy's mounted position disguised McKenzie's stature. As he rubbed against her outstretched leg like a faithful hound, she dropped a harness over his head and the great phallus jerked into motion. 'What's the PIN number, you groveling little turd?' When she hooked the bridle into an eyelet in the nylon foreskin the grunts grew all the louder, the machine bucked, jerked and dragged his flaying form to-and-fro like a rag doll. 'Just tell me the bloody number!'

'Don't. . . don't,' came the muffled reply.

'Now, Richard, all you have to do is tell me, and we'll let you go. 'You're not brave, stop pretending!' She turned up the jet, water pressure broke the straining leash and propelled McKenzie into the two-way mirror. Brandishing her whip Judy dismounted. 'Now dickhead!' she hissed as she stood over him. 'The bloody PIN number!'

Crosbie was watching from the surveillance van, he pressed the 'record' button as Judy pulled the hood from McKenzie's shaking head. 'You incompetent bloody fool!' she cried as he pressed his tethered wrists towards her. 'Where is he, where is Richard?' Squirming on his knees like a pitiful slave, he motioned to the two-way mirror.... 'Very clever, Richard, you can come out now,' Judy said, and kicked the policeman back onto his back.

Followed by Jeddah, Richard emerged from behind the glass with his hands high in the air. 'Truce! No recriminations,' he cried. Judy pointed to McKenzie, red-faced and fighting off paralysis. 'What about him?'

'Don't worry about that,' said Jeddah, 'I owe him one,'

Judy gleefully ripped the sticky tape from the sergeant's mouth, removing half a moustache in the process, and selected a king-sized appendage from the wall-rack display. 'Do you realize, mister big policeman boy, that you are now completely at our mercy?' Rab McKenzie's eyes gaped and glazed in terror. His last conscious image was Judy's lurid grin holding an ether-soaked towel over his face.

The mobile surveillance crew gathered around to watch Jeddah supporting the unconscious policeman's dead weight while Judy stripped him naked. She dressed him in leatherette suspenders and tutu, arranged a very interesting pose and brought out the camera. 'Well, big boy, do you know what I'm going to do to you now?'

Crosbie immediately recognized the composition. He breathed a muted sigh and twirled his pencil. 'Well, I never. I think we have our blackmailer.'

When Debbie asked if they should go in and rescue his sergeant, he stepped between her and the machine. 'What, and spoil the bloody fun? That guy tried to kill me,' he said, and switched the image to full screen.

It was dismal it was raining; it was Glasgow long after midnight when a lone figure was discovered hobbling awkwardly along the Gallowgate. Emergency services, who thought they'd seen it all before, were mistaken. They found a bulbous, bearded ballerina wearing a ludicrous outfit sporting a fantastic rear-end protuberance, repeating 'do you know what I'm going to do to you now?' over and over. They ferried him to Saint Patricks' University Hospital to be sectioned and indefinitely assigned to a padded room.

The Chief destroyed all the compromising photographs. He persuaded the newly appointed Fiscal to leave the blackmail charges on file and took early retirement on health grounds.

Crosbie set up home with Debbie, sublet his refurbished apartment to his old boss. Richard and Judy moved in with Gypsy over the treble A sex shop, and they all thought that would be the end of it.

Chapter Fifteen:
Day of Judgement

With Annie no longer in the land of the living, Gypsy took ownership of the downstairs sex shop. (It seemed only right). She snatched the registered letter from the postman, left him ogling the pixilating pussy rack and raced upstairs. After weeks of legal wrangling, the High Court Judgement had finally arrived. Judy eagerly opened the sheaf of court papers and speedread the legalese like a Philadelphia lawyer.

'In temperatures, estimated to have reached an excess of 3000 degrees Celsius, no earthly remains were recovered from the scene.'

'Bla bla bla…We knew all that!' Sifting through the pages to get to the conclusion, she held her breath, said a silent prayer and Richard sprang to her side.

'Notwithstanding the aforementioned reservations, we find for the petitioners. Therefore, we are summarily instructing the coroner to issue a Presumption of Death Certificate.

'Where does that leave us?'

'In the money, honey.' Judy immediately rang the coroner who told her that pending a final settlement a generous interim payment was on the way. The last part of her dream was finally coming true.

They closed up shop and headed to the Lavender club. The long-awaited celebration began in room 284, where they took turns to rodeo-ride the great black phallus in time-honoured fashion. The bearings once again seized, but the euphoric binge continued back in the 'Treble A' concept room. It ended with an inevitable reversion to type when they ran out of Viagra.

Richard was giggling in the bedroom, Judy relentlessly slagging him from the bathroom, and the phone rang.

'Get that will you, 'dickhead,' she shouted.' She was using that hurtful acronym more and more now, Richard put up with it because right after the big payday, she'd be out of his life forever.

Smiling, he picked up the phone. The probate clerk told him the final settlement had been suspended pending further investigation, and his mood plummeted. He banged the receiver on his bald head, then on the tabletop and bellowed, 'pending further bloody investigation, what the feck does that mean?'

The clerk replied that certain company accounts had been compromised. Refusing to elaborate, he hung up.

Judy ran dripping into the living room to see what all the fuss was about and the phone rang again. This time she snatched the receiver from Richard's grip and her jaw dropped. 'What the hell are you doing in the Bahamas Sadiq? What bloody evidence? Alive! How could that be? No no-no-no-no; she said, 'they're issuing a bloody death certificate!'

Shoulders drooped, she fell back into the chair, for the next five minutes, alternately nodded and shook her head in strained silence...

When Judy eventually put down the receiver, Richard clasped his hands together and conjured up one of his special cringing expressions. 'Refusing to issue a death certificate. How can that be, they were burnt to a bloody crisp?

'If they'd left any DNA on that bloody crisp, we wouldn't be having this conversation. They planned the whole thing, dickhead, that's how,' she said. 'They're alive and well. You must have ballsed it up somehow.'

What are we going to do?'

'I don't bloody know; they've got proof we tried to kill them. They're in the Bahamas. and if we don't go over there, they're going to the police!'

'The police! What are we going to do?'

Judy began to pace the floor. 'Shut up and let me think, dickhead! I should have known it when our bloody bank accounts were frozen.'

'What do they want?'

'We either go over there, or go to jail here, that's what.'

'The Bahamas! You're not suggesting I go, are you? I'm auditioning for the band. All I have to do is display my lack of talent, and I'm in.'

'That wouldn't be too difficult now, would it? If you stay here, you'll be auditioning for the prison quire.'

As usual, Judy had a homicidal fallback plan. . . Wearing her sexiest, skimpiest smallest dress she set off, as usual not bothering about underwear.

. . . Puckering from the Slash Inn doorway, she silenced a clutch of tongue-hanging barflies with a derisive index finger and strutted her stuff directly to the pool table.

Once the bar-side groans subsided, she stood between the two brothers and spoke to in low, serious tones. 'Remember me? I hired Sergeant McKenzie to hire you to do away with Richard Edwards, and I'm soon to be mega-rich.

Jeddah remembered her from the Lavender club encounter and crossed his legs. 'Well, what do you want from us now?'

'Dickhead Edwards, is history, there's someone else I want you to kill now, and I'm cutting out the middleman.

Jeddah was dumbstruck, last month's simple bribe-funded bender was turning decidedly complicated. He shuffled, scratched his arse, and tried to look nonchalant as he tore his eyes from her cleavage. Chalking his cue, he lined up for an easy black and missed. 'Who do you want topped, now misses, and what's it worth?'

Judy leaned forward and bent low to give him a better view. 'My husband Sam and Richard's wife, her name's Janet by the way. They live together now,' she added almost as an afterthought. Then she picked up the cue ball and didn't continue until the brothers had joined her at their favourite quiet table. 'Do we have a deal?'

'How much?'

Ten K and expenses for each kill.'

Tam couldn't stop himself from grinning, but Jeddah grimaced to hide a burgeoning smile. 'What about Richard?'

'Forget about him, now you deal with me directly. Instead of leaving you to your own balls up devices, I pick the time, place and method.' She tossed over a brown envelope. 'A small advance, balance payable on completion, of course.'

Jeddah rolled his eyes as she squeezed her boobs towards him, licked her lips and scanned his yearning face. 'You never know, there might just be a bonus in it for a good, slow kill. And you can forget about that idiot McKenzie, he's in the funny farm where he belongs!'

'Yeh better fill us in on the details then, misses?' Jeddah was trying to sound business-like.

'Time: approximately two weeks from now, place, somewhere in the Bahamas, exact location to follow.' She threw a second envelope on the table: 'itinerary, hotel reservations and travelling expenses.'

'What about method?'

'Still on the drawing board, right now I have a plane to catch,' she clicked her tongue, hitched up her skirt, bounced the graphite cue-ball across the baize and sauntered back towards the door. Tam turned to watch it pot the black, he turned back, and Judy was gone.

She caught the express to Glasgow International and went straight to the executive lounge. 'Sorted,' she told Gypsy. 'Make mine a large one.'

. . . Ten hours of 1st class 'Don Perignon' later, they were landing on the sunlit island of Grand Bahama. Smiling, flirting through 'passport control' and baggage checks, they made their way to the pick-up point.

Sadiq was sat behind the wheel of a classic Rolls Royce, but not the Sadiq of old. No longer fawning and servile; straight backed, and confident, this Sadiq pressed the 'boot release' and watched them load their own luggage. They climbed aboard to shower him with a barrage of questions: 'what the hell is going on. . . where are Sam and Janet. . . what do they want. . . why are we here?'

'What and where is easy,' he replied, 'why' is another story, but it's not my story.' Smiling into the mirror, he purred the engine to life and turned up the radio.

It was cold, wet and windy, (it was Glasgow!) only a stone's-throw from where James Crosbie was born. He still had a reluctant affinity with Springburn, and couldn't shake off the sense of nostalgia ambling down the main street. Nothing much had really changed: Betting shops bustling with activity. The Slash inn 'Men Only' bar still the smoke-filled time warp of raucous laughter, shoplifted contraband and tall tales, he remembered.

He bought the brothers a drink, and sat down between them in the back lounge to listen to the story so far. . . 'The Bahamas it is then.' he said. 'Buy some suitable clothes with the money she gave you. Did I just say buy? Oops'

'Who told you about the?' An 'under-table' toecap came too late to silence Tam.

Crosbie shook his head. 'You just did, son. Now if you're going undercover, you'll have to do better than that. I'm going to make a telephone call and if you buy me a large Jameson's, I may forget to ask you how much?'

'Undercover, eh,' Jeddah said while Crosbie was away. 'Double agents?'

'D'yeh no think he knows about dickhead's envelope?' Tam

said.

Jeddah thought about the question for a moment, shook his head, he forced an innocent smile as the returning inspector sat back down between them.

'Right lads, here's the plan: I don't suppose you own passports, no? Well, I'll see if I can rush them through for the both of you. Two potheads are better than one, so they say. I'll go on ahead and see you on the other side of the world. Any questions?'

'What do we do when we get there?' Tam said.

'You don't do anything; just agree to everything they say right up to the critical point.'

'Then what?'

'Then I appear with the Royal Bahaman Police.'

'So, we'll be wired up?'

'Wired up, miked up and camera'd up.'

'As long as you turn up,' Tam quipped.

'I will, if you two don't mess up, or try to keep any more secrets from me, you won't end up locked up! There are no more secrets, are there?'

If Crosbie was gambling on pure greed for their cooperation, he needn't have worried, this was to be the adventure of a lifetime. (The brothers would have done it for nothing!)

. . .The following week a Home Office currier hand delivered the passports and travel documents.

For two serial low achievers who'd never ventured west of Park Head, the journey to the airport itself, was an ordeal, let alone a trip to the West Indies.

They loaded a king-size hold-all with T shirts and shorts liberated from Primark's easy to pilfer shelves, and caught the overland express to Prestwick airport.

Exercising their 'duty free' shoplifting skills they began their funded binge in the 1st class departure lounge...

. . . When 'last call' sounded Tam led the way aboard the 747 Boeing in happy oblivion. Jeddah wasn't far behind. After stowing away his booty, he found sufficient distraction in the bikini pages of the in-flight glossy to take his mind away. Listening to the trolly dolly's instructions on what to do in the event of an emergency, all that began to change.

The pull of inertia sucked his features to eye-popping dread, and he reached for the sick bag. At 30,000 feet the plane levelled off, as did his condition, that was until they hit a series of air-pockets. Hyperventilation locked his jaws; cramped him into a fetal ball until a gentle soothing hum displace the roar of mighty turbines. He watched the golden sunset from his window seat, face to glass, until agitated sleep took him to that land of unlimited lager vouchers.

. . . Twelve hours later, the landing proved to be a bilious replay of take-off, and Jeddah had to be peeled from his seat. Once on terra-firma, he mustered enough composure to stagger blindly through 'Nothing to declare' and 'passport control' without a single word.

Empty bellied, parched, waving away a barrage of complaints, the brothers barged a path to the front of the sunlit taxi rank.

'Hotel Lauderdale, Jimmy,' Tam said tersely, as they climbed into the rear of the old Austin Cambridge saloon. Sensing a generous tip, a humble smile displaced the driver's initial deadpan, an expression that reverted when Jeddah regurgitated into his map pocket.

. . . Colloquially known as 'the Laundrydale,' the plush hotel was situated near Freeport on the Grand Bahama Island. Surrounded by olive trees, in an outcrop of orchids and jasmine, it was almost part of the landscape. With a predominately exclusive clientele of men in white suits' drinking Cointreau on the veranda, Graham Greene would have been in his element.

Odd wrong turners were never encouraged to stay, the staff, under instructions to turn away any 'bum-bagging' drifter who might accidentally happen by.

Tam and Jeddah may have looked like your typical 'white kneed hicks,' but a short-shrift reception and sour faces did little to deter them. In fact, it made them feel so much more at home.

Carrying a huge hold-all between them, they meandered obliviously past the scowling doorman. Didn't see the marble balustrades or crystal fountains, designed to capture early impressions, nor were they moved by the mosaics and gilt-edged landscapes that lined the foyer. Wearing lager blinkers, they were looking for their first Caribbean swally of this once in a lifetime, amazing holiday.

Sauntering past the registration desk to the cool of the lounge area, they bee-lined beyond the morning coffee drinkers to a well-stocked bar.

A man with Zapata moustache and sharp eyes, looked up from his Financial Times, then down at the bulging hold-all. The eccentric duo fitted no stereotype he knew of; which in his eyes, made them plausible drug barons.

'Two pints of your finest lager, Jimmy.'

The old bartender shook a quizzical head, and Tam put up two fingers, pointed to the cold shelf and broke it down into syllables. 'Bud-why- zah. to the power of two, son.'

The toothless old man slammed two bottles noisily onto the bar, to Tam's astonishment, he asked for no money.

When the solitary, keen eyed figure put down his newspaper to offer them another drink, Jeddah raised a brow and licked his lips. 'I think we're going to like it here,' he said and lapsed into his Highland fling routine mumbling 'I think I died and went to Parkhead,' to the tune of 'Comin' through the Rye'.

'I beg your pardon?'

'A couple of buds, would be pucka.'

Offering a friendly hand, their new benefactor introduced himself as 'Sadiq, resident laundryman, concierge, or financial facilitator if you will. Sadiq is Arabic for friend,' he explained in a hopelessly approximate accent.

'Aye, and Tam's Jock for prove it, I'll have another.'

Sadiq had reached the misconception he was addressing new 'soiled' money in need of legitimizing, a conclusion fueled by circumspection, which he put down to 'criminal guile.'

Judy's mood lightened on sight of Tam and Jeddah at the bar, and she told Gypsy not to worry. 'When the time is right my two Caledonian assassins pay the eunuch and old 'never had it' Janet a lethal visit, 'she said, 'and I'll be filthy rich.'

'And then?'

'And then, Gypsy, my darling, it's an island-hopping, bedroom bopping retirement for us.'

'What about Richard?'

'Richard who?'

Back at the bar, Tam decided to test Sadiq's generosity. 'A bit of puff would go down well, Sidney,' he said. 'You grow it in this part of the world, don't you?'

Sadiq looked at him dumfounded.

'Weed, man, wacky- backy, marri ju anna, pot. What about some Panama Red?'

'Ugh?'

'Lebanese, Acapulco gold, Purple Kush, Thai grass, Temple ball, Papaya punch or just good old Rocky!' Making 'pursed-lipped' puffing sounds, he mimicked the rolling of a joint.

Sadiq turned to Jeddah, who shrugged. 'Ganga, Sid, ¿hashish?'

'A ha! Do not worry. I will help you, my friends, but you must speak more slowly.' He rubbed his finger and thumb together and smiled. 'If you could give me some idea of the level of your potential investment?'

After a whispered conference and checking the immediate vicinity for eavesdroppers, Tam mouthed the word 'twenty'.

Of course, he meant a £20 deal of pot. Sadiq thought they were talking about 'money laundering'. 'Let us be very clear, we are talking about 20, with how many zeros?   Ah, I see you need to confer,' he nodded and wandered from the bar.

Jeddah screwed his face and whispered from the corner of his mouth. 'We've tried zero-zero hash, well let's just add a couple more zeros!'

Returning to a spate of Glaswegian incoherence, Sadiq gasped. Apart from the repetition of the word 'twenty' and a garble of 'zeros,' everything was lost in translation. He looked up at the expectant glint in Tam's eye, then down at the bulging hold-all. 'Forgive me, my friends,' he said, 'and you have it here with you now?'

Tam patted his pocket, lifted a thumb, and replied with typical Glasgow caution. 'Let's just say it's nae far away.' It was a response that sent Sadiq rushing to use the desk clerk's phone.

'A lot of fuss over a £20 deal, and this is just the guy who does the laundry,' Jeddah said, and ordered 'two buds.'

The toothless old barman served them up and disappeared into the sunlight. . . Half an hour later, he was refusing any payment for the 'Mars bar' sized puck he returned with, and serving up two more buds.

Jeddah took out the cigarette papers, licked his fingertips and went to work. Gypsy and Judy passed by, but he was too busy on a production line of 'five skinners, to notice the look of concern.

Tam picked up the hold-all and hurriedly followed them into the lift. 'Hey, this Sidney fellah's a right one, does he do the ironing as well?'

'Why is he making such a fuss of you two?' Judy snapped.

'It could be our smooth Glasgow repartee, or maybe he fancies doing our smalls, why?'

'Just don't get too close to him, that's all!'

'What the feck's it to you?'

'I'm paying the bloody piper, that's what!'

The lift doors opened; Debbie stepped inside and glanced at the slowly rotating dial. Smiling feebly at the three stone-faces staring back at her, she alighted at the next floor just for the relief. 'Don't get too bloody close, you're here to do as you're told,' she heard Judy hiss as the doors slid closed.

After stowing the hold-all safely under his bed, forty winks and a hurried cold-water swill, Tam was ready for a drink.

Toking away, cross-legged on the cold marble floor, his brother was still studying the fountain, (wondering why the hell he was studying a fountain). Sadiq was fussing over the vomit stains on his pants, and quipping in a foreign tongue.

'What a guy,' Tam thought, cleaning up already! He ordered a Bud and sat back to watch. Two more loaded joints, and Jeddah had passed the point of 'no return. Maintaining a 'limbs-folded' half lotus position, two attendants manhandled him into the lift. Tam laughed, but didn't blame Sadiq for refusing to see the funny side.

'Do not worry,' the Arab said sternly. 'It is easier to change a suit than a friend.' On that cryptic note he left.

While Gypsy and Judy were soaking up the pool-side rays, Tam was more than happy to spend the rest of that glorious day in the dingy bar. Fact was, he'd not yet been away twenty-four hours, already he was beginning to pine for the Glasgow grime.

Upstairs, his big brother was alternating between transcendental enlightenment and low-down manic depression.

In a unique display of abstinence, Tam declined the herbal generosity of Sadiq. 'I have to keep an eye on the big picture,' he said. 'Someone needs to!'

From their third-floor balcony James and Debbie were doing just that. Long after flamingos had retracted their proud heads into down, twilight noises fill the air: reptiles croaking as they snapped away at the mosquitoes, sand flies swarming in the nearby swampland. It somehow suited the dying twilight.

Debbie was determined to take advantage of the lull, 'heavenly,' she said as she spread herself across the recliner. 'Wake me when the war's over. This is turning out to be a perfect holiday. Oops, why am I sorry I just said that?'

Crosbie told her to 'relax.' For the first time in years, he was beginning to enjoy the feeling of freedom from the petty crime, corruption and despair of home. Even though part of him ached for a resolution to the whole mess, another part wanted the moment to never end. 'Tomorrow, Deb, we'll do a little exploring, but for now.' He reached out. . . For the first time in an age the whole night was spent without a care, and dawn was coming much too soon.

At that very moment, Gypsy, who wasn't used to playing second fiddle, was having second thoughts. Judy's insistence on wearing the metaphorical pants and her constant reference to the insurance money as 'mine,' was turning her head. It prompted a twilight walk in search of her mojo. She found it in the patch of swirling mosaic that Jeddah was studying on the bathroom floor.

Remembering that first encounter, it was her turn to take the initiative. She pounced: pulled the manacles from her hip pouch and once again cuffed him to the cold tap. They say that lightning never strikes twice, but a combination of blind panic and third world plumbing was about to prove them wrong! This time the pipework stayed intact. The fibreglass bathtub was ripped from its moorings, it flew in the air, upended and trapped them both beneath.

. . Tam meandered innocently down the hotel backstairs to take a look at the basement strongroom; years sidling the blind side of supermarket isles had made him a dab hand at 'innocent meandering.'

Clutching his first bud' of a new day, he crouched on the half-landing to watched the comings and goings with a growing interest. Sadiq passed several times, on each occasion punching out the same keypad combination, returning minus the bulging pouch with which he'd descended.

On one occasion, the Arab left the door ajar while he opened today's mail. Tam lay on his belly for a snakes-eye view, and opened his mouth wide: bundles of vacuum wrapped notes stacked high, currency of every denomination piled in neat tiers next to a digital counting machine. While this was happening, a bank of computers debited the accounts of online punters. Sadiq checked that the automatic labelling machine was spitting vacuum wrapped packages into a deep allocation basket, and he grinned.

Once Tam had seen enough, he scrambled back to the room, overturned the upended bathtub to find Jeddah and Gypsy tangled together on the sodden floor. 'Hey, bro,' he chortled, when he'd uncuffed them, 'you'll never guess what I just found. I don't know what he's punting down there, but he's raking in a bloody fortune!'

He went on to describe in great detail what he had just witnessed. Jeddah was in no condition to digest what his brother was trying to get across, but Gypsy took in every word.

His chonged out sibling sobbed like a child as the last remnant of damp hashish was wrenched from his grip and flushed down the drain.

'It's for your own good,' Tam said. 'You'll thank me in the long run. 'Money-money-money,' he sang that old Abba number while dragging Jeddah's limp body to the 2nd bathroom, and Gypsy parodied along. 'Money-money-money; on the bottom floor.'

After dunking Jeddah headfirst into the upright cold bath, they lay him on the bed to wipe away the tears. 'There, there, you'll be able to buy your own pharmacy soon.'

It was long after midnight before cannabinoids had sufficiently depleted to allow him his first legible utterance for 24 hours. Beginning with 'I'm starving,' followed by an indiscernible string of under breath expletives; ending with 'where's the pot,' (just before he lost consciousness again).

Another fitful six-hour sleep, he was still edgy, Gypsy coaxed him to something approaching normality with a stingy one skinner.

Over a gallon of scalding Java in the breakfast room Tam repeated the detail of what he had witnessed in the basement strongroom. A devious plan began to take shape: Gypsy was to keep an eye on the basement, while the brothers made their way to the nearest town to look for a getaway route.

It came as a wonderful irony that Sadiqi, the man they were planning to get away from was so glad to get them from under his feet, he offered them a lift.

Even before they left the hotel grounds, he was boring them with his much-lamented rags-to-riches tale. His classic Roller cut perilously through the milling community and glided to a halt on the main street. 'Don't forget our business,' he told them.

As soon as the much-relieved brothers climbed out, he put his foot down into a perilous U-turn: tyres screeched, pedestrians cursed. Two very parched young men looked back to see the car disappear into a cloud of dust.

Following their noses to a welcome waft of tobacco and stale ale, they ducked down the first seedy alleyway they came to. They had chanced upon a local hostelry. A six-foot high, three wide Neanderthal in the doorway growled in an indiscernible language that made them nostalgic for Springburn.

Tam asked, 'Is this shop open?' The sight of a back-bar lager selection over the big guy's shoulder answered for him, and Jeddah pushed unapologetically past.

Reminiscent of Glasgow's good old 'Sarry Head,' the decor was unadulterated by plastic or glitter of any kind: a shop of few pretensions, after their own hearts: the furniture entirely consisted of upturned half-barrels circled by milking stools, the bar-top no more than a huge chunk of unedged timber, perched upon kegs, spanning the sidewalls.

Tam concluded that the room must have been built around it, by the unwieldy appearance of the tattooed clientele, 'around them too!' he declared.

In a standard uniform of raffia hats, off-white vests and frowns to match, the regulars jealously guarded their drinks and glared at the interlopers.

'Two Buds, Jimmy,' Jeddah said. Grumpy locals promptly turned their backs as he elbowed between them and added, 'forget the glasses.'

'From the cold shelf, lah?' a surprising voice asked. Dressed in peaked cap and sawn-off denims, with skin not quite as dark as the rest; the man behind the bar had about him that same granite resilience, yet he wasn't one of them. 'My name's Agoro,' he said in an accent that belied the location.

Jeddah looked, in turn to the stoic regulars, then to his brother before he spoke. 'You feckin Scousers get everywhere!'

Agoro shook his head and laughed. 'Oh yeah, so do you bloody Jocks. What the hell are you doing this far from home, lads?'

The tension eased and Tam was pleased to note they were suddenly no longer under enemy scrutiny, 'lookin for a bevy,' he said.

'Well, you've come to the right place.' A broad smile preceded Agoro's warm handshake. 'You fellah's on holiday, yeah? You picked the right time as well didn't you, just before Hurricane

Charlie hits town.

'Hurricane Charlie?'

'Yeah, it's gonna be a whopper they say, so you'd better keep your heads down. I'm glad you came into my place; I'm grounded for the duration. They call me the flying Scouse-doctor around here.'

'Are you a real doctor?' Jeddah asked.

'No,' Agoro winked and poured three drinks. 'I'm a witch doctor.'

When Tam asked if he was ever going back to Liverpool,' you're having a laugh.' he replied curtly. 'The whole country's turned into a police state; you're knackered there unless you've got the right colour or the right dad: the Welfare System is dying, police are bent, MPs on the take, everybody on the make. the whole bleeding system's corrupt. And what happens if you try'n make a few bob yourself?' he asked rhetorically.

'Flog em, hang em!' Tam said, 'throw away the bloody key.'

Agoro finished his drink in one. 'Too right, lah, it's just the same here,' he laughed, 'only warmer.'

Throughout the epic binge that followed, the conversation veered from mild discontent to downright anarchy. After exchanging exaggerated anecdotes, the affinity that exiles often voice when they meet in foreign lands was enough to drive the locals home.

While Agoro was in the back room preparing a skillet of sizzling garlic pork and peppers, the brothers made a vital decision. . . . As soon as they'd eaten, Tam flashed Jeddah an encouraging look and came out with it. 'What if you knew where the local godfather's stash was, and he didn't know you knew?'

Agoro frowned. 'I'd say that you and your brother should be careful where you're going with this.'

'Ah c'mon, mate, it's only a 'what if,' Jeddah mumbled into his drink while Tam continued.

. . . 'What if you had, say half a million in dirty used notes?'

Agoro shook his head despairingly. 'I don't want to know.'

'Seen it with my own eyes in the hotel basement, pal. C'mon. What if? It's just a laugh.'

Agoro confided that he had probably flown in those very notes, 'from the Caymans to the hotel. 'Listen,' he said, 'I work for these people. You don't know who you're dealing with, what they are capable of!'

'Yeah, but what if?'

Tam's persistence finally paid off and Agoro gave in. 'I'd go back to Liverpool, and pull tongues at a few people, but it's not going to happen.'

'I'd buy the Sarry Head,' Jeddah said, and ordered another round.

Nassau International Airport had battened down ahead of the storm, Scallywag's relaunch at the prestigious Palace Hotel had to be cancelled. Call it providence, call it coincidence, the plane was diverted to Grand Bahama Island.

The probate lawyers required more time to release the Prentiss millions, but it didn't matter to Richard. Now a tried and tested member of the boyz-band, loving and living every minute, he just shrugged. 'Not a bad place to get rich!'

'Any new bod's in the line-up?' Judy asked expectantly. 'If we're going to be stuck here,' she selected her favourite implement from the rack, puckered, licked her lips and turned to Gypsy. 'We may as well make the most of it.'

'Sorry, you just don't do it for me anymore,' Gypsy said. 'It was all getting a bit 'much of a muchness anyway.'

'Aren't you forgetting how rich I'm going to be?'

'How rich you're going to be, exactly. She snatched the whip from Judy's hand and stormed from the room.

At first Sadiq was reluctant to let Scallywag perform at the Lauderdale, but the words, 'no fee' from the fat fellow rapidly changed his mind. Word spread around the island like wildfire, and a raucous hoard of fans gathered outside. While police were manning the main doors, the band were smuggled in through the trade entrance. (The fat manager groped Wang's arse on the way).

Using the hectic comings-and-goings that precede such an event as cover, Tam and Gypsy made several further visits to the basement strongroom. Jeddah had infiltrated the band's hash stash. (They were on their own now).

The roadies stacked-up to sound-check, and Scallywag took up position for onstage rehearsals. Gypsy tweaked the curtains to watch Wang and Richard simulating sex with the mike stands, hetero mode effectively reactivated, she wet her lips and pouted.

Fat manager stood behind and prodded her ear with a wet finger. 'Sorry, luv, they need all their energy for tonight's performance. Will I do?'

'I'm not that bloody desperate,' she said, (but she was). A limbo dancing nymphet was almost within touching distance, and that old sensual itch in need of scratching propelled her on that well-trodden path . . .

. . . Freshly preened and oiled, she lay on the bed and closed her eyes, the anticipation was becoming unbearable. 'Go for it, Rampant baby!' she squealed. Prepping for later, she aimed the gyrating rod with considered precision. Where like-minded sensualists had all too often fallen short, Judy hit the G spot, and managed to obliterate several taboos on the way.

The intoxicant air crackled with sensual impetus three floors below, and Crosbie gazed dreamily across the crowded dance floor. He was secretly mourning an unclaimed youth, until Debbie crunched him back to reality. 'Forget it, dear, you were never that young,' she laughed.

Fat manager turned off the house music and pushed his way centre stage. 'Ladies, gentlemen and others, you are about to witness a onetime first on this side of the planet, you, my friends are privileged. Now put your hands together for the one and only Scallywag!'

The thrum of a slow bass line, a haunting lead intro, a parting of the curtains, and a spotlight brought the star to life.

Legs spread, crotch cradled, Wang chortled and bucked on every tenuous step to the microphone. The crowd fell silent as he closed his eyes to raise his voice a whispered octave.

'I just want your bo-ho-ho-ho-ody,' he sang in gentle descant, and someone feinted in the front row. 'Gimme…gimme…gimme!' louder now, with more feeling as the lead guitar kicked in with a twelve-bar riff.

The backing group harmonized and crooned in the background. Richard's mime was as out of sync as his clumsy dance-steps, (but nobody noticed.) A staccato drumroll augmented the tempo from borderline-joyous to up-front hysteria. Pubescent screaming drowned out the indiscernible lyrics.

It left the audience at the fever pitch mercy of their Sharman leader, howling like a wounded bear, fending off flying underwear.

A roadie was extinguishing a flaming speaker with a fire

blanket, alarm bells echoed in the background, (and the band played on).

Wang and Richard groin-grounding their mike stands, backing singers behind, similarly engaged.

Pretending to be in the band Tam was fraudulently autographing a Lambada dancing teenybopper at the stage door. Judy and Gypsy, by now dog-locked on the third floor, (Jeddah missing all the fun).

That's it!' James cried, 'a decibel too far for me. What say we call it a night?'

'As long as there's a good wine and a cool bed waiting,' Debbie said. The lift arrived at the same time as the police, the music stopped abruptly. She pressed the 'hold' button expecting a welcome announcement on noise abatement.

The twenty strong line of 'British looking' bobbies, doffed their helmets and Velcro held bottoms to a man, and joined in the revelry.

'Now that's what I call community policing,' she said.

Swooning in total disharmony about 'testosterone love,' (raising one or two eyebrows, and plenty more besides,) Scallywag stripped to designer thongs. They were pushing the probity envelope, but nobody was complaining.

The sweet aroma of 'homegrown,' mixed with body odours to produce an aphrodisiac sensuality that suited the music, (suited the evening).

Hot-blooded Latin Africans took it as an early rehearsal for their forthcoming Boxing Day farrago. Cowbells and drums clashed with the falsetto drone of 'Do me up like a Christmas turkey' blurring from the house PA.

To minimize humidity, the main doors were opened, but the night air outside was as thick as soup.

. . . Four AM, the tempo was showing no signs of subsiding. James was steering Debbie through the flickering interior, a familiar voice drew him to one of the paper-thin doors, and he pressed his ear to the woodwork to pick out every word.

'I dinnae' feckin believe it!'. 'I'm talking telephone numbers here and you're still shitfaced stoned! Listen to me, Jed, I tell you I'm onto the big one!'

'I can't help it, bro, it's what I do, who I am. What would we do with all that dosh anyway, we couldn't spend it here, and Agoro wouldn't touch it!'

'We'll manage. I went back down there tonight to try a few more combinations. I'll get it in the end. C'mon, Jed, use your loaf, we'll never get a chance like this again.'

. . . 'Room service.'

Crosbie's bad Bahamian accent might have made Debbie smirk, but it was enough to fool Tam and he opened the door without looking. 'Have you ordered any booze, Jeddah?' A hand clamped firmly over his mouth and dragged him onto the landing.

Crosbie showed the white of a redundant knuckle and told him to get his brother. 'We need to talk in private.'

. . .He led them through the kitchens to a crumbling gatehouse relic of colonial days, that apart from the odd secret liaison hadn't been used for years. The mordant tang of stale sex and urine clung to Crosbie's nostrils, so he cut immediately to the chase. 'Did you know that these islands are still under sovereign control?'

'What does that mean?'

'It means I can have you arrested anytime I like.' The brothers looked at each other incredulously. 'Anytime,' he repeated, 'so start talking.'

Wise enough to know when they were beaten, they took turns to recount 'almost' everything that had happened since their arrival...

'Right,' said Crosbie, 'Tomorrow, you're taking us to meet this Agoro friend of yours. Now I suggest you get some sleep. I certainly need some.'

. . . An hour later found him looking out from his balcony across the swaying pampas. The blistering crimson dawn fought an uneven battle with burgeoning storm clouds to produce a thunderous biblical sky. (He was hoping it wasn't a sign).

Limbs of every shape, colour and girth were locked together, inert on the ballroom floor. A fitting metaphor for a battle lost, only they were bathed not in blood. It was spilt drink and congealed bodily fluids that tacked them to the marble, but like the debris of any Bacchanalian feast, someone's got to clear it up.

. . . The hotel staff grimaced as they struggled to negotiate the entwined masses: expensive perfumes lost out to morning-after flatulence as the hoard groaning revelers wriggled to life.

Judy and the fat manager were locked in a carnal embrace behind the drapes, Richard and Wang in similar repose, beneath a tablecloth awning.

The laundry maid pulled it from them and tossed it into her linen trolley. Richard tried to cover himself, but the maid had lost the capacity for surprise on such mornings, and went about her duties with a snooty indifference.

Stirring and innate on the ballroom floor, revelers had to look twice at their partners: men checked their empty pockets, women their handbags.

Only moments earlier Tam had staggered triumphantly back to the room to hide his twilight contraband under the bed.

The staff gave Sadiq a wide berth. Sat alone in the deserted breakfast room, he was punching out numbers with vehemence on his laptop, and they knew better than to intrude.

Unsure who would have to pay for the breakages, he paused to swear under his breath and added another digit to the total.

Unlike Agoro's bar, the hotel did have an auxiliary generator, when the electric storm shutters had hermetically sealed the guests from the weather, Sadiq took the opportunity to check the strongroom and complete the online orders. Sales were up on the month before. He told himself that as soon as the storm abated, he would visit the factory to pick up his bonus.

Pulling a Jiffy envelope from the nearest box, he fondled the top notes and looked down. Water had risen to his uppers. Gushing in from the air vent. it spread across the floor like a carpet.

He scanned the room in panic and began to run around in circles. 'Oh shit!' Taking off his shoes, he paddled across to stack the boxes onto desks and chairs, raced up the stairs and raced back down again to double lock the strongroom door.

Chapter Sixteen:
Lockdown

Jeddah told Debbie his brother was sleeping it off, and jumped in the back of the hired jeep. 'Don't worry, I can take you straight there,' he said. Judy watched from the veranda as they pulled away from the car park and wondered what the hell they were up to.

The fragrance of butterfly jasmine filled the blustering air as the 4X4 wended through the burgeoning wind towards the dusty capital. 'We'll come back, Deb,' James promised, 'when this is all over, whatever this is, we'll come back.'

The town was in complete lockdown: roads almost deserted, windows boarded, doorways sandbagged ahead of the storm. One or two determined locals, bent double against the gathering weather, were oblivious as the jeep passed them by and came to a halt at the blind alley.

Agoro was busy storm proofing ahead of hurricane Charlie, he had no interest in what was going on in the Lauderdale and wasn't expecting any business that day. The sky was still rumbling, so he left the front shuttered and fed the beer crates outside with yesterday's empties.

He didn't feign surprise or protest when Crosbie flashed his warrant card and followed him indoors. Shaking his head, he slowly poured himself a large rum.

Crosbie joined him at the bar, and Debbie stopped Jeddah in his tracks. 'We'll have a little chat over here, shall we?' She hid the order behind a smile and pulled him to a corner.

'What can I do for you?' Agoro said, pouring Crosbie a drink.

'It sounds like a terrible cliche, but the real question should be, what I can do for you?'

'Such as?'

Crosbie took out his warrant card again, and told Agoro in no uncertain terms that he would be fast-tracked to prison if he did not co-operate.

Agoro always feared this day would come, in an adverse way he even welcomed it, and poured two more. 'What exactly is it you want?'

'Everything you know about Sadiq, and what exactly it is you do for him. That will do for a start.'

'Nothing to it really, every week I run errands between the hotel and a factory on Monks Head Island; pick up product and deliver money, that's it.'

'Where does the money come from?'

Agoro paused to take a drink. 'All over the world, some sort of mail-order thing, Anyway, man, it's perfectly legal as far as I know.'

'As far as you want to know. Where does the money go to?'

'A factory on the island.'

Crosbie gave Agoro a look of mock surprise and shook his head. 'Factory, island? Okay we'll leave that for now. Who pays you?'

'Sadiq.'

'Who pays him?'

'I don't know.'

'Do you like prison food?'

Agoro reached for the bottle. 'Don't shoot the bloody messenger!'

Crosbie lowered his voice to a hiss. 'Not unless the messenger is holding something back. Now I'm not sure how involved you are, but you know a damn sight more than you're letting on.' He looked around and the others were staring. 'You're not high up on the ladder, son, I can see that. You've got a nice little thing going here, but will it still be here in ten years' time when you're released. You see, I just ask questions and if I don't get answers, I lock people up.'

'So, ask?'

'What is it you deliver? What does this factory make?'

A laconic smile splayed across Agoro's face as he took his time to pour two more drinks. 'Oh, you know, sexual aids, bedroom toys, that sort of thing.' Looking across, he studied Debbie's stoic reaction. 'I am just the messenger. I deliver the product and pick up E money. One round trip a month, that's it!'

'No, it isn't.'

'Oh, there is this.' Agoro fished a computer disc from his inside pocket and held it in the air. 'Weekly accounts.'

Debbie borrowed his laptop and opened the only file. After a cursory inspection she decided that ostensibly they were looking at nothing more sinister than a monthly sales analysis. 'Bedroom toys, seedy perhaps, not necessarily illegal.'

. . . Crosbie interjected. 'Bedroom toys? I don't think so. Is there any way of knowing who the end users are?'

'Not from this.' She tried to access the encryption at the foot of each column. 'It's asking for a password.'

They both turned to Agoro who nodded his head. 'Nothing too complicated, 'Italics, lower-case, bold and underlined,' he said and typed in '2 8 4 s l i d e o n.'

Just look at this, James,' Debbie said. A stream of accounts spewed onto the screen and she recognized some of them: 'Wee Willie Wonga, Pope-headed blurter, Double-headed, Crown headed, Gland headed, and of course the fabled Rampant Rod, each have their own section.' She pointed to an inordinately large entry. 'I know these things are in demand, but five thousand pounds for a . . .'

Twirling his pencil again, Crosbie interrupted. 'What exactly is it, Agoro, what's he really selling?'

'I honestly can't tell you. I pick the stuff up and drop it off. That's all she wrote!'

'Okay, when's your next pick up?'

'Sunday.'

'Room for a couple of passengers?' he said, and Agoro nodded solemnly.

Jeddah could see that some conclusion had been reached, he sat down on a barstool between the two men. 'Lesh have a drink?'

Crosbie told him to go back to the hotel to wake up his brother. 'And keep away from the bloody basement.'

Lights flickered, the floor beneath them rumbled, followed by a loud crash as the empty crates outside blew over.

Agoro began clearing the bar top up of all the empties. 'He's going nowhere! Someone help me, this'll be a big one!'

Between them they lifted the mighty oak bar-top from the upturned kegs, turned it on edge to carry it outside and slot it into place across the front shutters.

No sooner was it secured, than the wrought iron cleats holding it began to vibrate in the face of a ninety mile an hour gale. When the power failed Agoro primed the storm-lamps with paraffin. 'It's going to be a long night, he said, 'I suggest you all get comfortable. Help yourself to the bar.'

Jeddah didn't need to be asked twice, his mouth was watering by now. The removal of the bar-top made the liquor much more accessible and he made straight for the Budweiser shelf. . . Half an hour later he regressed to that incoherent drawl that James Crosbie detested so well. Harping on about 'the wearing of the green'

And 'it's a grand old team to play for,' his voice lowered to a drone of indiscernible expletives and he passed-out, face down on a beer-soaked table.

Crosbie settled under a storm lantern with Debbie, but with no auxiliary power supply, the laptop was running out of power. She took a snapshot of the accounts and made do with mobile phone and a notepad. 'From what I can see, they're using the factory to front some kind of wholesale distribution operation,' she said.

'Drugs?'

Debbie nodded. 'Cocaine I'd say, given the proximity to South America.'

'How?'

She pointed to a line of figures. 'They advertise their wares on the Dark Web, genuine buyers order from there, but if they include this code,' she drew an inverted Y on the page. 'And of course, five thousand pounds, they receive a very special package, clever, yes?'

'But how do the punters know what's on offer?' Crosbie said.

Debbie shook her head. 'You're the detective.'

Slobbering at the mouth, Jeddah was groaning towards consciousness slurring 'lesh had a drink.'

Agoro ignored him to serve the others with soup. 'Sadiq is a good man,' he said calmly. 'If you hurt him, you hurt me,' he glared on his way back to the kitchen.

'Now that's what I call loyalty,' Crosbie said, 'but somehow, I don't think that he should be worried. It's whoever pays Sadiq's wages, I want.'

Tam turned off the fire hose at the back of the Lauderdale basement, kicked in the ventilation grill and smiled through the gap before squeezing inside. Ankle deep in water, he trudged across the floor. He had just enough time to pass out two boxes and pull the vent back into place before Sadiq returned with the janitor.

Surveying the disarray from the doorway, Sadiq cupped his chin and held out a hand, 'It's stopped,' he said. 'Leave that here just in case.' The janitor dropped the submersible pump and was promptly ushered from the room.

Tam fought his way back along the gravel path and buried his loot beneath a pile of ashes in the old gatehouse. Angling his body into the storm, tree by tree, against the driving rain, he made his way to town.

Beer crates, patio furniture and uprooted ferns rolled like tumbleweed along the main street. Foundations are designed to resist the forces of gravity not the uplifting elements of a whirlwind. Less substantial adobes were actually ripped from their footings and sacrificed to the storm.

The wind whipped his feet from the boardwalk and tossed him into the air like a helpless manikin. Locking his fingers around an anchored newel post, he screamed for help!

Agoro heard his cries and dragged him into the lee of the alley. The wind almost sucked the side door off its hinges as it slammed shut behind them.

Tam leaned across a table gasping for breath while Agoro secured the door. 'You pick a bloody good time to come visiting, lah. What the hell were you doing out there anyway?

'Oh, excuse me,' Tam said, 'you don't get many typhoons in Springburn!'

'Hurricane,' Agoro corrected, 'and there's more to come.' He tried to smile and Tam said he was sorry. With the exception of his slurring sibling, they circled the pool table to share a bottle. 'At the mention of one of his trigger word's Jeddah peeled his cheek from the table, opened one eye and mumbled, 'lesh av a wee dram.' (It was going to be a long night).

Agoro told them he had always got on with the 'Jocks' in the armed forces. When Crosbie asked if that's where he learned to fly, he went on to explain that he had to endure seven years of institutional racism in the RAF before he won his wings.

'Where did you serve, son?'

'Egypt first, I was cashiered after the Falklands, but I couldn't find a job in Civvy Street. 'Now I fly a Cessna between the islands, there's no pension scheme,' he held a glass of white rum up to the light, 'but there are compensations. What about you, inspector?' (There was a biting irony to his tone).

Crosbie offered a half-hearted salute. 'Her Majesty's second battalion, son, Northern Ireland and Hong Kong, but it wasn't all bad.'

Agoro set a lighter tone to the conversation by relating several hand-on-heart barrack room anecdotes of his own. 'They taught me a lot, most of all, that the world didn't end at the top of Upper Parliament Street!'

'I'll drink to that.' Crosbie raised a glass and recounted an incredulous army story involving camels, illicit whisky and cricket bats.

The others laughed, but Tam was unmoved, he had his mind on other things. After finding one of the boxes in the gatehouse crammed with neatly packed dollar bills, he knew he'd had the biggest result of his life. It began to dawn how wealthy he had just become: a state of posttraumatic grandeur was making his pulse race, and he just couldn't concentrate. Greed masquerading as logic decreed that the money had become his personal property, (and he wasn't about to share). There was no way he was going to give any to a fecked up alkie like Jeddah, after all, he had done all the perpetrating!

He smirked down at his chortling burping sibling who farted unashamedly; it only served to underscore his feeling of superiority.

Taking on the decorous traits befitting his new status, he tutted. 'I'll try a brandy, have you got any of those Havana cigars; the ones rolled on page three thighs?'

Agoro handed him a single skinner, which he proceeded to puff with a little finger in the air. 'How much is the property around here then, pal?' Leaning back to enjoy the sweet elixir of affluence, he put the glass to his lips. The practicalities of converting all those dollars into sterling in Glasgow were put on hold.

The Lauderdale kitchen staff had been sent home for Christmas on full pay. Chef prepared a lavish banquet of lobster, pigeon peas and pork with all the trimmings. A two-gallon punchbowl was filled to the hilt with Sky Juice: a local concoction of sweet milk, gin and coconut water. (Bellies stuffed and wine flowed).

Sadiq added a liberal sprinkling of crushed blue powder to the mix and tapped his glass. 'Ladies and gentlemen, and others, the airport may have been closed until further notice, not so the bar.' Wearing a fiendish glint, he fed the waiting flagons from the doctored mix with a silver ladle. 'Eat, drink and be horny, I mean merry, or do I?'

Wang closed his eyes to savour the growing sensation in his groin. 'I think you mean horny. I'm ready to party!'

Richard was feeling it too. (If he had any hair, he'd be letting it down).

Gypsy was playing footsy with Sadiq under the table, toes slowly moving upward. Adjusting his crotch, he shouted 'here's to adversity,' and raised a glass.

'I'll drink to that!' She dipped her flagon directly into the punch bowl, wiped her mouth with a mitten clad hand, burped and cracked a knuckle painfully.

Once more Richard's libido began to wonder, he slipped a casual hand beneath the hemline of her peasant skirt and dug his nails in deep. 'Doesn't that hurt?'

She didn't react, simply cracked another knuckle and burped again, only this time louder. 'No point if it didn't.'

Sadiq refilled the flagons. 'Tomorrow, Insha'Allah, I would like you all to accompany me to Monk's Head Island, weather permitting of course. There are people there who would really like to meet you.'

The crushed Viagra was taking its toll on Judy too. Licentious lip-licking images flashed through her one-track mind as she scoured the wall mounted South Sea chart for Monks Head Island and fanned her face. 'Where is it, and what is it, a sort of sex commune?'

'Our destination is not on any map. Let me say sexual predilection plays a major part,' Sadiq added cryptically and stood to adjust his gusset. 'We meet in the lounge at noon,' he said. 'Tonight, however, you are all to be my guests.'

Judy ran a tongue around open lips, a seductive calypso-beat fueled her panting curiosity with what he was carrying inside those baggy harem pants. Liberated and lubricated, the fantasy of a filling in a menage-á-trois sandwich heartened her. 'It's chic to shag a sheikh, I hear.'

'Spread-legged on the penthouse billiard table, Wang blew ganga smoke to the florescence and groped his way from knee to knee.

'What good is sitting alone in your room?' he sang. For an encore he lay across the baize, and one by one began to slowly peel away the layers; one by one his backing band dwindled until he was once again alone. 'Life is a cabaret, old chum,' ended on a disturbingly flat note. Midnight bells were chiming; tears dripped onto the chalky baize.

Richard and Gypsy were the last two upright on that dancefloor far below. Calypso had permeated the humid air, it floated on sound waves to settle in a frisson deep under Richard's skin. A guttural groan began somewhere in the pit of his stomach as his blabbering lips quivered to a rumble. Eyes jammed shut, the only sound immitted was a pre-orgasmic 'Ahhhhhh.'

Gypsy finished for him: 'Ahhhhh know exactly what you need, babe.'

Judy was rummaging through her leatherware stash in the penthouse suite, Sadiq, about to make that age old mistake of trusting his ego at the expense of libido. 'The time has come InshAllah,' he whispered. Flirting with himself in the mirror, he wet his index finger to assuage a wayward eyebrow and stepped back for a full frontal. Only then did he realise just what wasn't happening. Alcohol was having that age-old effect. He screwed his eyes and jerked wildly to no avail; only then did he begin to panic. 'C'mon Apollo, c'mon c'mon,' he urged frantically, but sensed no movement. 'C'mon c'mon, my old friend,' he was begging now; 'please do not disappoint me.'

He tried to force his mind between the centre pages of some distant glossy, but it just wasn't working, he began to pray to Allah and then to curse his will. 'Oh, why do you do this to me?' he asked rhetorically, but could think of too many reasons, so he resorted to promising everlasting devotion to the Koran. 'If you grant me this one respite from the curse of the grape, I will be forever your humble servant!' But Allah wasn't to be fooled.

When Judy re-entered the bedroom, Sadiq was mumbling into his pillow. She assumed he was uttering some pre-coitus incantation when he was, in fact, talking dirty to himself in a last-ditch attempt at arousal.

Naked and carrying a selection of adult toys she moved in for the kill. 'C'mon, big fellah,' she squealed and tugged at the bedclothes. 'Let's see your obelisk, then.'

He fell silent, clutching the silken sheets to his midriff and averting his eyes he slid from the bed muttering, 'I need the bathroom.' Padding away, chin on chest, slipping the vanity bolt, he turned on the taps and fell back flogging a dead horse. 'Oh no,

Apollo, not when I need you the most.'

After several more minutes he conceded to the brewer's curse, and slinked silently and dejectedly away through the party door.

'Well, it looks like I'm lumbered,' Judy said after drop-kicking the bathroom door open. 'Not to worry.' She selected one of her favourites and turned on the turbo-charger. 'Or perhaps 'lumbered' isn't the right word.'

The calypso juddered to silence in the dancehall, but Richard was too caught up in the occasion to notice, and kept his body molded into Gypsy. They circled the empty dance floor until he realised the band had gone to bed, then he made his play. The evening was screaming out for a prosthetic finale, and he pulled her tighter, spraying hot spittle into her ear, he told her he had a plan. Leaving her sipping martinis in his bedroom while he slid on his slide-on, then to administer the rogering of her young life, seemed doable. 'I think a bonkable finale is in order. What say you?'

'Go for it!' Gypsy cried. Struggling through the deserted foyer they found it difficult to walk and hold each other so close. Assuming they were the only guests still awake in the building, Richard confided his pet elevator fantasy, Gypsy confessed it was a schoolgirl dream of hers too. Immediately going to work on his belt, she pushed him into the lift; they both fell to the floor, grappling for dominance: Gypsy on a mission, Richard struggling to keep his phallic reputation intact.

Sadiq backed in, fell (arse first) on top of the startled couple, genitals jammed hard against Richard's cheek. Gypsy squeezed free and forced herself into the corner.

Trapped beneath a pair of enormous Arabian testicles, Richard's words of protest were reduced to a strangled splutter. 'Pftt, pftt, excuse me! Do you, pfft, mind! Feckin gerrrofff!' he finally managed.

For the first time acknowledging the squirming figure beneath, Sadiq looked down. 'Oh, I do apologise,' he said and used Richard's groin as a fulcrum to regain a more modest pose.

Unhindered by dangling extremities, Richard's muffled cry rose to a disproportionate screech of pain.

Clutching the bed sheet to his now astonishing erect erection, Sadiq looked down in anger. 'A bit blinking late now, Apollo!'

With a great phallic image emblazoned on her memory bank, Gypsy unconsciously reached down. 'Or maybe not.'

Richard shook his head as he hopped from the lift. 'After what I've just had jammed in my gob, I'll leave you to it.' He closed his eyes, and twitched his nose to blindly follow the feint scent of Chanel through the deserted hallways.

. . . Eventually he found Wang, fetal on the pool table: lipstick engrained on a tear stranded cheek, one hand tangled in the balk pocket netting, the other down his trousers, he stirred and rubbed his eyes. 'I thought you'd gone all hetero on me,' he said

Richard picked up a discarded cue and reached for the chalk. 'Well, there's nothing like a gob-full of unwanted scrotum, to remind you of just what you're missing!'

Gypsy pulled Sadiq off balance out onto her veranda, without any pretense of foreplay she spreadeagled and looked to the sky. 'C'mon big boy,' she cried. At that very moment a fork of lightening pierced the crimson clouds, and she wondered was it an omen. . .

Watching that same angry sky through a crack in his barroom shutters, Agoro had that very same feeling and drifted off to sleep thinking 'what if?'

. . . Early the next morning Crosbie and Debbie help him to take down the shutters. Last night's electric semaphore had given way to a sunrise that blasted through the window, it filled the barroom with a golden glow that stirred the sleepers to semi consciousness.

It took a cup of scalding Java to fire Tam and Jeddah to their senses, another to get them upright and an ultimatum from Agoro to start them moving. 'You two aren't invited, but the rest have exactly four hours to get back here or I'm going without you,' he said, as they shuffled despondently into the sunlit street.

Crosbie fired the engine of the 4x4 and they set off for the Lauderdale in silence. . . A little over half an hour later he picked the guilt edged invitation from reception and held it to the light.

At no extra cost, the management cordially invite you and your good lady to be wined and dined at the old colonial mansion situated on Monks Head Island. We would be honored if you would assemble in the lounge at noon. Transport to the airfield will be provided.

'Looks like they knew before we did,' Debbie said, stretching out her foot from the foam. (Crosbie said nothing).

Chapter Seventeen:
Monk's Head Island

Richard and Judy sat back-to-back on the back seat, Gypsy had cried off with crotch fatigue, but Sadiq seemed fine as he slid in the front smiling and winked at the driver. Crosbie and Debbie were the last to climb aboard. They sat tight-lipped as the Silver Shadow pulled away, and Judy nodded politely, 'we meet again, inspector.' She grinned, then pulled a face behind his back.

The half-hour journey was spent in tense silence, Debbie didn't know quite what to make of it, so she just sat back to enjoy the scenery. Ten miles later the road became a lane, the lane, a chisel-stone track that led on to the airfield: lined with black mangroves and overhanging banana palms, its runway hidden from all but ariel view.

They bumped to a crunching halt, where Agoro waited at the foot of the Cessna's fold-down steps. He produced a pack of deflated life jackets from the side hatch and handed one to each of the passengers. 'I am required by aviation law to issue basic safety instructions, purely routine, just a precaution,' he assured them, 'so here goes,' he said and held his own jacket out. 'Pull the yellow hoop to inflate, blow the whistle if you're in trouble, keep your seat belts on at all times, unless I say different. Enjoy the flight.'

Sadiq took the co-pilot's seat, Crosbie and Debbie immediately behind, either side of the aisle. This left Richard and Judy once more with the rear seats to themselves. Each pretended to study a flight-glossy, straining in opposing directions, while Agoro went through his safety procedure. After making sure all seat belts were fastened, he finished his pre-take-off routine and instrument checks. 'Hold onto your halfpennies!' he shouted, 'here we go!'

Retracting the flaps, he grasped the throttle and taxied onto the two-acre runway. Picking up speed into the wind for maximum lift-off, the Cessna took to the air and zoomed laterally beyond the trees into the clear blue sky. 'Okay!' Agoro shouted over the racing engine, 'our destination is just over 100 miles due south, we will arrive in a little over fifty minutes, so relax and enjoy the view.'

At 2000 feet, the pull of inertia equalized, the plane levelled off, the thrust went from the engine noise and the passengers began to relax.

Crosbie looked down at the slowly disappearing landmass below, and felt that strange sense of foreboding: once again he was flying over occupied Egypt and into enemy territory. His knuckles clenched; the nearer to their destination the more intense this feeling of trepidation. He looked to Debbie gazing forlornly from her portal, took her hand and squeezed. She tried to return his smile, but there was worry behind her eyes too. 'We'll be fine,' she said, 'don't worry we'll be fine.'

'You can take your seat belts off now,' Agoro shouted over his shoulder, and Judy was the first to react.

She pulled the release and immediately crossed the aisle. 'You don't mind if I swap places with you, do you? Richard makes me want to vomit, bad karma you know.'

Crosbie declined for the same reason, but the point was well made. 'Some people have that affect,' he said. He could see Sadiq smiling through the gap, and nudged Debbie. 'At least someone's enjoying the trip.'

. . . Twenty minutes of loaded atmosphere later found them refastening their seatbelts. The plane dipped; Monk's Head Island was rising like Atlantis from the mist. 'Hold tight!' Agoro shouted, he banked for a landing pass, and dived steeply to follow the contours of the volcano.

Oozing from its gaping mouth, ancient extrusions of lava had cut concentric furrows that circled the huge chasm. The Cessna's polarized screen had neutralized the glare from his view and he gripped the controls with a new urgency.

From the air, the surface looked too rough to facilitate a landing, but the larva ruts had been artificially filled to form a deceptively flat plane.

Clearing the surrounding ridge by yards, the aircraft rose gently and veered to follow the contours. 'A lost world,' Agoro said and lowered the landing gear. 'Touchdown in three minutes.'

The pulsing beacon of a radio mast blinked blue and then red, he lined up his descent between it, and the setting sun. The monks called this 'Le terrain du diablo,' he said as he compensated for the push of geo-thermals with his joystick.

Crosbie looked down into the open mouth of the crater. 'Land of the devil!'

A kaleidoscope of green and yellow flashed by the windows as the Cessna's nosecone dipped. The passengers recoiled as machine and silhouette met on the windswept surface. Agoro lowered the flaps and threw the brakes. The Cessna bumped along to a stop and he cut his throttle. After turning off the instruments, he told everybody to unfasten their seatbelts and passed down the fuselage to lower the exit hatch.

The inverted stairway dropped noisily onto the strip. As protocol demanded he stood at its foot and helped his passengers to alight.

Richard and Judy seemed to have forgotten their feud; arm in arm, they followed the others to stare in awe into the mouth of the seething volcano. Sadiq didn't join them, he'd seen it all before.

Crosbie and Debbie looked into the vast caldera. Agoro told them it had been dormant for years, 'considered defunct,' he said, 'but if you look carefully, you'll see that this baby's only sleeping, these things never die.'

'Just like old soldiers,' Debbie said, and looked to Crosbie. As if to underline the point, a tiny fissure broke from somewhere deep in the depths to release a plume of sulphur dioxide into the air.

When Sadiq told Agoro he was to accompany them to the mansion house Agoro wasn't too happy. 'I can come back for you,' he said, 'I've got a bar to run.'

'Forgive me,' the Arab smiled, 'but I must insist. 'Your bar will look after itself.'

Agoro knew this was more of an instruction than a reassurance, and there was little he could do. His compliant silence was broken by the encroaching rattle of metal on metal.

. . . Half-hidden in an arch of ferns and bramble, a narrow-gauge carriage trundled upwards, cables straining in the undergrowth. It shuddered and bumped uneasily to rest at a pair of steel buffers, and they all climbed aboard. Assisted by gravity, at a rate of descent regulated by no more than a simple handheld lever, they began their funicular journey. The carriage picked up speed into a sparse ravine and they held on for dear life.

At the exact halfway point, the rattling chassis, burst from the undergrowth and slowed. Snapping and cracking newly sprouted green chutes from the adjacent track, an identical empty carriage passed them on its way to the summit. Clearing the sheer rock-face by inches, they careered through a hand-hewn tunnel into the cavernous interior, and squealed to a halt in the dark.

Standing out from the red rock like an abandoned movie

prop, a pair of steel elevator door swished silently open. A loom of overhead cable fed the hanging lamps that dimly lit the way, not a word passed between the passengers as they crammed inside. Sadiq smiled and Agoro shuddered as the lift doors closed.

Crosbie stood at the back holding onto Debbie's hand. Richard and Judy exchanged anxious glances as a strangely familiar voice crackled through the speaker.

From the viewing deck deep inside the mountain, Sam Prentiss was looking down with a certain relish. 'My friends, do not be concerned. Imagine you are travelling through time and space to Avalon. Enjoy the trip.'

The fully functioning factory below was operating to maximum capacity, he smiled contentedly and put down his microphone to watch.

. . .In every two-minute cycle, titanium digits were transmogrifying raw polycarbonate into humanoid organs. With the ability to lift a bus and the finesse to peel an egg, robotic sentinels waltzed in perfect symmetry around the feeder umbilical.

. . . A cyborg freeze-moulded base polymers into testicular orbs, and loaded them with a white crystalline substance from a chromium hopper. Once the micro circuitry was implanted and the bridal strap elasticized, the scrotal seam was vulcanized.

Sam was fondling a finished sample of his product with considered pride as he watched. Above the drone of swishing bionics, a synthesized voice alerted him to a problem a flashing red light highlighted where it lay. It triggered a pair of callipers to pluck the troublesome unit from the assembly line and drop it into a vat of molten plastic.

Sam squirmed, he looked at his watch, then at Sadiq, who appeared smiling on the overhead screen. 'We're all here, sir.'

Janet activated the CCTV. A sneer played on twisted lips. She raised a glass to the guests as they trundled from the funicular track to the Mansion House. 'Here's to divine comeuppance,' she said, and they both sniggered.

The last remaining monument of a shameful slave-trade was built on the lee side of an abandoned anchorage. Depicting all Agoro loved about the tropics, paintings of Lucayan Indians that could have been his ancestors frolicking on a sunburst beach, lined the dining room.

Three of the West wing walls were screened in idyllic oils, the remaining wall, almost completely of glass, offered an unfettered view across the cay.

Agoro was admiring the flamboyance of flamingos dancing on the waters beyond when Crosbie joined him. 'What do you think?' he said under his breath and pointed to a shadowy figure, grinning from behind a traverse gully.

'I think we're in trouble. Keep smiling and look at the chandelier.'

'Cameras?'

'Too many for comfort, and a five-lever high tensile lock on the door, appropriate for Toxteth, maybe, but a nineteenth century mansion, I don't think so.'

Richard and Judy were pigging out on peppered quail eggs from the lavish buffet, but the others were not eating. Debbie drew Crosbie's attention and whispered that she had seen armed men on the parapets. She was tugging him toward the glass when a voice interrupted from behind.

Minus his thick moustache and coverall, Sadiq appeared decidedly Anglo Saxon. He smoothed down his Saville Row suit, pulled at his cuffs and cleared his throat. 'This mansion once belonged to the Duke of Windsor. They say it is where he and Mrs Simpson entertained their German friends. Our hosts have a great admiration for the aristocracy, you know.'

The brick faced waiter behind him was too clumsy with the tray he carried to be following any vocation. An involuntary tic lifted his distended brow, a nose-job, at best a partial success, betrayed a pugilist past.

'Oh, you must excuse Oaks, he's not comfortable with strangers,' Sadiq said.

The big man put down the tray, shuffling his huge bulk between them, he moved across the room like a shadow boxer to open the door, (and there they were!)

Resplendent in outfits that once belonged to the wayward royalty, Sam and Janet entered grandly. Her gown was a perfect fit, 'Successful bid at Christies,' she boasted, but Sam would later confess that 'the duke was a bit of a short-arse, and his stuff had to be re-tailored.'

Bedecked in plaid and chiffon, they perused the room behind Sadiq's formal introductions. . . 'And last but not least of course we have Richard and Judy, of whom you've had the pleasure,' he said, unaware of innuendo.

Janet paused, took off the pince-nez spectacles and shook her head. 'Ah, Benedict Arnold, and Matta Hari,' she sighed, 'our would-be assassins.'

'Janet, I...'

'Oh dear, Richard, you're not going to grovel are you, please don't.' She waved him off with manicured fingertips, diamond bangles swinging on her wrists, then turned to Judy. 'It all worked out well in the end, dear. Were it not for your uninspired little plan at the clinic, Sam and I would never. . .'?

. . . 'We would never have met, had you not planned our murder,' Sam said, 'it's as simple as that; for that reason alone, we've decided to let you live, for the time being,' he added under his breath with a mischievous air. 'No such luck for the police inspector and his eminent doctor friend, I'm afraid. As for the turncoat pilot . . .'

. . . 'Especially, the turncoat pilot,' Janet said, 'most disappointing.'

Agoro shook his head despairingly and Richard wrapped his act of great surprise in a clumsy guilt-displacing ruse. 'You dirty traitor!' he cried.

Showing no such pretence, Judy turned to Sam. 'But why, when, . . how?'

'Why is easy, my dear, money and revenge, obviously, when's another story!' Sam was angry now. 'You gave us the idea when you spiked us with Viagra, expecting us to die playing exploding bloody salamis! That only leaves us with 'how!' he shouted.

'We brought you here to repay you that's all, you'll find out how soon enough,' Janet sneered. The chilling nuance to her tone left Agoro cold as she turned to him. 'We are aware that you've been helping the policeman with his enquiries, also, that you downloaded certain confidential information, for which you will pay the ultimate price. In the meantime, the rest of you can enjoy our facilities.' She nodded to Oaks, and he felled Agoro with a crunching blow to the kidneys.

Sam walked slowly over to nudge the prostrate man with his Oxford brogue. 'We paid you well and you betrayed us!' Staring down contemptuously at the writhing figure on the floor, his smile broadened, his eyes widened. 'You, Judas, will be confined elsewhere while we contrive a fitting end to your treacherous life. Take him away!'

Crosbie pushed forward to help Agoro to his feet. 'Stay strong, son,' he whispered.

Before Agoro could respond, Oaks was dragging him from the room.

. . .Sam raised a calming hand. 'I do apologise, inspector. Now I'm afraid we must leave you for a while, but if you should need anything. I'm sure Oaks will oblige. Try the quail eggs, they're really quite exquisite.' He offered his arm in an exaggerated motion to Janet, who likewise accepted, and linked him from the room.

Ignoring Richard's solicitude, Crosbie picked up a bottle and two glasses, he followed Debbie onto the piazza and slid the doors closed behind them.

Anxious to keep a healthy distance, Richard and Judy stayed where they were and did their best to ingratiate themselves with Sadiq.
. . . The Arab listened patiently to their solicitations of innocence and reassured them he would pass their sentiments on. 'But right now, you need some rest,' he said. He instructed Oaks to escort them to their room, and left without further ado.

Debbie could see what was happening through the glass partition, 'Don't be too hard on them, James,' she said. 'They don't seem to know it, but I'd say they're in worse trouble than us!'

They sat together on a tiled mezzanine at the warm water's edge to watch the courting flamingos bill and coo. Either side of the shallows the horseshoe escarpment offered no lateral view. Under no instructions now to stay hidden, armed guards crouched on the rim, chain-smoking and laughing through their boredom.

Crosbie followed the path of a discarded cigarette end as it bounced downward off the mildewed angles. 'Can you see that?' He pointed to a decrepit boathouse hewn into the cliff face.

Debbie put on her sunglasses and peered across. 'What good's a boat to us, James?'

'Look up and a little to the left.'

The flash of Agoro's distinctive 'orange' shirt billowed from the cladding just above the boathouse gates, and she angled her compact mirror to the burning sun.

Crosbie took off his shoes and waded ten yards closer. The razor-sharp coral bed forced him back to the piazza, but by then he had seen enough to know Agoro was still alive.

Spurred by Debbie's mirrored signal, Agoro honed his diver's knife on the lime-stone wall, gritted his teeth in the darkness and gouged away at the wooden floor. Bruised and bleeding, but unafraid; determination left no room for fear, he took a deep breath and plunged the blade downward.

. . . An hour later, Oaks returned to escort Crosbie and Debbie to the grand baronial lounge. Fittingly it was the very room where another treacherous couple once planned their disaffection.

Two leather Chesterfields in the mahogany panelled room were angled to an enormous marble fireplace: patterns of mottled flame rippled onto a mock Tudor tapestry that hung above. Sam and Janet occupied one couch and offered their guests the other. 'We've decided to placate your curiosity,' Sam said. 'As you must appreciate; genius doesn't exist until it is recognised.'

'Rather like lunacy?' Debbie sneered.

'Women can be so tedious I know,' Sam sighed and turned to Janet. 'Not you, darling.' He pressed a button on his console, and the lights dimmed until the room relied entirely on the dappled gas glow The tapestry rolled upwards to reveal a bank of multi-sectioned flat screens, each one depicting a different phase of an impressive production line.

Sadiq played host with the sherry, while Janet provided the commentary. 'Welcome to our world, chief inspector. You will notice, the process is completely automated: raw plastic pellet at one end, product at the other.' She paused to give her audience time to take it all in . . .

Crosbie looked intently at the wide screen panorama of a factory running at full capacity.

Sam touched another control on his console. One half of the screen was taken up with multi angled views of the liquefying process, the other half, a line of completed units passing through a Spectro-scanner. Every so often a buzzer sounded; a camera zoomed in on some minuscule flaw before a calliper plucked the offending unit from the production line. Another frame displayed an enormous reject bin emptying into a vat of molten plastic. Sam leaned back into the leather. 'Nothing wasted,' he said as he sipped on his cut-glass. 'I do hope the lady isn't embarrassed at the sight of all these appendages?'

'On the contrary,' Debbie replied. 'I find the concept of sexual inadequacy fascinating, and you are, understandably perhaps, somewhat of an authority, but aren't you missing something?'

Sam stared suspiciously around the room and checked his groin. 'For instance?'

'For instance, the real reason we're here, and exactly what you two lunatics are peddling inside these pathetic toys!'

Sam exchanged wry smiles with Janet. 'That's for us to know and you to find out. Do try to be less tedious, your time is far too precious to waste on vitriol.' He spun the tumblers and opened an attaché case on the low table. Inside were two completed penile prostheses. Janet cradled one from its nook and held it lovingly to her cheek.

'Janet is holding the reason we are all here, bear with me.'

He went on to explain how they had 'cheated the reaper,' as he put it, 'by the merest of chances.' Picking up the remaining sample, he compared it with Janet's. 'Look the same, don't they? but one is quite literally a timebomb, the other a dream machine, and if someone hadn't bitten through the synthetic sac?' Winking at Janet, he raised the sample to his lips and feigned a bite, 'neither of us would be here to tell the tale. You're obviously aware of my unfortunate accident.' Sam touched himself suggestively and sighed. 'Well, necessity and invention, my dear chap, soon put that more than right.' He blew Janet a kiss, then kissed the gland head. 'Did you know that Adolph Hitler only had one testicle?'

'Yes, and if I remember rightly, he dropped that too,' Debbie smiled. By now she had decided her hosts were completely unhinged.

'You have plenty of money,' Crosbie said to change the subject. 'Why get involved with narcotics?'

'Narcotics? Now you are beginning to bore me. Put your bloody warrant card away, inspector, cocaine is just as much an aphrodisiac as a narcotic. 'Come on, mister policeman, what would you hide inside a plastic prosthesis? Think laterally, what better place to hide a sexual aid than inside a sexual aid? In plain sight as it were, but there's more!'

'Priapus was the Greek god of procreation,' Janet said. 'You, doctor, will be familiar with the name?'

'Priapism? yes, a vascular disorder that results in prolonged unwanted erections. The supply to the smooth muscle is muted, the blood cannot escape, and it's very, very painful.'

152

'Very good, doctor, but just imagine the effect combined with a chemically induced compulsion to copulate.

'It makes you randy, so what?'

'We have discovered a compound isotope that reacts with cocaine to induce sustained priapism,' Sam said. 'Climacta! we call it.' He smiled like a Cheshire cat, cupped his hands into a megaphone and spoke in his best newscasters' voice. 'We interrupt this neurone transmission with the following announcement...Go forth and multiply!'

Janet giggled, poured herself another drink and continued. . . 'Once copulation has begun, the spent juices are re-absorbed, and without an antidote the cycle repeats and repeats until?' She looked to Debbie.

'Cardiac and pulmonary arrest?'

'Correct! Unless an adrenaline compound was to shock the vascular system back to normality. We call it 'over-cumming,' oops!'

'Just what is the point?' Crosbie said.

'Addressing the overpopulation of our planet, that's the point. Don't you see?'

'No.'

'Increased life expectancy, coupled with multifaceted sexuality has resulted in a population explosion, an explosion, if unchecked will eventually collapse our eco systems,' Sam said.

'How

'Overuse of land, greenhouse gasses, increased waste production, pollution, water contamination. resource extinction, there's a few more 'how's' for you.' Need I go on?'

'What about why?'

'Because we can, that's one why! Levelling up the bonking field, another.' Call it saving humanity if you like, but that sounds a bit too theatrical. Serves 'em bloody right anyway. Now I am bored.' Covering his mouth with his hand to mimic a yawn and stifle a giggle, Sam summoned Oaks to lead the prisoners away.

Agoro was still wrenching at the splintered boards. Gouging away in the dark; his purchase increased, and the wooden floor began to shear, when his working space grew wider, he squeezed his aching form between the joists. . . A scintilla of refracted moonlight beckoned him to cast his fate to chance, and he let go...

The 100-year-old rotted deck below, collapsed to a mulch on impact and sent him tumbling into the bilges. Taking some time to collect himself, knee-deep in silt, he climbed from the barnacle wreckage to edge through the slats of the crumbling boathouse door.

Finger-touching the way along weeping mildewed walls, he dragged himself onto the carved landing out entrance to a long-abandoned wine cellar and crawled inside.

Sandwiched between empty bottle racks, a retractable panel slid open to reveal a disused dumbwaiter. Knees to chin, he somehow cramped his weary limbs inside. . . A deep breath, a silent prayer, he heaved on the pulley to draw himself upward, inch-by-agonising-inch.

Crosbie stood to one side, and raised the heavy bedpost high into the air as the ancient hoist creaked closer. The creaking stopped, as did his heart when the panel slid slowly open. . . a hand appeared from the knot of contorted limbs inside and Crosbie poised for a strike.

. . . 'Stop!' Debbie shouted. Confusion was quickly displaced by concern as Agoro's bloody form fell to the floor and unfurled at their feet. She sat him upright to attend his wounds as best she could.

. . . Ten minutes later Crosbie was banging on the door shouting for 'help!'

The guards were all in the basement watching adult movies and Oaks drew the short straw. Out of cigarettes, in need of a drink, he cursed at the pleading voice from inside. 'What the feck d'yeh want?' he screamed through the solid hardwood door. 'I'm not a feckin bell-boy!'

'You need to take a look at the lady!' Crosbie shouted back. 'I don't think your bosses will be too happy if she's not well enough to torture in the morning!'

This confused the dullard into thinking, and he didn't like it. 'Okay, stand back and no funny business!' He slowly turned the key in the aging mortice, opened the door just wide enough to see that his charges were at a safe distance. Crosbie was wiping Debbie's brow as she lay still on the bed, huddled against his chest.

Uzi first, Oaks tentatively slid a foot inside
. 'What the feck's. . .'

The bedpost thundered into his cranium and his world went black.

. . . He came around, trussed motionless, crammed helplessly inside the appropriately named 'dumbwaiter.'

Sam and Janet were sitting comfortably on their vintage leather chairs. They were mulling over the days' events, when in walked Sadiq with the news of Agoro's escape.

Janet told him not to worry, 'CCTV is a wonderful innovation, don't you know?' She picked up her favourite decanter, sat back, pressed a button on the console and the wall mounted screen once again lit up.

. . . The main artery of the south wing was covered by close circuit security cameras, as was the approach to the living area, where the three prisoners moved cautiously from frame to frame. Crosbie and Debbie stayed close behind Agoro, Uzi in one hand, trying door handles with the other.

Sam and Janet were thoroughly enjoying the spectacle, and watched with growing excitement until the prisoners were almost within touching distance, then Sam plunged the room into darkness.

. . .The catch gave under Agoro's grip, and he turned to the others. 'Quiet,' he hissed, eased the carved mahogany inward and held his breath.

Three prisoners were trying to focus when Janet flipped the light switch, raised her hands high and symbolically applauded. 'Surprise surprise!' she squealed.

'Bravo!' Sam cried and lifted his Luger pistol.

Agoro took careful aim with his automatic weapon, the others took cover behind him. 'Mine's bigger than yours,' he said.

'That's true in more ways than one,' replied Sam with a smile. 'You don't think I'd trust a fool like Oaks with live rounds, do you?'

Agoro lifted his muzzle to the ceiling and clicked on an empty chamber. He spun around to find the real 'dumb waiter' sporting a formidable bruise on his forehead and snarling menacingly in his direction.

Two more granite faces arrived, they filed into position, and Sam relieved Agoro of his useless weapon. 'Well, it's been fun, old chap,' he said, and nodded to Oaks. 'Take them down to the shop floor.'

Hands pinned tight behind his back, Agoro flexed as Oaks bobbed and weaved and drove a ham sized fist deep into his solar plexus before dragging him from the room. The two henchmen followed with Crosbie trussed between them.

Sam called Debbie by name and said his outfit could use another logical mind, and she paused in the doorway. 'I don't think so, you wouldn't know what to do with one!' She was grabbed from behind and forced to her knees, and Sadiq's protests fell on deaf ears.

'Playtime's over now. Take them away,' Sam growled and turned to Sadiq. 'You had better decide which side you're on!'

The production line had been reprogrammed and calibrated to a new weight/volume ratio; Sam had devised a different fate for each of the prisoners: Debbie was to be freeze-moulded, Crosbie vulcanised and Agoro recycled. (If things went wrong there was always Oaks).

In the comfort of the baronial lounge, he picked up the CCTV remote to watch the fun: Crosbie and Debbie were shackled to the conveyer. Agoro came around, half-buried beneath a mound of condemned product in the reject bin, Janet moved closer as it began to tilt.

'Get out!' Crosbie screamed, but his voice was lost in the mechanical whine of hydraulics. 'Get out!'

Toppling forward, Agoro grabbed at the rim to peer over the edge. Recycled units flying over his head into the boiling miasma below, were instantly vaporized. Recoiling from the searing heat, he tried to spread his weight against the sides, but he was losing purchase.

'The pipes, grab the pipes!' Debbie roared.

Agoro sacrificed what little grip he had to gravity and grasped a flaying airline. Swinging like a helpless manakin, he bent his frame just enough to deflect his path from certain death and dropped to the side of the sizzling tank.

The broken hose thrashed around the room like a frenzied serpent, its gunmetal spigot smashed into the contact breaker and came to rest in the vat of molten plastic. An eerie 'hisssssssssssss filled the darkened factory like a ghostly sigh of relief, as all the machinery ground to a halt.

On hands and knees, he crawled beneath the static conveyer to unshackle his friends.

Sam had watched from the viewing deck until the factory plunged into darkness. 'Guns it is then!' he shouted angrily. Safety catches off and psyched up, his entourage followed him to the production line. He paused on the threshold to let them pass. 'Take no prisoners,' he bellowed loud enough to be heard inside. 'And shoot to kill!'

In the ensuing panic three prisoners made good their escape, jamming the factory door behind them.

Sam sent tracer-beams into every nook and cranny, but they were nowhere to be seen. When he turned on the auxiliary supply, the airline belched to life in the bubbling vat of plastic, and sprayed the room with a shower of molten pellets. Undaunted, resolute, and staring straight ahead, he marched untouched through the white-hot meteor storm to the observation deck to turn off the power, and pressed his face to the monitor.

A stray globule compromised the circuitry, sending the robotic limbs wrestling to a mass of tangled steel: their servos blew, a twisted monolith of metal formed before his very eyes. While this was happening, a hopper burst and filled the air with a compound of highly concentrated Climacta.

Henchmen danced and screamed as they plucked the burning splatters from their clothing. Sam made himself a solemn promise. Growling through clenched teeth; eyes bulging, froth bubbling from the corners of his mouth, he screamed, 'I swear that I will personally pull the fecking trigger!

There was no need to lock the door on Richard and Judy, a Climacta enzyme in the quail eggs neutralized any inclination to escape. They were bucking and twitching in the throes of their sixth orgasm when Richard rose, bum-first onto Sadiq's loaded hypodermic.

. . . Adrenalin evacuated the Climacta from his bloodstream. It desensitized the whole of his lower body and rendered him from rigid to flaccid in less than a second.

It had a comparable deflating effect on Judy; she fell back to the floorboards in a state of extreme torpor. 'Wow,' she gasped. 'I could get used to this!'

'Tough, 'cos that's all you're bloody getting,' Sadiq shouted. He left them rummaging for their clothes, and strutted as bold as a bobby along the deserted corridor.

. . . Finding the others flummoxed at the steel elevator door, he pushed between them. 'You won't mind if I change sides, will you?' They stood back, he swiped a card across the sensor and the doors slid slowly open. 'I think I've had enough of those two bloody lunatics!' he said, and they all piled in behind him.

At its lowest point in the tunnel below, the funicular carriage was ready to begin its ascent. They paddled across, jumped aboard. Agoro released the hand brake, but the carriage refused to move. 'The linkage must be down,' he said.

Wielding his AK 47, an automaton guard suddenly emerged from the blackness. Ankle deep in the water between the rails he made a noisy point of cocking his gun, and demanded they put their hands in the air. Enjoying his moment of supreme power, he smiled when the 'shoot to kill' order crackled from his headset.

Traversing the line of startled faces, his barrel levelled on the defiant leer of Crosbie.

Chapter Eighteen:
Couple for life?

Agoro circled his fingers around the armor plating of the overhanging cable, wrenched it into the water, and the lights blew in a flash. The gunman crashed into the mud, trigger finger shuddering at the same speed as the deadly electrons coursing through his body.

. . . His weapon discharged into the roof of the chamber at twenty rounds a second and seized at the same instant as his heart.

Janet saw it all on her monitor. 'Don't worry they can't get off the island,' she assured Sam and dabbed an antiseptic onto his arm. 'I've got something for you, my little Rambo,' she smiled and reached for the syringe.

A cloud of aphrodisiac particles filled the production line air, but the guards were all too busy trying to avoid the front line to notice. Not so Sam, preacher-like, he raised his palms for the full attention of his flock. 'They can't get off the island. All we need to do is keep them moving, they'll head for the Cessna where I'm organizing a reception committee,' he laughed and told Oaks to take his best man to the landing strip. 'Any questions? No, good. The hunt is on!'

The men pretended to rally to the cause, but the Climacta had kicked in by then, and they shuffled about looking busy, while trying to settle the growing phenomenon in their pants.

Agoro looked back at the torch-lit posse as they assembled in the dark, then at his own disheveled band, and he sighed. 'C'mon, get a bloody move on, we've got a lot of ground to cover.'

Judy was struggling to reconcile his serious mood, with a residue of Climacta still popping at her neurons. On sight of a guard face-down shuddering in the mud, reality bit her on the backside. A new determination, took hold, and she discarded her stilettos to hobble barefoot across the shallow waters. 'Cumming,' she gasped.

The escarpment was so exposed, it seemed only sensible to keep to the ravine, which at least offered some sidelong cover, and they all fell into line behind Crosbie. The winding gully traversed a swamp of mangroves. It opened out to a great flurry of flamingos dancing in some kind of carnal daisy chain. 'Didn't I read somewhere that they partnered for life?' Debbie said as a bird jumped off one accommodating hen to mount another, and then another.

Sadiq confessed he had seen nothing like it before, but Crosbie suspected the truth, and quickly changed the subject. 'If we follow the coastline to the other side of the plateau we should be there by dawn.'

Still not completely free of Climacta imbalance, Rickety-legged Richard and barefoot Judy weren't so confident.

Phosphorous playing on the moonlit breakers, and palms waving in the evening breeze seemed to soften the mood; when prickly coral gave way to crystal sands, they found the going a little easier and began to settled down. (That was all about to change).

. . .The ground beneath them rumbled like a peptic stomach, Richard squealed like a baby and Sadiq told him not to worry, 'it happens every so often.' he said, but he had never felt such a strong tremor before. The deafening silence that followed was broken by the thunderous roar of 100,000 scurrying wings. Every bird on the island simultaneously took to the sky and blocked out the sun.

The colony of iguanas couldn't have cared less, wild goats glanced lazily from their grazing then returned to the cud, it served to regulate the mood.

'There's nothing to worry about, it happens every so often,' Sadiq repeated, but he didn't believe it himself. . . It might have been easy to forget their grave peril, but he had witnessed Sam and Janet's slow decline closeup, and knew they would stop at nothing.

. . .He had joined them when it was no more than a cottage industry, then they hit the Climacta jackpot, and the money rolled in. The rest, as they say, is history, but personal overuse had directly contributed to their crazy decline. He was so glad he had steadfastly refused to overindulge, that's when he began to rethink his position in the grand scheme of things.

Beneath an arch of overgrown trailing greens, an early warning curtain of bottles, cans and sun-bleached bones, hung from a ribbon of twine. It blinded the entrance to an abandoned bivouac.

Agoro suggested it might have once been the hide of an Obeah rebel, passed on through the generations.

A blackened iron kettle lay in the dirt beside what was once a fireplace, meagre possessions strewn carelessly all about. Apart from a good stock of tinned food on a ledge too high for ruminants, few personal belongings survived. Crosbie took an ancient blunderbuss and a flare gun from the mud-wall ledge and creaked open the action. 'I'll bet this old thing still works.'

Legs akimbo like a saddle-sore jockey, Richard shuffled into the clearing. Judy was behind him, still barefoot, naked from the waist up, wearing nothing more than the remnants of a shredded skirt.

'Phew!' Holding her nose, she traced the pervading stench to a rotting blanket on the ground. Tentatively nudging it back with her toe, sent a dozen rat-like creatures squealing into the bush. She screamed and ran to Agoro who kept her at arm's length.

'Nothing to be scared of; Hutia are harmless,' he laughed, 'taste a bit like pork, actually.' He pushed Judy away and handed her his Swiss army knife. 'If you want to do something useful, see what's in those tins. I'm going to check on the plane.'

. . . 'I've got an idea,' Richard said after he had left, 'remember that radio beacon? Well, what if we shoot the mast with this cannon?' He held up the blunderbuss, 'when somebody comes to fix it, we'll be rescued!'

Debbie laughed. 'Are you kidding? It took two years for someone to fix the streetlight outside our house!'

Sadiq took the sample case from his shoulder pack. 'On its own it doesn't prove much, but it's a start,' he said, then he produced the floppy disc. 'This has every transaction PIGME ever completed, Cayman account numbers, suppliers and Climacta distributors on five continents: names and addresses, the works!'

'What's in it for you,' Crosbie asked cynically, 'immunity?'

'I think that would be a fair exchange, don't you?

. . . Regal and imperious, Sam stood in the leading funicular car wearing the late duke's ceremonial dress: medal ribbons stretched under the weight of unearned bronze, three-cornered hat decorated with the skin of a snake. Straining the polished brass buttons of his scarlet tunic, he puffed out his chest and cried, 'once more into the breach!' to Janet, sat smiling behind a black lace fan.

When they hit the steepest incline, the uphill leg of the journey ground to a halt. Bearers had to dismount and make their way on foot as the carriage rolled slowly upwards. They trooped alongside pushing and tugging through hostile undergrowth to the crown, and scrambled onto the running board for the last few level yards.

Sam held his sabre high, he picked up the old brass telescope, and tossed his monocle into the rough. 'They'll be here,' he said, 'and when they do - ah ah!' Mimicking the report of a machine gun, he aimed a pointed hand into the bush, blew on his fingertip and returned the imaginary weapon to its imaginary holster.

. . . With an increasing sense of the danger ahead, Agoro carried on toward the very source of his fear, (he had no choice). Hidden beneath a shield of bramble and ferns he watched from a safe distance. When he had seen enough, he crawled back beneath the bracken, broke into a lumbering trot along a curved line of palms to the clearing, and sat on a tree stump to recover. 'Well, we can forget about flying out of here,' he whispered when the others gathered around. 'They've got a bloody arsenal up there!' He went on to describe what he had seen on the landing strip, and the mood plummeted.

Crosbie took an inventory of the provisions, he concluded that if they ate the wildlife, they could survive indefinitely, and set about preparing for a long stay.

Agoro disagreed. 'We won't have to wait long before they come looking for us, and that's when we take the airplane!' He made it sound so simple, but in truth, didn't have a clue how.

As well as a can of light oil, Debbie found powder and shot, and spent what was left of daylight cleaning the old brass gun.

Judy discovered a case of Campari and popped a cork. Agoro sniffed it and told her that the special flavour was from a local tree, farmed just for its aromatic bark.

That night they sat around the glowing campfire, drinking and reminiscing. Agoro engrossed his audience with tales of witchcraft and magic. 'Alagba was the leader of the 'Egungun' Obeahs who brought their own African bush-lore to the Bahamas,' he said. 'He invited all the strong young men to join a rebellion. Wearing coloured goatskin, they painted their faces with pigment and frightened the shit out of the British. Even the slave traders kept their distance.'

'What happened?' Debbie asked.

'Spears against guns, what do you think?'

'Were they all wiped out?'

'Not quite, a few fled to the outlying islands. They say that some still live in hides protected by snake-witches.'

'Are you saying that this is one of their hides?' Judy asked. What was left of her skimpy dress had ridden almost to the waist and when she saw him looking, she puckered.

Agoro turned away and shook his head. 'I don't know, but I do know a snake-witch when I see one. I'm going to bed.'. . .He awoke to a too silent dawn and joined Crosbie on the same tree stump. Coffee was on the boil, and he took a cup. 'Notice anything peculiar?'

Crosbie looked around and studied the opaque sky for a moment. 'No birds?' he said and cupped his ears. Usually drowned out by the dawn chorus, land animals could be heard scurrying in the undergrowth. 'Weird.'

'Notice anything else?'

He stood still and felt the slightest of reverberations underfoot. 'The volcano? I think we'd better bring our plans forward.'

'What plans?'

Agoro fixed Crosbie in a quizzical stare. 'You're the old soldier.' .

Crosbie, who knew all about the value of jungle camouflage, painted his face with red clay from the shores of the lagoon and donned a cape of green and purple ferns. Agoro followed suit; together they setoff through the bush.

. . .An hour later they crawled to a thicket vantage point overlooking the railhead, and watched Oaks emerge from a tent to hold the funicular carriage door open.

'Time for us to go, sir,' he grunted, and made a production of rattling the aircraft's ignition keys in the air before handing them over.

Sam leaned from the lead car, turned towards the rumbling chasm and threw the keys into the inferno. His eyes were red and wild, he ran his fingers through disheveled hair, shouting 'leave them to the volcano!'

Agoro watched the carriage disappear downhill before sliding backwards into the bush. 'Who needs an ignition key!' he said. 'I'm from Toxteth?' He smiled and patted his Swiss knife as they broke into a canter back to the hide.

The mirror-like surface of the lagoon began to ripple: an

angry earth grumbled like a wounded bear before the water returned to glass.

The others had felt it too, the mood had turned to anguish; Judy didn't try to pretend. 'We've got a baby blunderbuss and a flare-gun with one charge against the Woolwich bloody Arsenal!'

Debbie sighed. 'We might be walking into their trap, but what choice do we have?'

'Good bloody plan!' Judy said cynically as they set out uphill towards the landing strip. They hoped to arrive under the cover of darkness but there were no clouds, the moon was almost full, the land lay silent, numbed . . . re-energizing.

'Wait here,' Agoro whispered to the others, as he dropped down and belly-crawled towards the tent.

Crosbie followed him and crouched between the guy ropes to peer inside: a bottle, corkscrew and a 'good luck 'note lay in the centre balanced on an upturned wooden crate.

. 'Dom Perignon, very civil of them. Shall we?'

'Why not?' Agoro gripped the shoulder of the bottle to engage the corkscrew and paused. . . A tiny fleck of red between the slats of the crate caught his eye. A simple spring-loaded device attached to the percussion cap, was primed to detonate a bundle of gelignite beneath.

The smile suddenly left his face and he turned to the others waiting in the bush. 'Get the hell out of here!'. . . Sweat ran in rivers down his arm and saturated his grip, but he daren't move a muscle.

Crosbie looped the free end of a guy rope around the bottleneck and bound it to the crate. Trailing the line through fingertips, he backed away in silent prayer...

Agoro slowly unfurled his cramped fist, eased it gently from the bottle, wiped his brow on his shirt sleeve as he carefully edged towards the others, and lay down to watch the fireworks.

Everybody on the island heard the blast when Crosbie let go of the rope. The khaki tent shot high into the air ahead of a ball of searing flames, the crate came fluttering down in tiny matchwood splinters . . . Seconds later, the canvas reappeared like a distant parachute in the sky. It slowly descended towards the mouth of the crater to hover above some invisible forcefield before floating gracefully across the great divide.

Crosbie took a large wrench from the Cessna toolbox. He disconnected the ginny wheel that held the funicular belt drive, effectively demobilizing the narrow-gauge.

Agoro checked the landing gear and flight controls, and found everything in order. 'As far as I can see they've sabotaged the radio, and that's it!'

Crosbie frowned, 'I don't like it, it's too easy. They bet an awful lot on a bottle of wine.' He did a cursory inspection of the immediate area, but missed the tiny camera fitted to the navigation beacon.

Watching from the observation deck, Sam whispered an instruction into his handset, a hatch in the fuselage sprung open and out climbed Oaks with his sidekick brandishing an AK 47.

They dragged Agoro from the cockpit, ordered everyone to 'sit down,' and Oaks told his man to 'Shoot anything that moves!'

Spanning the ginny wheel with his tree trunk arms, he threaded it back onto its spindle and pointed to Agoro, 'You, Tonto, get the tools and put the belt back on!'

Agoro rose to his full height, he no longer wore his cape, but the red mud that had dried to war-paint on his black cheeks made a formidable impression. 'Bollox,' he sneered.

Oaks held his gun to Debbie's head, he cocked it and Agoro slammed the lid of the toolbox open. 'Okay, big fellah, take it easy.'

While this was happening, the henchman changed position for a better view of Judy's thighs. She shifted to improve the angle, and he began to lick his lips.

Crosbie slowly reached behind to redirect the business end of the blunderbuss. An eye twitched towards the movement, and Sadiq interjected. . . 'What are you going to do with us?' he shouted.

'We're taking you all back to the mansion house, then everyone dies,' Oaks replied. He stepped into the first car, rested the barrel of his semi-automatic on the back of the seat and took careful aim. 'Right! I'm not even going to count to three now, Tonto, if you don't get a move on, I'm going to shoot your friends one by one!'

His henchman attempted a grin and cocked his weapon.

In a final gesture of conciliation, Agoro slowly lifted the heavy wrench. 'Nearly there,' he said, and smashed the business end into the henchman's skull. When Oaks rushed forward, Crosbie fired the ancient gun and peppered his face with shot.

The sheer impetus sent 200 pound of steroid assisted muscle bucking onto the rear car. The jolted carriage moved backwards and shook him to life.

As he grabbed for his weapon Debbie fired the flare gun and seared the flesh from his face. He screamed as the car hit the steep incline and whooshed from sight in a plume of flame.

The ground was shaking underfoot. Crosbie pulled away the chocks, and ferried everyone aboard the Cessna.

It took Agoro no time at all to bypass the ignition, but he couldn't activate the autopilot. 'I must be getting rusty,' he said. Not bothering with the equipment check, he told everybody to fasten their seat belts, fired the cylinders, and the plane shuddered violently. 'That's the bloody mountain,' he shouted and fired the cylinders again. . . The engine kicked in; he levelled his nosecone to the curved horizon and pulled back the throttle. . .

Sam Prentiss waited for the optimum moment to detonate the first charge, and a red blast spurted chunks of magma into the fuselage.

Swerving to avoid the huge hole that suddenly appeared in his path, Agoro tried another angle, but the same thing happened, and then again and again, until the runway was no more than a pepper pot of rubble.

With just enough room for one last maneuver, Agoro spun the wheels on their combined axis. It ended with the tail almost touching the rail head, the nose hanging perilously into the gaping mouth of the volcano. A charge, detonated yards away, provoked yet another angry response from the mountain.

Agoro gripped the controls. 'Thermal lift! Remember the tent?' he shouted over the rumbling din.

'Oh Shit!' Richard screamed as yet another explosion rocked the aircraft. 'We're all going to die!'

Crosbie strapped himself in next to Debbie. 'We are if we stay here, that's for sure!!' he yelled. As the explosions converged into one continuous roar, it was impossible to distinguish geological from ballistic, and he grasped Debbie's hand.

Richard was having his face slapped by Judy, Sadiq praying to Allah. The Cessna wheels began to turn, slowly at first to established traction, it began to pick up speed. 'We only get one shot,' Agoro said, and pulled the throttle back as far as it would go: rubber skidded to smoke on the scorching hot surface, a tailfin clipped the volcanic rim, it sent the plane on a downward trajectory and Richard began screaming again.

Fissures spat up plumes of molten rock, an eerie crimson glow suddenly displaced the natural light. Boosted by the intake of tepid air, the engine raced to maximum velocity as the Cessna plummeted!

. . . Geo-thermals collected under its wings to keep them just above the bubbling depths. . . Agoro could feel the heat of the smoldering undercarriage through the souls of his trainers; smoke was seeping from the centre console. 'Ahhhh Almighty God help us!' he roared and strained at the controls.

. . . After what seemed like an age, his plea was answered. The tiny plane was somehow lifted from the gaping inferno, sucked from the jaws of hell on a cushion of torrid air, it cleared the far incline of the crater by mere inches and Agoro eased off his throttle. The engine coughed and spluttered through the fallout, but pre ignition kept it running to pull the Cessna to the clear blue horizon.

A 'cup final' cheer erupted from the passengers. Monks' Island faded to a dying ember in the mist: Crosbie tightened his grip on Debbie's hand, Agoro thanked God, Sadiq praised Allah, Richard and Judy wept with relief.

Before the last radio-mast was sacrificed to fate, Sam watched the Cessna disappear into the mile wide volcano jaws, that was the last he seen of it, but he couldn't be sure. The mountain roared again, the volcano erupted and spewed out molten rock that oozed down the escarpment to fill the tunnel system. Steel elevator doors disintegrated and opened the way for the deluge of lava that destroyed everything in its path.

. . .A volcanic cloud rose to blot out the sun for ten square miles: within an hour the mansion-house had become another Pompeii. (It was time for Sam to implement plan B).

. . . With nothing more than the instincts of a homing bird, Agoro checked his watch against the position of the sun, and eased the Cessna an approximate due north. The rising thermals had cushioned the three-ton machine to a comfortable altitude and he began to relax.

Within sight of the mainland, he prepared to engage the landing gear, but something was amiss. 'The tyres have melted!' he shouted.

As the aircraft began to lose power, Crosbie circled the

passengers and tugged at their harnesses. The words 'don't panic' would do little to abate their fears. 'Hold tight,' was all he could think of, and left it at that.

The injection seals dissolved and flooded the cylinders with high octane fuel. This resulted in a sporadic firing that pulled the aircraft to an acute list, (its wingtip almost skimming the water.)

Leaking fuel ignited, Richard looked through the portal at the flashing flames and began to howl like a wounded bear.

Agoro opened his throttle. 'Will someone shut him up, we're losing an engine.!' The one parachute that Oaks hadn't sabotaged was under the pilots' seat, he reached down and tossed it to the whimpering man. 'Here's the deal: you either put this on and take a jump, or you shut the feck up!' Naturally enough, Richard opted for the 'shut the feck up' option.

Agoro grappled the controls with a new determination. 'Anybody else?' When nobody replied, 'we need to lose some weight fast,' he told them.

Crosbie symbolically thrust the parachute out first. Sadiq followed with the fire hydrants and baggage, Richard slid the sample bag under his seat with his shaking foot.

'Not enough!'

For one delicious moment all eyes turned; Richard could do no more than cringe and pray.

Crosbie reached over to tear the fuselage lining from above his head. Finally, he managed to disengage the heavy retractable stairs from the inside. He plunged them into the ocean, and the Cessna began at last to level off.

'Now let's all go home,' Agoro said calmly. Referencing the position of the sun with the time of day, Grand Bahama eventually appeared on the horizon.

At a thousand feet above sea level, just as Nassau airport came into view, their second engine spluttered to silence and they rapidly lost altitude.

Air traffic controllers pressed the panic button, and ducked instinctively as the listing Cessna cleared the control tower by a hair's breadth. Alarms sounded as it dipped and lurched violently before losing its flaps on the perimeter wall and dropping like a stone. Wheelrims gouging a hundred yards of runway, it spun like a top on its undercarriage before snagging on a column of landing lights and snapping like a carrot.

Emergency Services doused the flames at one end of the wreck, and watched in amazement as Sadiq's leg emerged from the other. . . Crosbie and Agoro were keeping Debbie upright between them, Sadiq followed close behind. Richard fell to the ground, clutching the package beneath his coat.

Judy felt for terra-firma with her bare feet before the rest of her followed. Wearing what was left of her shredded skirt, she tottered in front, legs splayed out like a broken marionette.

Customs officers had them as just another crew of ill-fated gung-ho cocaine smugglers. Once Crosbie showed his warrant card, their attitude changed dramatically. 'What a miraculous escape you've had,' the consulate said, 'but what on earth were you doing on that God forsaken island in the first place?'

'Just took a wrong turning,' he replied.

'What the hell are you up to?' Debbie asked after the diplomat had left.

Crosbie was very careful with his answer. 'Let's just slow down here, Deb,' he said,' at least until we know exactly who our friends are.'

'Are you saying that he could be one of them?'

'What I'm saying is, let's not mention a few things until we're sure!'

One other craft had left Monks' Head Island ahead of the deluge that morning. Keeping four foot above the razor-sharp flint, a lightweight Hovercraft shinnied south to the deep waters of the South Pacific.

The next day when they met up in the Lauderdale lounge, Sadiq said what they were all thinking. . . 'There's a small fortune in the strongroom here, I suggest we've all earned a share.'

'Wait a minute, the money's dirty,' Debbie said.

Crosbie stood and turned. 'Let's not be too hasty here, let the man speak.'

'It's not our money.'

Agoro, who till now had listened in silence, felt the need to interrupt . . . 'The question is, who does the money belong to: the D E A, Customs and Excise, or the bloody Tax man?'

'Perhaps the question should be, who deserves it?' Sadiq added hopefully. 'Who's to say it even exists? Look, we're giving them the computer disc, they'll be able to confiscate millions, if not billions in hidden assets, but they won't know anything about the cash in the basement.'

Agoro rubbed his chin thoughtfully. 'Just how much are you talking?'

'Twelve million, give or take.'

'I'm for taking.'

'So are we,' Richard and Judy said in unison.

Crosbie found a pencil to twirl. . . Everyone in the room looked to him for a response, but he refused to be hurried. 'Dirty money,' he repeated and shook his head. 'I don't know.'

Agoro couldn't control himself, he took the pencil from Crosbie's grasp, slowly and deliberately snapped it in two. 'Well, I do bloody know! Look, these people tried to make a pan of Scotch broth out of us, remember! We've been beaten up, locked up, blown up and fecked up by them. We're owed, and excuse me, where I come from dirty money still buys a loaf!'

'He is right, Sadiq said. 'Think of ourselves for once!'

Crosbie walked slowly across the room and stooped to retrieve the broken ends of his pencil. Reconnecting the jagged pieces, he examined the join for a long time before pulling it apart again. 'Let's put it to the vote, who thinks we should tell them about the money in the Lauderdale?' His bottom lip pushed out when not a hand was raised, and he slowly nodded. 'If it's not broke, don't fix it.' Flinging both halves of the pencil into the paper basket, he took in every face in turn, until he came to Debbie. When she nodded, he smiled and then everybody smiled. 'Okay,' he said at last, 'but it's got to be done right!' The next flight home isn't for another week. That gives us just enough time.'

Chapter Nineteen: Paradigm shift

The Lauderdale bar shutters were down, and the wayward brothers were 'morning-after' parched. If they weren't committed lager-louts, and if they had the sense they were born with, they'd have gone back to their room to recover. But they were, they hadn't, they didn't, and a lifetime of over-indulgence, drew them back to Agoro's place for a hair-of-the-dog curer.

This time their entrance drew no more than a cursory glance from the locals. In body-language reflecting his scurrilous mood, the overweight grey-vested bartender Agoro had left in charge, scratched his arse and swatted the sandflies that buzzed across his vision.

Tam ordered 'two buds from the cold-shelf, and' Jeddah kicked the jukebox when it refused to digest the wrong coin: it drew a menacing scowl from grey-vest, who growled and slammed the bottles angrily onto the counter.

'Bollox to you!' Jeddah snarled and kicked the juke box again. Tam rescued the situation with a Bahamian dime and warned his brother he was being watched.

'Little Old Wine Drinker' crackled in the background and Jeddah announced he was 'going for a Jimmy Riddle!'

'Just one hangover away from luxury retirement,' Tam told grey-vest. 'Soon to be feckin nouveau riche!' Then he put his fingers to his lips. 'Shh,' he whispered as his brother staggered back. 'Don't tell our kid, 'cos I'm a greedy baz.'

Wonted indifference would normally prevent Jeddah from wondering what went on in his absence, but when his Glasgow nose smelled double-cross, it was a different story. He checked Tam's smirk in the back-bar mirror and pulled him to one side. 'Would it be fair to say that you usually do the worrying for the two of us and I do the bashing, and I rarely, if ever, ask questions?'

Tam couldn't disagree, he nodded and slurped. 'Fair to say, eye.'

'Well, bro, here we are stuck on the other side of the feckin planet without a pot to pish in, and you're grinning like mah ninny! Is there no something I should know?'

Looking down from Jeddah's scowling eyes to the white of his clenching knuckle, Tam weighed up the odds, grinned, tutted and forced a smile. 'You're only right, bro, I wanted to surprise you,' he lied, and went on to fill in all the details of the great heist, except of course when it came to the location of his ill-gotten gains. All he would say about that was, 'it's safe as hooses.'

'Stick it where the sun dinna' shine!' Jeddah said, ordered another Bud and moved along the bar.

After being unceremoniously dumped by Richard, Wang was on his third Bud of the day. 'I can't live without him,' he bawled. 'Life has no purpose.'

Grey-vest leaned across and patted him on the back. 'Worry not, me fren? De Obeah man can fix yeah.' When Wang asked where this Obeah man could be found, he was told to go to the next village. 'Worry not, he gonna find yeh.'

In walked Gypsy with a serious glint in her eye. She still had unfinished business with Tam, as long as she could afford his company, he played along. 'You never know your luck in a big titty,' he grinned, snuggled up and tweaked her arse.

This seemed to annoy Jeddah. 'I'm getting away from this lovey-dovey shite,' he said, and volunteered to escort decidedly suicidal Wang, on his quest. Grey-vest directed them to a shanty neighbourhood on the far edge of town. (As soon as they set off, he picked up the phone.)

. . . Stumbling out into the sunshine, they made their way through a maze of picket matchwood left by the storm. It eventually gave way to cinder-block adobes built in chaotic rectangles on the lee side of a small hill. Embarrassed at Wang's blubbering, Jeddah reasserted his masculinity by kicking out at an offending mongrel nipping at his ankles. 'Hey, pal, d'yeh no ken the Obeah-man?' he shouted across the street.

Old Tom, who could be anything you wanted him to be (for the right price,) was waiting for them. Toothless gums sucked at his cheeks as he leaned on the balustrade. 'If yah lookin' for da Obeah-man, well he found you!' He reached for his funny shaped stick, rapped it noisily along the surviving spindles. and tottered forward. 'Is yah troubled, me frens?' he asked in his best patios.

Jeddah turned in his tracks, gathered up the slack in the shoulder of Wang's coat and thrust him forward. 'It's no me, d'yeh ken? I dinna believe in all that shite, ma wee pal here reckons he needs yeh.'

The old guy kicked the yapping mongrel from his path and beckoned them both into his parlour with a crooked finger. He tied a string of bottle tops and chicken bones onto the end of his funny shaped stick, sat down and waved it over his head. It felt ridiculous, but it had worked in the past, old Tom saw no good reason why it shouldn't now. He began to wail in an improvised version of Obeah language, which today consisted of a babbling mixture of groans and phony patios whines, strangely conducive to his daddy of a hangover.

'Bollox,' Jeddah said, 'any cold beer?'

The old guy sent the unbeliever into his kitchen while he brought up the small matter of a fee.

'No problemo,' Wang fanned his plastics across the table like a pack of playing cards.

'Close your eyes, yah troubled fellow, and tell de Obeah-man yah story.'

While Wang was rambling on about unrequited lust, old Tom selected the only card with four-digits scratched into the celluloid. He rattled his funny shaped stick over to the window to examine the pin number in a natural light. 'Tell me more, habibi,' he said, and punched the details into his I phone.

Wang prattled on; 'I know Richard's just a low-down slut and he can't help it, but why should I suffer?'

The old man had gotten the gist by then. 'Why indeed, me fren?' he wailed. 'So yeh want dis man to only have wadjet zen love eyes for yah?' By now he knew there was a £100 daily limit on the card, and told Wang that the treatment would run into several days.

Jeddah returned with a can of lager, idly picked up the funny shaped stick, turning to remonstrate, he knocked over a biscuit jar from the occasional table. The mongrel hound flew to gather up the waste, it caught its coat on the dangling chicken bones and dragged the stick from Jeddah's grip.

The old guy could twist anything into a sign, but this was an unexpected bonus. 'Ahm do be tellin' yah, man, de dog-witch knows.' He pinched the scrawny mutt by the ear under the pretext of stroking it, right on cue it emitted a ghostly howl. 'Yah not feck wit de spirit.' Pointing the dog's nose toward Jeddah, who was laughing so much, he dropped his beer, he pinched its ear again, causing it to howl even louder. 'Now yeah got dah mout on yah!' he moaned. 'Yah gotta buy back yah soul!'

'I'm skint, pal.'

Deftly switching his attention back to Wang, Tom lifted an eyebrow. 'De sperrid's back with dis one now, he be sweatin!'

Wang put a hand to his leaking brow and shook his head. 'He's right, I am!' It was ninety degrees in the shade, but he wasn't thinking logically. 'What's a sperrid?'

'De walkin dead, yeh poor troubled soul, de walkin dead.'

'Oh my god. What can I do?'

'Yah gotta confront it, man. First, we take the billy.' He handed Wang his funny shaped stick, arm-locked the squirming dog into submission; after carefully scooping the weeping mucus from its eye with his thumbnail, the mongrel scampered back to the broken biscuits.

'Yah gotta confront it, man,' he repeated, he dug his fingers deep into Wang's clenched eye socket to apply the sticky goo and swung the stick in circles to an improvised jig. 'Yah will see de sperrid through your third eye and he will help you. The seven keys of power are now yours!'

174

Perspiration and mucus combined to a veil over Wang's vision, (the more he rubbed the more it smeared.) The room began to spin, a curtain fluttered in the breeze, and he fainted.

The old guy sent Jeddah in search of another beer and leaned over to whisper in Wang's ear, 'he is old and he is young.' Hearing Jeddah returning from the kitchen, quickly added, 'he is dead, yet he breathes.'

Wang awoke spluttering and wiped his eyes. 'Did you see it, did yah see de sperrid?' old Tom asked and frowned knowingly. 'Ah,' he sighed.

'Ah, what?'

Tom gestured toward the door. 'Ah, you must walk barefoot on the stony beach to keep the sperrid at bay until . . . Now begone! Return only when the sun has set.' (He knew full well that the beach was at the opposite end of town to the bank.)

Jeddah was almost certain that the whole thing was a con, and he detoured to the local liquor store, after which he obeyed Tom's instruction 'almost' to the letter. . . Resting weary limbs next to a case of submerged lager; a gaggle of lycron speedos on one side, beer stall on the other, wasn't the most unpleasant way to spend the remainder of that sunny day.

Old Tom wouldn't have disagreed, having withdrawn his first £100 from the Bahamian International Bank he was halfway through his second bottle.

The sun eventually set on a very fruitful day for him, and he was almost annoyed when the stupid white men returned to interrupt his siesta. I say 'almost,' because he just about managed not to laugh as he looked down at the bruised and swollen feet of his benefactors.

Two very bedraggled specimens stood before him, exhausted, drunk and leaning against each other to stay upright. Explaining that each island had an Obeah centre where the sperrids walk, he told them this one was near to the Lauderdale, and arranged to meet them there the following evening, 'to lift the curse,' as it were. Waving Wang's cash card momentarily in the air before it disappeared back into his back pocket, he said he would have to keep an article of theirs to stay 'in touch.' Much too preoccupied with having to wait until after midnight to make his second withdrawal, Tom forgot to tell them they were walking the wrong way.

Two thoroughly depleted men hobbled down the street supported by each other's weight. As they circled the hilly outskirts in search of the town, Jeddah lost his footing in the dark. Collapsing spread-legged into a heap, he lost consciousness thinking about lycron speedos. (Wang seized his chance.)

. . . An hour and a half later he helped Jeddah to his feet and poured him into a yellow taxi.' The next time he woke he'd have almost no recollection of his sojourn into same sex sex. Even though he ached in places he never had before, he refused to think the unthinkable, but try as he might he just couldn't muster up a bad mood.

Tam was in similarly high spirits. An evening that had begun interestingly enough, got even better when he escorted Gypsy and her gold card to the casino. Till then the nearest he'd been to leisure gambling was a smoke-filled betting shop in Springburn.

Coloured chips and a spinning roulette wheel were a bit more up-market than ten bob each way on the favourite, but the 'don't get too greedy and play the short odds 'principals were just the same.

Things were going exceedingly well: Gypsy distracting the croupier with her tits while Tam placed another late bet. 'I could get used to this,' he said, and wrapped his arms protectively around a small mountain of winnings, but he failed to take his own advice. Instead of laying off the long odds with even money bets, he went for 'broke,' as they say, and that's how he ended up.

They sang Tam's favourite Abba 'Money' song all the way to a table at the Starlite Cabaret Club. Intoxicated, by the endless limbs taunting from the stage, he didn't object when Gypsy's hand explored his groin, and was foolish enough to believe her promise this time 'to be gentle with him.'

Saying he needed a 'Jimmy Riddle', he talked her into the scenic walk back to the hotel. What he really needed was to check on his buried treasure. Braving the burgeoning storm, he excused himself and slunk into the old gatehouse.

The mordant stench was a bit too much, even for Gypsy, and she raced on ahead, 'to prepare,' she said.

Conceding that different things turn different people on, Tam breathed in the air with a certain relish and dug up the treasure with bare hands. Endorphins running wild, he fought through the flurry of airborne ash to bury his face in the paper money.

Old Tom's headlights picked out his ghostly form emerging from the gatehouse, covered in grey, chin on chest, arms pumping triumphantly in the air. Convinced he had just seen a living-dead sperrid, he braked before zigzagging into the bush. Sparking up a loaded joint, he queried the star peppered sky for a sign. 'Then it's true, de sperrids do walk.'

. . . All through that night, he postulated upon the times he'd cashed in on those old African legends. Come the dawn, he had resolved to do anything to make amends, anything that is, short of returning Wang's bank card.

After catching his own ash-caked reflection in the tinted foyer glass, Tam decided to use the back stairway, and found Gypsy's room without too much trouble. Wearing nothing but latex, chromium and a licentious grin, she delivered him directly into the foaming bathtub.

Submerging his happy grin until his skin began to crinkle, he dragged his aching body from the perfumed depths to peer into the joss-stick lit, bedroom. Soggy three skinner dangling from the corner of upturned lips he trudged towards the inviting glow and looked down. 'Oh, feck no!' Amphetamine shrinkage hadn't quite worn off, and he couldn't rise to the occasion.

. . .Several different kinds of nausea lapsed him into a coma-like trance and he collapsed into a twitching heap at the foot of the bed. . . He came to, spread-eagled, manacled hand-and-foot to the brass rails. Gypsy was circling with her deviant box of tricks. 'Now then, little fellow, let's see what we have here?' she said, and his heart skipped two beats.

. . .In the penthouse suite six floors higher, 'Do me up   like a turkey' was playing in the background as Jeddah lay in similar repose, loosely tied to Wang's four-poster, fighting off any inclination to smile. 'I don't know about this gay lark,' he said. 'it's all new to me.'

Wang yawned, bit into the first knot and turned onto his side, muttering 'it was new to us all once. God loves a tryer,' just before he fell fast asleep.

Jeddah listened to the snoring till he could stand it no longer, twisted himself free, kicked Wang in the balls and left by the back stairs. Ducking inside the gatehouse to avoid the burgeoning storm, he found old Tom squatting in the ashes. Oblivious to the swirling wind that filled the air with a grey mist, he was juggling a wad of chewing tobacco around his one good tooth.

'Where's mah wee mate's plastic?' Jeddah snarled.

Rambling incoherently something about 'living dead sperrids,' old Tom handed over Wang's cash card.

'Anything else to declare?'

The old man gave him the fraudulently withdrawn hundred dollars and dropped back onto his haunches. 'The third eye is now mine!' he chanted.

'Keep it,' Jeddah stuffed the money in his pocket and went back to his own room to sleep it off.

. . It was almost noon when he finally made it to the breakfast room to find Wang, Tam and Gypsy in a huddle. 'Who'd have thought,' Wang lamented, 'one brother bonking an S&M queen, the other straddling the gender line?'

. . . The embarrassed silence was broken by Tam. 'Don't tell me you're coming out, our kid?'

Jeddah threw Wang's gold card across the table, and scratched his head and his arse at the same time. 'How can I bro,' I'm no sure I've been in?'

'Wang smiled seductively. 'Oh, you've been in alright, he laughed and Gypsy laughed.

Jeddah was finding this non-violent, gender-neutral side increasingly uncomfortable. He came from a place where men wore the trousers, not eyer-liner, and he wasn't amused. 'I'm keeping the peace this time, bro,' he said, 'but it's no easy.'

After checking that everybody was looking, Tam lifted his sweater to show a golden piercing through each of his nipples and one hanging from his navel. 'I've got another, but I'm nae saying where, so I won't take the pish, if you don't!'

'Deal!'

Thunder began to rumble, storm clouds gathered, they raced each other to the bar, laughing and recounting the previous night's admissible follies. It looked to be the start of another epic binge until Jeddah mentioned his morning encounter with old Tom.

'He was where?' Tam spluttered, dropped his pint and scrambled down the steps. Ducking his head into the sandstorm he forced his way into the driving rain across to the gatehouse.

A funnel of wind had whipped a vortex around the dancing figure at its centre. 'Begone, yeh foul spirit,' old Tom cried and waved his funny shaped stick high in the air.

Tam had arrived just in time to watch the last of his fortune, bill by bill, sucked through a whirlwind of swirling ash and wafted skyward. When Jeddah finally caught up with him, he was openly weeping at old Tom's feet.

'De sperrid has left now, weep no more!' the old man cried as the last of the paper money disappeared into the storm. Then he backtracked into the darkness, never to be seen again.

Tam fought the cyclonic gale all the way back to his room, emptied the minibar, and collapsed face down on the sixth-floor balcony. . . Awakened by the incessant pounding thunder, his eyes snapped open to the golden glow of sunrise, and it didn't make sense. Jamming them shut, the thunder roared once again, he realised the storm was taking place inside his head. Shivering in a cold sweat he stumbled to the bathroom mirror. The only remedy for the pitiful image that confronted him was an early 'hair of the dog.'

Storm clouds had conceded to an eye-piercing light, so the brothers took the dimly lit back stairs to the breakfast room. It was there that Gypsy and Wang hit them with the latest double whammy. (The airport had reopened and they were both flying back to Glasgow with the band that very afternoon.)

'Last Call' came over the airport tannoy and Gypsy winced. 'I hate to leave you, honest I do, I'm needed at the Lavender club you see.' She linked a long black nail into Tam's favoured piercing, tugged him closer, stuck a tongue in his ear and whispered that there would always be a place for him there.

Wang told Jeddah to sing if he was glad to be gay, and tweaked his arse at passport control. Watching the plane take off, Tam wiped away a tear. 'What are we going to do now, bro?'

There's only one answer to that,' Tam replied, and with what little was left of their windfall, they set off for a last Budweiser pilgrimage. (It seemed only right!)

'Still off on business. I'm in charge until he comes back.' the Neanderthal doorman grunted when they asked where their friend Agoro was.

'Bollox to this for a game of soldiers,' Tam said, 'let's find a user-friendly bar.'

They were just about to leave when the big man pulled the cover from the pool table. 'Oh, we might as well have one while we're here,' Jeddah said and slapped a note onto the bar top.

To ward off encroaching sobriety, Tam took a large swig, grinned sluggishly, and pointed to the pool table. 'Hey, bigyin, d'yeh no fancy a wee wager?'

The grey vested giant nodded, ambled from behind the bar, without once smiling, he slowly chalked his cue. Tam racked up the balls, he won the toss and after a decent break, intentionally fluffed an easy eight-ball. His opponent potted it, shrugged, picked up the five-dollar bill and traipsed back to the bar.

Tam winked and staggered around the table. When he deliberately miss-hit the cue-ball into the corner pocket the big man chuckled . . . The sting was on! 'What the feck are you laughing at, fat arse?' he slurred, 'I'll play you for a hundred dollars if you like!'

The money was counted out under their noses, and Jeddah fell silent. He suspected they were being hustled, but Tam wasn't worried, he was after all, a player of some repute in the Glasgow suburbs.

A scurvy crew of onlookers hurriedly circled the table. After every shot they mumbled their Bahamian commentary and then hushed. A respectable period of safety play followed while the combatants got the measure of each other. (The game was on!) . . .

Tam escaped every trap, in return lay a few of his own, until there were only three balls left on the table. Winking at his brother, he gently rolled the cue-ball behind the last remaining red. The spectators fell silent as he raised his hands in mock apology and danced a celebratory jig back to his chair.

In appreciation of such a fine snooker shot, the giant nodded and tapped the edge of the table with his palm. . . without taking his eyes from the baize, he slowly and deliberately chalked up. Calculating the angles, he moved the spectators back with his great fat arse and lifted the butt of his cue high into the air.

Jeddah coughed loudly, but it didn't put grey-vest off. Stepping back from the table, he re-chalked his cue before resuming the passé position. He took his shot; every breath in the room was baited as the cue-ball pirouetted agonisingly slowly in a wide arc. . . it trundled along the balk cushion to kiss the eight-ball home.

The crowd clapped and cheered. Fat man mimicked Tam's apologetic gesture and stuffed the notes into his greasy pocket. Smiling for the first time that day, he issued a French curse and bent back into his newspaper.

'That's it!' Tam took off his own watch, tossed it onto the counter and ordered two Buds. 'Skint and sober is not a workable combination, but well played,' he said and took a drink. He was willing to leave it at that, but the weight of ridicule from the regulars was beginning to tell.

When he discovered his fat arsed opponent was a three times Bahamian pool champion he began to twitch. 'Shut the feck up! Yeh feckin barms!' he growled, but the regulars laughed all the louder.

For the benefit of another late arrival, the giant brandished his wad for what was to be the last time and leered over at the brothers. 'Chow,' he grinned and raised his glass.

'That's it!' Jeddah regressed to type and aimed his stare menacingly. The bigger man drew a pickaxe handle from beneath the counter: his grin turned to a taunting scowl.

Knuckles clenched and smiling mischievously Jeddah approached the bar while Tam held the door open behind him. 'You'll no need that, pal,' Jeddah said, and dropped his hands to his sides. 'I ken you're a hard man.' His cringing manner seemed to appease as he leaned forward and whispered. 'You hustled our kid good, and we respect you for that.'

Aye, you turned the tables, laddie,' Tam shouted from the doorway, 'You're a pro and that's the truth.'

Jeddah held up a placating hand. 'No offence, okay? I can see that you're an assassin and I'm really, really scared,' he smiled, 'but there's no real need to take the pish.' The giant was confused and shook his head as Jeddah leaned further to explain. 'It's okay, I'm in the business too, semi-retired you might say, but I like to keep ma wee hand in. You'll have heard of the Jackal? well I'm the Jockal, pleased to meet you!' The giant shook his head in confusion and Jeddah added, 'well if you've got to explain the joke,' and offered his hand.

As the big man reached out to take it, a well-placed head-but caught him cold. On his way to the floor, he was relieved of the cash and the two Scotsmen hit the sunlit street to the echo of police sirens.

. . . Amorphous shapes on fungus-ridden walls hinted at past atrocities; a million microbes danced in the single shard of sunlight from the tiny, barred window.

'As prisons go it could be worse,' Tam said, but Jeddah failed to see how. 'At least we get running water.' When he went to the basin and turned the taps nothing happened. 'Well, somewhere to pish anyway,' he said as he unloaded his bloated bladder into the multi coloured sink. . . Too late, he was pissing onto his own shoes through an unplumbed waste pipe.

'Well, it can'nae get much worse,' he laughed as the bundle of rags in the corner farted loudly, followed by a more ambiguous noise.

. . .When the huge grey vested bartender got back his winnings, he dropped the charges. His only condition, the 'Springburn lager louts' kept away, and that suited Tam and Jeddah fine.

Despite promises of abstinence the lure of amber nectar was challenging their resolve, as they staggered dreamily towards the Lauderdale.

Sadiq, now the proud owner, was waiting at the bar, looked them up and down. 'Allahu akbar, Intoxication is the work of Satan, so resist!'

'Feck sake, after what we've been through, Satan'd be a wee walkover,' Tam replied, 'but the annals of working-class crime are crammed full of ill-fated drunken missions, so we're resisting!'

Later that evening Crosbie and Debbie were in the lounge juggling their various options when Jeddah and Tam ambled past without so much as a single sideways glance.

'Those two are up to no good. That's the second time today our errant neds' have passed an open bar,' Crosbie said. He knew they were up to something, which next to their plans he assumed must be trivial, but when they refused a free drink, he wasn't so sure. . . If he hadn't had bigger fish to fry, he'd have challenged them there and then.

Under scrutinising eyes across the room, Tam attempted a smile, Jeddah made a production of yawning and remarking how sleepy he was. They took the lift to the first floor and shinnied back down the drain pipe.

. . .After burglarising a nearby plant-hire yard, they heaved the heavy compressor to the rear of the hotel. . . A burnt-out magnetic auger and pneumatic-jack hammer later, they finally gave up.

Watching them shuffle, puffing and panting from behind the basement, knowing the money they were trying to steal had already been shared out, Crosbie couldn't help but sympathise.

Under new 'Money laundering' laws, clearing banks were mandatorily obliged to report large cash deposits and transfers. He knew they couldn't just waltz through 'nothing to declare' carrying suitcases stuffed with cash, so he had to come up with another plan.

. . .For two days, he wrestled with the logistics of legitimising such a large sum . . . and then it dawned: the answer had been staring him in the face. He called in a favour from a friend in the Foreign Office to send a diplomatic pouch marked 'Exhibits.'

Knowing exactly where to find Tam and Jeddah, he plonked two Budweisers on the bar between them. 'Do you want the good news or the bad news, boys?'

'If not for shite news, we'd have no news at all,' Tam said and took a hefty swig. Crosbie told him they were booked on the same flight to Glasgow, and Jeddah wasn't sure if the news was good or bad. He couldn't help feeling a certain affinity with the two wayward sons of Springburn. 'You'll nae be subject to any criminal charges,' he told them, ordered two more Buds and slipped them each a fifty spot.

The flight home was very much a mirror image of the outbound journey for the brothers. They returned to their Springburn tenement in a predictably inebriate state, wondering if it had all been a trip too far . . .

Crosbie met Richard and Judy in a Gallowgate bar and handed over the diplomatic pouch containing half the proceeds. They had already decided what to do with their newfound wealth, but he made it a condition that any plan should include Gypsy and two streetwise Neds.

Wheels of corruption were greased; funds laundered, bribes abounded, the Lavender club's late-night gambling and liquor licence rubber-stamped.

Planning permission was granted, the whole area became a high-viz, hard-hat zone. Before the demolition crew moved in, the giant phallic appendage was sold off to an S&M club in Soho, the two-way mirror and the John Holmes cut-out, to a Cleethorpes nunnery.

Over the coming weeks 1000 tons of rubble was transhipped to a Gorbals landfill, Lavender rafters stripped to the eaves, the whole area closed off to Sunday traffic.

. . .Two mammoth cranes worked in tangent to lift an enormous glass dome over adjoining rooftops, and lower it, inch perfect into position.

Followed by an army of suits carrying blueprints, the trades moved in, painted over the graffiti and relined the walls with 3D erotica. Worn out fetish accoutrements were replaced with state-of-the-art paraphernalia, field-tested and signed off by Richard and Judy.

As the frenetic pace began to ease, architect's Volvos gradually replaced builder's trucks, and the final makeover began.

Crosbie declined an invitation to be guest of honour at the 'grand opening,' but it triggered his idle policeman's mind. Even though he tried not to want to know, curiosity got the better, the detective in him began to juggle the improbabilities. At every given opportunity he and Debbie found themselves driving past. . .

. . . After only three months the Lavender dream was almost a reality, but they would never get to see the finished product. By then they would be raising a glass to the new club's success from the safe and distant Nassau harbour. 'What was the point in carrying all that money to the other side of the world when we have everything we need right here,' Crosbie said.

Carrying a tray of chilled Campari, Agoro came from behind his new bar to join them. 'I'll drink to that!'

Chapter Twenty:
Opening Night!

High-end deviants came from far and wide for the grand opening of the New Lavender Club. Advertised on Facebook, eBay, Amazon, even the Dark Web, online membership fees were exorbitant enough to deter all but the unfeasibly rich: a sultan from Bahrain, a family of Russian oligarchs, a lottery winner from Liverpool; (a cartel of hedge fund Tories paid extra to remain anonymous).

Who needs gambling when the Champagne's a hundred pound a pop?' Jeddah whispered behind his fist.

Rubbing his hands in glee, Tam chuckled. 'Let's not forget the five grand membership.'

'Let's not!' Tamken,' Richard shouted.

'I've telt yeh, it's nae Tamken. It's just Tam, ken?' Tam said. Richard just scratched his arse.

Along with the mega rich takers, in their element, the wealthy sad and deviant in denial, emerged from their closets and cram-packed the main lounge. In feathers, studs, leathers and plastic, they stared down in confused disappointment. The great center-piece they'd been promised was no more than a liquid crystal orb taking up most of the lower floors. It had been bombarded with electrons to show a tropical sunset, lapping waves, and nothing more.

Notably underwhelmed and fast becoming frisky in the heat of prickly rubber-wear, overzealous guests milled and bleated like petulant stars.

Judy waited for the optimum moment of discontent; on her signal Tam threw the switch. . . Suddenly, the orb became transparent and lit up the labyrinth beneath. The hoard surged forward as her posh commentary boomed through the radio mike. 'Each concentric corridor represents one of "Dante's nine circles. The more devout will be aware that there are three main categories of punishment according to Dante: fraud, incontinence, and violence. Now we all know what fraud is, in fact, most here call it 'tax-avoidance.' In the interests of health and hygiene we have to discount incontinence, so what are we left with? Well, see for yourselves!'

She tapped her cudgel on the rail and the bawdy audience drew a communal breath.

. . .Jeddah was on the door checking tickets to the tune of, 'Sing if you're glad to be gay.'

Tam had the job of encouraging guests towards the foible of their choice. 'Ladies and gentlemen and others, just what is your wee preference?' Legs astride at the entrance to the games room, he broke into classic rap:

'Now we've got spankers, thankers,
whippers and wankers,
rubbers, leathers, shackles,
gaggers and huggers.
Doers, don'ters, maybe and fakers,
shakers, bonkers, givers, and takers!'

Doctor Hook's 'Don't Give a Dose to the One You Love Most' boomed out from the house speakers while he took a long toke and geared up for the final verse:
'Crown heads, Papal heads, Paisley heads, Dick-eds.
Gonna get your rock off, gotta get your socks off,
Dinnae be shy and you'll soon get high:
Buckfast brecky, gerit doon yeh necky,
fiddlin' yeh lecky, you know why!
Shopliftin' griftin' chokin' tokin',
Hissin' Sid and Bongo smokin'.
Rasta pasta Sumo Sue after.
Springburn lodgers,
DODGY TODGER DODGERS!'

Resplendent in second-skin leather, perched suggestively on a hydraulic ram, Gypsy slowly ascended from the centre of a hazy grey mist: thigh boots straddling a frozen block of carbon dioxide, raven locks swirling.

Cracking a golden nine tails with an arrogant flick of the wrist, she flayed the silver-sprayed nymphet squirming at her feet.

'Want some of this, peasants? The gossamer only delivers symbolic blows, (but for an additional sum?')

To give the voyeurs time to pay extra she babbled on about 'lustful souls tossed in the tempest and 'unrequited lust' and took a deep breath.

'Take a look!' She motioned to the 'stocks and pillory' section in the outer circle and shook her head. 'Out of bounds, I'm afraid,' she shouted. . . Just as predicted the crowd went ballistic, until she made a production of caving in under pressure. 'Okay, you've talked me into it, but terms and conditions apply.'

Pulling a bunch of direct debit forms and disclaimers from her bum bag, she added with finality, 'cheques, only if accompanied by a current bankcard if you please.'

. . .Ten minutes later and two floors below, she was relishing the chastisement of her first paying customer.

'You naughty. . . thwack. . . naughty. . . thwack. . . boy,' she cried as Scallywag's 'Chains of love' blasted through the speakers. 'What are you?'

'I'm a naughty. . . thwack. . . naughty. . . thwack. . . boy,' Wang bellowed as he curled into a groaning ball, to rapturous applause.

(He had just won a first in fetish folklore that nobody could ever take from him.)

Winking at Jeddah, Judy licked her lips. 'C'mon big fellah. What about it, they say you should try everything at least once before you die?' she shouted over the radio mike.

'Don't take this personally,' Jeddah replied, 'it's just that the thought of straight sex doesn't do it for me anymore.'

'Who said anything about straight sex?'

'Walk on the wild side' was playing. Richard wandered aimlessly down to the lower levels, he perched on the plastic ducking stool to collect his thoughts, picked up a cast-off rubber suit and held it jokingly to himself, (just to see how ridiculous it might look). 'Let's see what these perv's get out of it, eh?'

Deciphering the zip arrangement, he lay on his back and lifted his legs high in the air. 'Silly buggers.' A hidden hook snagged on his pubes and he felt the icy cold draught to his nethers. With an almighty effort he curled upwards to wrench himself free, in the process, smashed his head into an overhanging steel shackle.

. . . He awoke handcuffed to a Perspex rack, metabolism frozen in that priapism half-life that only ever happens by freak accident, an untameable state of arousal impossible to physiologically duplicate. (Judy pounced!)

Never having been out-bonked before, she tried every trick in the 'Acrobatic Sensualist's yearbook, and then some new ones. She squatted and she groaned, moaned, bucked, bounced and squirmed every which way imaginable. Finally, like a weary cattle drover at the end of a long drive, defunct and saddle sore, she dismounted and undid Richard's cuffs.

Still locked in that proud, erect state, he cupped his hands arrogantly behind his neck, thrust out his buttocks and grinned.

Judy made him promise (on pain of castration,) not to tell a living soul of her abject orgasmic failure. In return she would pledge eternal devotion and treat him with a respect befitting the flesh and blood equivalent to her beloved Rampant Rod...

Laying a loving head on her shoulder, Richard smiled, his earlier brush with defilement had somehow made him appreciate the value of such a malevolent partner. . . Their mutual incapacity for guilt had drawn them back where they belonged. (Together).

Judy tweaked his arse and winked. 'What about an early night, big fellah?'

. . . They waited until everybody had left, and raided the fetishist display cabinet before dancing all the way down the back stairs.

. . . Gypsy and Wang were waiting with Tam and Jeddah at the main street taxi rank: a night cap and a foursome in the Treble An apartment seemed very much in order.

A black cab loomed from the shadows. It sped past them and squealed to a halt beside Richard and Judy emerging from the alley. 'Home,' Judy squealed between tongue-out smooches, 'and don't spare the horses.'

. . . The large driver looked into his rear mirror, smiled at the entwined couple on his back seat, engaged the central locking system and tilted his cap over the scorch marks on his face as he turned off the main road.

Afterword

Writing The Todger Dodgers has been a wild, laugh-soaked rollercoaster through the chaos of human ambition, vanity, and desire. What began as cheeky satire quickly turned into a mirror reflecting our obsession with reinvention, technological, emotional, and moral. Every character, from the hapless Dick-Ed to the delightfully devious Judy, carries a spark of our shared madness. Because, let's face it, progress and insanity often share a bed. If this story made you snort, blush, or grin mid-page, my mission's complete. Thank you for coming along for the ride, may laughter always steer you through life's most magnificent cock-ups.

Published in Collaboration with Noble Legacy Publishing

www.noblelegacypublishing.co.uk